YOU HAD ME AT CHÂTEAU

PORTIA MACINTOSH

Boldwood

First published in Great Britain in 2024 by Boldwood Books Ltd.

Copyright © Portia MacIntosh, 2024

Cover Design by Alexandra Allden

Cover Illustration: Shutterstock and iStock

The moral right of Portia MacIntosh to be identified as the author of this work has been asserted in accordance with the Copyright, Designs and Patents Act 1988.

Every effort has been made to obtain the necessary permissions with reference to copyright material, both illustrative and quoted. We apologise for any omissions in this respect and will be pleased to make the appropriate acknowledgements in any future edition.

A CIP catalogue record for this book is available from the British Library.

Paperback ISBN 978-1-80426-729-5

Large Print ISBN 978-1-80426-730-1

Hardback ISBN 978-1-80426-731-8

Ebook ISBN 978-1-80426-728-8

Kindle ISBN 978-1-80426-727-1

Audio CD ISBN 978-1-80426-736-3

MP3 CD ISBN 978-1-80426-735-6

Digital audio download ISBN 978-1-80426-732-5

Boldwood Books Ltd
23 Bowerdean Street
London SW6 3TN
www.boldwoodbooks.com

For my wonderful family

1

'As the sun began to set, and the beachgoers disappeared with it, all of a sudden it was just me and him. He reached out and tucked my hair behind my ear. He didn't say a word to me, not with his lips. He said it with his eyes. The touch of his fingers as he grazed my face. That deep, heavy sigh that made his chest rise sharply before slowly sinking again. I could tell that he wanted me, and I wanted him too, but here? On the beach? I knew that we shouldn't, and I think he knew too, but he didn't care. And then he did say it with his lips. He leaned in and kissed me, removing all doubt. Why had I spent the last year thinking he just wanted to be friends? Friends don't kiss each other like this, they don't lay each other on the sand, slowly pull the string of their bikini, loosening it behind their neck... but this just felt right. Well, right then it did. But you never really know what the future holds.'

Silence. Stone-cold silence. Silence is never good – not in response to something like that. My God, actually saying the words, I'm cringing so hard, and yet she's saying nothing.

'Jen?' I prompt her. 'Are you there?'

'Yep, I'm here,' she replies, chirpy as ever.

That's the thing about Jen, her tone is exhausting. Even when she's telling you something that's bad, she delivers it like she's telling you that you just won – let me just switch to my TV game show host voice – *a brand new car.*

'I thought there might be more,' she adds.

'No, no more,' I reply. 'Well, I mean, that's the end of the chapter.'

However difficult it might be to write a book, genuinely, it's a billion times harder to bring yourself to read it out loud to someone. I even struggle reading it to Jen and she's my editor. I don't know, it's weird, because once the book is published you want everyone to read it, but at this stage, opening up that part of your brain for someone in real time, it's scary. It's almost like they might be able to find their way in, and see more than you want them to.

'Right, okay,' she says, pausing for a moment. 'I'm just skimming through what I have in front of me.'

What she has in front of her is my first draft and, if I were to give it a working title, I'd call it something like: *50k of Shite.*

Things were so great with my first four books. I wrote them so quickly – or at least it felt like I did. It was series, called *Always a Bridesmaid*, with each book focusing on one of the four bridesmaids in a friendship group, set over a summer full of weddings. They were such fun romcoms, set in beautiful locations, with dreamy leading men and the pages were just bursting with jokes and romance. And they were a hit! So much so that Jen offered me a contract to write another series and I bit her hand off. It turns out though that it's not so easy to just, you know, knock out another hit.

They say everyone has a book in them, but hardly anyone has two. That's kind of how I feel about my series.

The first one practically wrote itself. Of course, I had the idea before I turned it into a series of books. Now I have the book deal, for another four-book series, and I need to come up with the ideas. It's nowhere near as fun this way round.

Of course, if this were something I just did for fun, I could figure it out. However, it's not only my job (and therefore my only way to eat and keep a roof over my head), but being contracted to a publisher means sticking to certain terms and timelines.

My book – my shitty 50k – needs turning in again, in a couple of weeks, and it needs to be 25k longer. That's why I'm on the phone with my editor, because so far our (and by our I mean her) best idea is to write flashbacks to make up the extra.

'I did have another idea,' I tell her. 'And I have a good chunk of it for you to read.'

'Oh?' Jen replies.

'The thing is, it's a bit of a different genre, and—'

'Amber, let me stop you there,' she interrupts me. 'You're a romantic comedy writer. That's what you should be writing. Actually, I know what you need to do, and I think you do too – you need to write the spicy scenes. That will make up the extra.'

I mean, I'm not sure I've ever read a romcom where an entire third of it was just shagging, but this has come up before, where Jen has suggested I spice things up. The thing is, I don't have a problem with it existing in books, I'm a sex-y person (contrary to what my love life suggests), I just can't write horny scenes to save my life. Romance – yes. Comedy – my God, I am unrelenting, on and off the page, when it comes to cracking jokes. Descriptive shagging – honestly, I can't. I just suck. And not in the way Jen wants.

'Well, we still have our meeting booked in,' I start.

'Do we?' she replies. 'Oh yes, of course we do.'

You can tell by the tone of her voice that she's forgotten all about it. I did think it was weird, that she asked for a call.

'So, how about I send you the other thing I've been working on, because it is still kind of a romcom, and you could glance over it, and if you think it might be stronger, maybe we could... pivot,' I suggest.

Silence again. And then...

'Okay, yes, send it over,' Jen replies. 'But, Amber, think about what I said. We need to get this draft wrapped up before Christmas, or we're going to lose all the spots we've scheduled for getting the book through the different stages, and then, well, we don't want that, do we?'

No, obviously I don't want to breach my contract any more than I want to press pause on my income, but I have to write a book that I'm proud of, right?

'We don't,' I confirm. 'See what I send you. I think you'll really like it.'

'Okay but, in the meantime, finish the scene you just read to me,' she demands. 'Keep it going, after the kiss. Spice things up! You won't regret it.'

We say our goodbyes, leaving it at that.

What Jen doesn't seem to understand is that I don't think I'll regret it, it's that I can't really do it in the first place, and what is even worse than not feeling like a sexy writer is not feeling like a good writer at all. I feel so overwhelmingly, almost dangerously uninspired.

I think it's time to shake things up. I just hope Jen agrees with me.

2

Are you ever having a bad day, or doing something difficult, or just generally feeling rubbish and you think to yourself: I wish my mum or dad were here, to make it better? I think that all the time and yet, it's funny, because my parents seem to have the knack for making things a bit worse.

'Okay, kids, I need you to listen carefully, because we have some news,' Mum starts, pausing to take a deep breath. 'Your dad and I are pre-divorcing.'

'What?' I squeak.

'Really?' Tom, my brother, says at the same time.

'It's important to us that you realise that sometimes things just don't work out,' Mum continues. 'But we need the two of you to know that it's not your fault. Is it, Johnny?'

Mum gives Dad a sharp jab with her elbow.

'No, no,' he quickly joins in. 'It's not your fault.'

Wait, hang on a second.

'Pre-divorcing?' I say, because that's a new one to me.

'Yes,' Mum says, her face serious, but the hints of a smile flickering at the edges of her mouth. 'It's basically an intent to divorce, later, when we've worked out the best course of action.'

'But wait,' Tom chimes in. 'What about Christmas?'

Tom's innocent but seemingly ill-timed question breaks through the seriousness of the moment. Mum's face visibly shifts from that of a calm therapist to that of a woman who has been pushed in front of in a queue too many times and is about to finally snap.

'We're getting divorced,' Dad tells him plainly. 'We're not denouncing Christianity.'

'You mean renouncing,' Mum corrects him. 'And, seeing as though it's *so* important to you, Tom, we thought it would be good for us, as a family, to spend Christmas together one last time.'

'So Santa will know where to leave our presents?' my brother jokes – at least I think he's joking.

I allow myself a little snort.

'It's nice to see you're taking it so well,' Dad half-jokes.

'Sorry, I've just never heard of a pre-divorce,' Tom replies. 'Are you, like, actually doing it?'

'Yes,' Mum says, clearly and plainly. 'Unless things get better.'

'So you're not actually divorcing?' I check.

'We're *pre*-divorcing,' she says again. I still don't get it.

I just stare at her, my thoughts racing with a million questions, but there is one obvious one that I have to ask first.

'Why are you getting divorced?' I ask, the words feeling heavy in my mouth. 'Or pre-divorced, or whatever the correct term is.'

Mum's expression softens. She looks a little sad that I'm even asking her the question, but her tone remains firm as she meets my gaze.

'It's just not working,' she explains simply – there is a regretful edge to her words too, though. 'Neither of us is happy.'

Jill Page, my mum, with her impeccable posture and professional demeanour, shifts in her seat for a moment before regaining her composure. Despite retiring early from her job as a solicitor, she still carries herself with an air of professionalism – one that she probably could have retired too. Sometimes, when she tells us things, it's as if she's about to deliver a report rather than just, you know, talk to her kids.

I'm not expecting her to only wear twinsets and pearls and spend her days knitting – or any other silly stereotypes – it's just that her power suits and her girl-boss bobbed hairdo aren't as necessary as they used to be. I wish I could get her to relax a little.

'It's been a long time coming,' Dad admits, offering us one of his trademark friendly smiles. 'But hopefully you understand.'

Johnny Page, my goofy, fun-loving dad, is in his early sixties as well. He has kind eyes behind his glasses, and a sense of style that matches his demeanour – he's so laid-back, he's horizontal. Unlike my retired mum, Dad is still working as a tree surgeon. He always jokes about never retiring, claiming he'll only hang up his boots when he falls out of a tree or when the world runs out of greenery. He's a huge sci-fi nerd whereas Mum much prefers a cosy romance, and that's just the start of how polar opposite their personalities and tastes are. When you think about it, it's a miracle they've lasted this long.

'What your dad and I need is for the two of you to be really brave, okay?' Mum says, her tone as determined as it is sad. 'We can all get through this, but you kids need to be strong. Do you think you can do that?'

'Mum, we're both in our thirties,' I reply, deadpan, because I'm starting to think that she thinks we're ten and thirteen, when in reality I'm thirty, Tom is thirty-three, and we're both fully grown adults who flew the nest over a decade ago.

'I know,' she says softly as reality catches up with her. 'But it still must be hard for you both.'

'Can't you work it out?' Tom asks optimistically. 'If this is only a pre thing. Maybe give things another go, for old times' sake?'

Dad shakes his head sadly.

'We've tried, mate,' he says, and there is just something about Dad being serious that makes things seem genuinely terrifying. When Dad isn't joking, things are bad. Honestly, even when he did the eulogy at Grandad's funeral, he was getting laughs.

'This seems out of nowhere,' I point out, my mind racing to make sense of it all. 'And Christmas sounds like it's going to be super awkward.'

'Just to confirm, the actual Christmas dinner will be unaffected, right?' Tom checks.

His priorities are just fantastic, aren't they? I'm not sure he's taking this seriously. I'm not sure I am either, to be honest, because I'm still not sure what 'pre-divorcing' actually means.

Mum's shocked expression speaks volumes.

'I thought you two would be more distraught,' she admits – she almost sounds disappointed.

Tom shrugs in a way that shows the apple hasn't fallen far from the tree.

'We're all adults,' he says simply. 'You guys can do whatever you want. Or pre do whatever you want, or... whatever.'

'Amber?' Mum prompts me. 'What do you have to say about all of this?'

'Assuming Christmas dinner is unaffected,' Tom reminds me, as though it makes a difference.

'Yes, can we all shut up about Christmas bloody dinner,' Mum snaps.

I can see the corners of my dad's mouth twitching, as though he's dying to laugh at Tom, but he knows it isn't the time.

I swallow hard, to try to shift the knot that has taken up residence in my throat.

'Obviously, I'm upset,' I begin, because *obviously* I am – no matter what's going on, I hate to hear that they're unhappy. I just need to make sure that I say the right things. 'And I don't fully understand why it's over. And of course I would rather you stay together... but I respect your decision.'

Deep down, I'm clinging to the hope that maybe they haven't fully thought this through yet, and that when they do, they'll change their minds. After all, they've been married for over thirty years, and they've made it this far. What a shame it would be to throw it all away now.

Mum's expression softens, although she still seems unsatisfied.

'It's important to me – to *us* – that you kids understand that it's nothing to do with you,' she continues, getting the conversation back on track. 'This is grown-up stuff.'

I try to suppress a smile, knowing all too well that it wouldn't be appropriate given the circumstances. It's just jarringly funny, and kind of cute, that Mum is telling us in the same way she would have done twenty years ago.

'How about I take you both out for ice cream,' Dad jokes, lightening the mood. 'You've taken the news like good kids.'

I see something shift in Mum's eyes. This surge of something that looks like it's bubbling to the surface.

'Everything's a joke to you, Johnny,' she snaps, as whatever it is finally boils over. 'And *that's* why we're splitting up.'

Mum practically jumps from her seat and storms out of the living room, leaving the three of us sitting around the coffee table on our own.

Tom picks up a cream cheese and cucumber sandwich, his appetite clearly unaffected, and takes a huge bite.

Yes, obviously my mum catered telling us that she and my dad are getting a divorce.

Dad sighs heavily.

'You kids should stay single for as long as you can,' he suggests with a jokey smile, though you can see a hint of sadness behind his eyes. Then, as if to distract himself from the reality of the situation, he asks: 'So, what are you two doing this evening?'

I glance at Dad, a smile creeping across my lips.

'I have a date,' I confess. 'But, if it's any consolation, those usually end with me continuing to be single, so...'

'Ah, don't be daft, you'll have a great time,' he tells me. 'Ignore me, I'm an old cynic.'

'Good luck with that,' Tom says. 'And by that I mean tell him: good luck with that. That being you.'

Do brothers ever grow out of winding you up? Because Tom has been my brother for thirty years and, I swear, he's only getting worse. Still, aside from being siblings, we're friends too. We both work in London so we hang out all the time, and I know that, if I ever needed him, he would be there. He just might crack a joke while he was there too.

'Tom, why don't you stay for dinner?' Dad suggests. 'It'll be less awkward with you there.'

'Why doesn't Amber stay?' Tom replies, vaguely panicked at the thought of sitting at a dinner table between our warring parents.

'Because Amber has a date, she just said,' Dad replies.

'And speaking of which, I need to get going,' I say, smiling to myself as I leave Tom to deal with this one alone. 'I'll see you guys later. Good luck.'

I direct those last two words at Tom. He shoots me daggers.

Yes, the weight of my parents' impending surprise divorce is weighing heavy on my shoulders, but there are plenty of other things on those bad boys too. I need to get a few other things off my plate, before I can add this into the mix, and one of those things (and the easiest, if I'm being honest) is this date tonight.

Suddenly I'm not feeling all that romantic, or optimistic, but we move. Let's just hope I'm luckier in love than my parents, huh? Somehow I doubt it!

3

If there is one dating rule that I have always stuck by, it's that I would never, ever, *ever* under any circumstances be set up on a blind date. I believe my exact words would usually be something along the lines of: it would have to be a cold day in hell, before I would let someone set me up with a stranger.

Well, it turns out, it doesn't need to be a cold day in hell, just a chilly December evening in London. Let's just say that my love life has been pretty quiet lately, and by 'pretty quiet' I mean non-existent, and by lately I mean for a really, really long time. Sure, I've been on dates, but they never seem to go anywhere, and I don't really think it's me (not most of the time, at least), or the lucky, lucky men who get to date me, but things just never seem to click for either of us.

I've tried meeting people myself, but I don't quite have the confidence to essentially pick people up in the street, and I don't exactly give off the confident, approachable vibes that would make the men come to me, if I'm being honest. Oh, and of course I've tried the apps. I've tried them, uninstalled them, tried them again and uninstalled them again – and so on and so on.

Really, the only two things I haven't tried are going on blind dates and taking part in a reality TV dating show, and with the latter being so very far out of my comfort zone, I'm left with no choice other than to give being set up a go.

Still, I almost backed out, right at the last moment. I don't know what I was hoping for – perhaps to bump into Chris Hemsworth on the journey to see my parents, who would of course fall in love with me, at first sight, and he would somehow know about my blind date and he would tear off his shirt, and get down on his knees, and beg me to go out with him instead. Didn't see him, though, didn't even see anyone who looked like him, or looked at me, so here I am.

It's just a coincidence, that I'm living in a loveless world after learning of my parents' impending divorce (excuse me, pre-divorce), so perhaps I should just be thankful that I've got this date lined up this evening. A little bit of hope is exactly what I need right now, to try to take the edge off the bleakness.

Sometimes even I find it hard to believe that I'm a romance writer – seeing as though I can only conjure it up on the page, and not actually manifest any in my real life. You would think it might serve me well, to know the tricks of the trade, to have tried and tested things on the page, like I'm running scientific simulations. Sadly, I've always found the com to be more my strong suit. As for the rom, I don't know, I don't even feel like I'm doing a good job on the page at the moment. I know that I should just finish this draft, in the way that Jen wants me to, but for some reason I just can't make it happen. It's not writer's block necessarily, more that the creative side of my brain is protesting. It refuses to let me work on it. The second I try to work on my book, I freeze up. That's why I'm so keen to get Jen to read my other draft. God, I hope she likes it. Although it does need a lot more work, because a big chunk of it isn't actually written yet.

With less than a month to go until Christmas, I'm not sure what's easier, going on a good date or finishing writing my book? The latter, for sure. Not that it's easy, not at all, it's just I've seen evidence that I'm actually capable of that one.

I rushed back to my apartment after my parents dropped the bombshell on me, and got ready for my date in less time than I would have liked, but I figured it was better to turn up looking vaguely presentable, but on time, than to spend ages on my hair, make-up and outfit, only to make a bad impression by turning up late. So here I am, not looking my best, but on time, and there's no sign of the guy anyway.

And now I need a stress wee – fantastic. It's funny because when I'm at home, in my writing pit, I will drink and drink (mostly coffee, never enough water), and not move from the spot for hours, and not need the loo all day, but as soon as I have any sort of social obligation, my body fires off signals left, right and centre, so I'm off to the loo, I guess.

I'm in a bar called Charliez, one that I haven't been in before but it seems nice enough. Like all bars in December, it's super busy, with clusters of people pumped to the max with festive cheer, so at least I know we won't need to worry about awkward silences. It could still be awkward, obviously, but at least it won't be silent.

It's one of those places with a room full of individual toilets that can be used by anyone – good, because that means more toilets, so no crazy queue for the ladies' while fellas fly in and out of the gents', but bad because it significantly increases your chances of sitting on a seat covered in splashes.

I sit down and take my phone from my clutch to check my messages from my cousin Amy again. It's Amy who has set me up with her friend Ray – she pitched him to me as a fellow writer, someone I was bound to get along with. I don't think I know of any men called Ray who are under sixty. The name makes me think of my dad's former bestie (they fell out over a STIHL saw – something my dad *STIHL* goes on about, and no, I don't know what one is either, I think only Dad can tell his thousands of saws apart) who was called Ray – and then I suppose there's Ray Winston, Ray Charles and Ray... Mears? Best I can do. None of them make me think of a young bloke turning up (thirty is generally still categorised as young, right?) but Amy assures me that this Ray is my age, and that he'll be carrying a single red rose, so that I can spot him – something that feels impossibly corny, like the kind of thing I would write into a scene for a date that was doomed from the start.

I put my phone back in my bright pink clutch bag. I thought a bit of colour was necessary, after throwing on a white shirt and the tailored black trousers I found conveniently screwed up on my bedroom floor – because I was worried I looked a little bit like I was going to a wake. So I straightened my long blonde hair and I layered on the eye make-up behind my white thick-rimmed glasses in the hope it would jazz me up somehow.

Standing up, as I go to pull my trousers back up, I notice something in one of the legs. Is that...? Oh God, it's a pair of knickers, and a worn pair at that. I probably took them off with my trousers the last time I wore them and, like the catch that I am, left them there. I was going to say thank God I noticed in here, as though there was ever a likelihood of me taking my trousers off this evening anywhere apart from here in the loo or at home alone. Of course, I've no sooner pulled them out of my trousers (like a really shit, kind of kinky magician) when I've dropped them in the wet sink. Amazing, just fantastic, not stress-inducing at all. Obviously I've got no choice but to wring them out (thankfully they're not soaking wet) and stuff them in my clutch bag, because I can't exactly leave them in here, or flush them down the loo, and now that they're wet returning them from whence they came (my trouser leg) is off the table. Stunning. I'll probably forget I put them in there too and find them weeks later, when I've forgotten all about today (look at me writing this date off already) and least expect it.

As is typical of London, if you go deep enough into anywhere expensive enough, it can make you feel like you don't belong there, and that's exactly how I feel here in Charliez. Well, if you subscribe to that mentality, which I don't, but there's always that worry that you'll be forcibly removed by those who do. The dress code here appears to be: unaffordable. Everyone else is in their designer outfits – everywhere you look there's a Balenciaga B or a pair of Gucci Gs. Meanwhile I'm doing my best to make sure that the label isn't sticking out on my Zara shirt and that no one manages to eyeball my bag as something I picked up from Topshop a million years ago. Who am I kidding? I'll bet no one in here ever set foot in an original Topshop. What I've been telling myself is that I'm hoarding items – and I have been since I was a kid – so that I have a collection of clothing that will eventually be considered vintage which I can make a fortune from selling. And that's my excuse, for why I still sometimes sleep in one of those Miss Selfridge tie-dye love-heart T-shirts that were all the rage in the nineties, and I'm sticking with it.

Charliez is all about elegance with a hint of – how do I even describe this? – purposeful tackiness. It's supposed to be jarring, I guess, as you cast an eye around the room and try to make sense of the décor. The polished mahogany, the plush animal-print velvet, and the chandeliers that look like they belong in a ballroom but, for the purposes of the venue, have been refitted with disco lights. I know, it sounds awful, but somehow it works perfectly, shining down over the beautiful clientele and their overpriced cocktails. Oh, and with it being Christmas, the place is decked out for that. This is an old building, with super-high ceilings, so they've gone for the biggest tree they could get, over-loaded with the most decorations they could squeeze on there, resulting in something that would give the Rockefeller Center a run for its money. The bar is lined with tinsel – yes, tinsel, the old-school kind your gran brought out every year when you were a kid – and you can hardly take a few steps without finding yourself underneath a piece of mistletoe. It's coming down like snow, suspended in the air, putting a huge amount of pressure on the folks below – although people appear to be ignoring it for the most part.

Still no sign of my date. I push my way to the bar to order myself a drink, and smile as I glance over a Christmas-themed cocktail menu that offers drinks like a Sleigh My Name and Yule Only Live Once – bloody hell, at £32 a drink, yule only buy one once too. The young barman who serves me manages to do so in a way that barely acknowledges I'm even here. He looks so miser-able, in a way that I'm starting to think might be part of the job, because he practically makes my drink with contempt. There's no way a drink can taste good when it's thrown together with such little effort, and yet... wow, it's amazing. I want to say that it tastes £32 good, but maybe that's just another thing I'm telling myself to make myself feel better.

I see a man making his way through the crowd, a single red rose in his hand. Ah, this must be Ray. My date. Holding his soli-tary rose to let me know that it's him – something that sounded sort of romantic, on paper, but in real life looks sort of sad.

I know, you should never judge a book by its cover, but if it weren't for the rose, Ray seems like the kind of guy you could easily overlook in a crowd. He's got that sensible, slightly unkempt look that only a writer can truly pull off. His hair, a nondescript shade of brown, is messy, like he's just run his fingers through it while contemplating his next paragraph. He's wearing a jumper that could only be described as comfortable and jeans that are neither too tight nor too baggy.

I often wonder if I look like a writer. I mean, I'm sure I do when I'm actually writing, wearing what I like to call my 'house bra' (a big, squishy thing that does nothing for me or my boobs), an oversized T-shirt and my PJ bottoms, with my long blonde hair scraped up into a bun on the top of my head – to be untangled at a time when I have, well, time – and then there's my glasses. Tonight, though, I'm dolled up for my date, so the glasses are the only part of the writer ensemble that made it out of the house, for obvious reasons. I love over-the-top glasses. I figure, if I need them, I may as well rock them. They're as much a fashion accessory as my bag or my earrings as far as I'm concerned.

It's probably a good sign that Ray looks as out of place in here as I feel, because it makes me feel like we might have more in common than simply being writers.

I grab my drink (or what little is left of it) and hop down from my stool. I should let Ray know that I'm here, and I'm me, to save him from aimlessly wandering around the bar with a flower.

'Ray, hi, it's Amber,' I say brightly.

Ray snorts.

'When Amy said it was a blind date, you know it was the date she was referring to, and not me, right?' he replies. 'I know it's you. I can see.'

I'm instantly stopped in my tracks because I wasn't expecting him to say, well, anything apart from hello. Is he joking or...?

'Oh, er, sorry,' I apologise – because *of course* I apologise. I'm always fucking apologising, with no real idea why. I wish I could stop. 'I thought, with it being a blind date, and me only knowing you were you because of the flower, I didn't think that you would know that I was me... if that makes sense?'

'That barely makes sense,' he replies, narrowing his eyes at me. 'And *you're* a writer?'

He's either a total arsehole or going for some kind of 'treat 'em mean', extreme negging strategy. Or he could be joking, I suppose, but I don't really get it.

'Yep,' I say simply.

'Well, I've sorted us a table, and I've ordered us some food,' he announces. 'They do these sharing platters here – amazing – so, let's sit down, and order some more drinks, yeah?'

Okay, this is more like it. Perhaps his nerves were getting the better of him too, and he's settling down now.

'Okay, let's do it,' I reply. 'You should try one of these drinks. Honestly, they're so good.'

'Tell you what, why don't you ask the barman to send us over two more, and charge it to our table – table 13,' he suggests.

I smile before doing as instructed. I catch up with Ray at table 13 – unlucky for some, but hopefully lucky for me tonight. Oh, and I mean that in a good-fortune way, not a 'get lucky' way, I hasten to add.

'So,' I say, sitting down across from him.

'They're big glasses,' he points out, nodding towards my face.

I push them up my nose.

'Oh, yeah,' I say with a laugh. 'I like to make a statement with them, I guess.'

'They didn't look as in-your-face in your photo,' he tells me.

'They're more on-my-face,' I joke – then I realise what he just said. 'In my photo?'

'Yeah, I had Amy show me a photo of you, before I would agree to come,' he says. 'You never know who is going to turn out to be a bit of a moose.'

He smiles briefly, almost flirting with the idea that he might be joking, before snapping back to his straight face.

'Are they real glasses?' he asks.

'Yep,' I reply, reaching behind my ear to wiggle the arm on one side, making my glasses bounce on my nose.

'I mean, do you genuinely need them?' he clarifies.

'Only if I want to see,' I reply, trying to joke away the awkward vibes. 'I'm good, until about arm's length, and then things get blurry.'

'I wear contact lenses,' he tells me, and somehow it sounds like a suggestion.

'I gave them a go but I couldn't get on with them,' I confess. 'I could get them in okay, but I found getting them out at the end of the day a nightmare.'

'I find that glasses aren't always appropriate,' he points out.

'Oh?' is all I can think to say.

'Yeah, I mean, come on, are you planning on wearing them on your wedding day?' he replies.

'Steady on, buddy, it's only our first date,' I joke. 'But, hey, at least the frames are white.'

Ray pulls a face.

'Not that I'm asking, but it's good to know these things,' he explains. 'Dating in your thirties isn't easy, is it?'

I feel that.

'It's a bit like trying to do your present shopping on Christmas Eve,' he continues. 'All the good stuff is gone, so you just have to make do with whatever is left.'

I'm relieved when a waiter turns up with our drinks and our charcuterie board because, again, I cannot tell if Ray is joking or not, but he *must* be.

'Wow, this looks so good,' I tell him.

Ray takes a sip of his drink and pulls a bit of a face.

'The drink is... interesting,' he replies.

This is not going well at all, is it? Perhaps if I try something else.

'So, what do you write?' I ask him.

'Novels, like you,' he replies. 'Well, not exactly like you, obviously. I write historical fiction so it's a lot more involved than just coming up with the stories. It requires extensive research – trips to the library, to historic sites, to interview experts.'

'I love a research trip,' I reply.

'Yeah, but I'm talking real ones, not visiting a beach for "inspo", for wherever you're setting your latest roll around in the sand,' he replies. 'It's not that I don't do sex but, when I do, it's not for fun.'

I know that he's referring to sex in his books but, honestly, I wouldn't be surprised if that carried into real life too.

'I don't really write sex scenes,' I confess.

'I thought you wrote romance?' he asks, one eyebrow raised inquisitively.

'I do,' I reply.

'But... no sex? I thought that's what these books were all about?' he says, and I can tell from his tone that he means it.

'I mean, I think of myself as more of a comedy writer than a romance writer,' I tell him. 'It just so happens that my books have a strong romance arc, so marketing them as romcoms is the best way to go – well, that's what my publishers tell me.'

'Well, what do publishers know, hey?' he replies. 'Sex sells. You want to think about it. It's what women want these days.'

My jaw drops ever so slightly.

'I'm sorry – are you mansplaining women to me?' I ask. 'And my job? And... and...'

I notice Ray's eyebrows shoot up and, if I didn't know better, I would say he looked almost scared.

'I... I... I wasn't, I would never,' he insists. 'Is everything okay? You seem a little...'

Ray's voice trails off. Ah, shit, is this me? Am I just determined to have a bad date tonight? Perhaps I should be honest, show him that I'm a genuine person, I'm just having a bad day.

'I'm sorry,' I say with a sigh. 'I pretty much came here from my parents' house, where they sat me and my brother down and told us that they were getting a divorce, so my mind is all over the place. So, that might be why I seem a little... off.'

'I was going to say "intense",' he replies. 'But, wow, that's rough. Did they say why they were divorcing?'

'I guess they're just not happy together any more,' I reply with a sigh. 'I don't know, it all sounded so confusing.'

I take a big gulp of my drink. This is the last thing I wanted to get into but perhaps it will be good to talk about it?

'No wonder you don't think of yourself as a romance writer,' he points out. 'Between your parents, and your own love life, there's not much to feel inspired by, is there?'

I don't know if Ray is trying to insult me, or whether his speciality really is just saying the wrong thing at every opportunity, but I don't need this. To borrow Ray's analogy from him, it's not Christmas Eve yet, so I don't need to settle for 'whatever is left' tonight.

'I'm guessing the sex isn't there either then?' he continues.

Yep, that's my limit.

'Listen, sorry, but I need to go,' I tell him – apologising yet again.

'Oh?' he says, and he sounds surprised, which is hilarious. Does he think this is going well? 'But you've hardly touched the food – it was expensive.'

'I'm sure it was,' I reply. 'Let me give you some money for it.'

I'm on my feet now, hurriedly fussing with my clutch, so that I can give him some cash and then get out of here as fast as I can.

As I pull out my purse, my still kind of wet knickers fall out of my bag, landing on the table in front of him. For a second or two, Ray just stares at them.

'What, er...?'

I think he might finally be speechless.

I snatch them up, quickly stuffing them in my bag.

'Sorry, sorry, that's from... before you got here,' I blurt, not making any sense.

Ray's eyebrows shoot up.

'Oh,' he says, his voice so much higher than it has been so far.

Oh. Oh God. He thinks I mean something far, far different to what I actually mean. Ah well, he was implying I was sex-starved a moment ago, and I am, but I don't want to spend another second on this date so I may as well own it.

'Anyway, bye,' I tell him.

He doesn't even say goodbye.

Wow. I really, really didn't expect to show my date my knickers tonight, and yet here we are.

Bloody table 13. I couldn't have got more unlucky if I'd tried.

4

I thought I'd been on disastrous first dates before but it turns out I didn't know the meaning of the word. Well, a boring date here, an incompatible man there – none of it seems like a big deal now, not when you compare it to finding a dead body!

Jen looks up from her iPad. For a moment she just stares at me, almost like she's studying me.

I smile hopefully.

'What do you think?' I ask her.

I've been nervous about this meeting ever since Jen called me in for it. Well, when your editor says she wants you to come into the office to talk about your new book, panic sets in, and after talking to her on the phone it only made today going well seem all the more vital. That said, I had a very interesting conversation with myself on my way here (in my head, obviously) while I was on the Underground, where I eventually decided that, you know what, I believe in my other idea. I just need to let Jen read it and I'm sure she'll feel the same.

'A body?' she blurts, leaving no room for interpretation. 'That's a bit dark, isn't it?'

'Well, yes, but it's still a comedy,' I reply. 'And there's still a romance arc in there. I just thought it might be fun, to go down the crime route, and have some fun with that.'

'You had a very, very successful four-book series,' she reminds me. 'A romance series – why would you turn to a life of crime now?'

I purse my lips for a second, to resist cracking a joke.

'I just love fun murder mysteries,' I reply. 'And I think I have a great idea for a series. TV shows like *Monk*, movies like *Knives Out* – there's always been a market for it. So I'm thinking why not bring a little of that to the romcom market.'

'Look, Amber, I hear what you're saying, I do, but that's not what readers want,' Jen explains. 'They want exciting.'

'It does get more exciting,' I chip in, trying to find my confidence again. 'There are more bodies.'

'No, Amber, what I'm saying is that the kind of body counts you're talking about are not the kind people care about.'

Jen raises her eyebrows to let me know it's a sex thing. Oh, boy.

'Right,' I say simply.

'If you're wanting to be more, I don't know, adult, then I stand by what I said on the phone,' Jen says. 'Readers love the spice.'

'Oh, I don't know, I...'

'I'll tell you what,' Jen talks over me, her eyes darting back and forth between me and the glass wall behind me. 'I'm going to give you a book, one with lots of spice, and you're going to read it and then give it a go. Just, I'm sure this is great, but forget murder, add in some spice to your almost completed draft, and see where we are. Okay?'

I can't help but pull a face.

'But you've only glanced at it for a couple of minutes,' I point out.

'Sorry, we're just so busy today, it's not really a good time,' she tells me and now she's making no effort to hide the fact that she's looking beyond me.

'But you called me in,' I remind her.

Jen's eyes snap back to me and I see her realise that I'm right.

'Okay, yes, that makes sense,' she says. 'Why don't you come back after lunch? I'll have more time then.'

Suddenly it occurs to me that Jen is glammed up today. She's one of those thirty-somethings who exclusively wears trousers and a top, trousers and a top, trousers and a top. Sometimes it's nice jeans, sometimes it's a fancy blouse, but it's always trousers and a top. Not today though, today she's wearing a yellow dress, strappy red heels, and a face-full of make-up – the kind that says she's out to impress. Now that I think about it, everyone here today looks like they're dressed in their best. Well, everyone but me, in my black skinny jeans and my oversized black and red stripy jumper. I did take the time to curl my long blonde locks, and I always wear a face-full of make-up because I feel naked without it, but my chunky black boots can't compete with a strappy heel. I wonder if it's their staff Christmas party later or something.

'Erm, sure, okay, I can do that,' I reply as I pull myself to my feet. 'What, just come back in a couple of hours then?'

'Yeah, that would be perfect,' she replies. 'I'll have something for you by then.'

I'm not exactly sure what she means by that but I guess I'll go with the flow.

'Okay then, I'll be back,' I tell her as we leave the small glass-walled meeting room, but Jen is off. I notice her run over to one of the other editors.

'Is he here yet?' I can just about make out her ask giddily.

Ah, so it's like that, is it? Someone more exciting than me is coming in. Someone famous, I'll bet, because, honestly, it feels like they're publishing more celebrity-penned novels than 'regular' writer ones these days, and it's not that I mind it, and I get that for the publisher it's a no-brainer because these people come with a built-in audience, but so many of them are ghostwritten. And, again, I don't mind it, but the people writing these books are often author friends of mine who just didn't get the backing for books published under their own name. Sometimes I wonder if that's what the future holds for me. I don't exactly have the freedom to write what I want as it is. I would hate to write books to order for other people.

'Hey, Amber, just a second,' Jen calls after me as I reach the lift. 'Here, take these. Examples of spice done well. Give them a go, see if you think it's something you can do.'

'Okay, thanks,' I say, taking the three books she's holding out in front of me.

Alone in the lift I examine them. Obviously they're all authors who are with my publisher so one of them I know, one I've met and another I know of. I can give them a go, sure, but writing sex scenes isn't something that comes all that naturally to me, so I've always just sort of danced around it.

Well, if I've got some time to kill, I may as well grab some lunch. I need to figure out what I'm going to say to Jen, when I go back, so that I don't leave completely unhappy.

And I know just the person to ask.

5

'"His pounding member swells in my hand as I spit on..."'

'Words I *never* thought I would hear my brother say,' I talk over him, cutting him off.

Tom laughs.

'This is putting me off my panini,' he says, his lunch in one hand, a book in the other.

Tom and I are tucked away in the corner of a café near his work. It's the kind of place that seems to be used exclusively by businessmen and women, none of whom seem to stay longer than it takes them to grab a caffeine fix and a sandwich to take away. The service is frantic but efficient, like a well-oiled machine that goes at a million miles a minute. No one looks up from their phone, as they order their artisanal latte and quinoa salad, but no one expects them to. There's a constant hum of activity – baristas shouting out orders, the hiss of the espresso machine, and snippets of business jargon being barked around. Oh, and then there's me and Tom, sitting in the corner, reading the mucky bits in romance books while I dig into the avocado bagel that's going to stop me getting on the property ladder until I'm in my forties.

He's currently reading excerpts from *The Harder the Heart* by Kelsey Kane. I'm yet to meet Kelsey, she's a debut, but there's already talk about them making her horny professional golfer romance into a movie.

'I would've made more use of the balls,' he tells me.

I stare at him blankly.

'Like, the golf balls, ball puns – I thought you were the writer,' he jokes.

'Sorry,' I say with a laugh. 'I'm just... frazzled. The last thing I thought she was going to do was send me away with a pile of horny homework and expect me to flick through it over lunch.'

As soon as the words leave my lips, I realise what I've said.

'Don't,' I quickly insist.

'Oh my God. "He fills me with his—"'

'Fore!' I call out, stopping him in his tracks. 'I can probably guess.'

'Seems more like an eight, from what I'm reading,' Tom jokes. 'Eat your bagel. I'll do your homework for you.'

Tom is a corporate lawyer, and a good one at that, so I figured if there was anyone who could send me back into my meeting with Jen armed with a bunch of buzzwords to get me what I want, it would be him. He's also someone I can always count on to cheer me up, when I'm feeling down in the dumps.

He picks up another book. *Summer at Cove Bay* by L. E. Price.

'Well, for starters, before we even get to the mucky stuff, I'm pretty sure a cove is just a type of bay, so that's a silly name,' he points out. 'Still, let's give it a chance.'

Tom thumbs through the pages until he gets to the subject matter we're after.

'Wow, Chapter Three, we're going for it,' he tells me. 'Let's see. Oh... oh, oh, God.'

'Don't make it sound like you're joining in,' I joke.

'It's a solo scene,' he informs me. '"I wasn't expecting the new lifeguard to be so hot, but I need him, I need him to save me. My knees are weak, my heart is beating behind my big breasts. Just thinking about his rock-hard abs makes me flick my—"'

Tom pulls a face at the page.

I sigh and roll my eyes.

'That's not...'

'A man wrote that,' I tell him, reading his mind.

'Well, that makes sense,' he says. 'I assumed L. E. Price was a woman.'

'I think it's on purpose,' I reply. 'There was thriller writer, Dickie Woodrup.'

'That's never his real name,' Tom practically cackles.

'Well, Dickie Woodrup by name, Dickie Woodrup by nature,' I joke. 'It was sort of an open secret in publishing that he was kind of a sleaze – he grabbed my arse at the summer party a couple of years ago. Anyway, I guess one day he grabbed the wrong arse, people started sharing their stories about him, no one wanted to read his thrillers any more – and suddenly, as people were rereading them, it was becoming apparent exactly how creepy he really was – so that was that for Dickie. But you can't keep a bad man down, can you, so now the new open secret is that he's quietly writing romance novels to pay his bills.'

'Well, he's not very good,' Tom points out.

'Well, that rarely stops men who want to succeed,' I joke.

'And there's me thinking publishing was boring,' he says as he sips his coffee.

'No, no, we have our sex pests too,' I tell him. 'It keeps us on our toes.'

'I wanted to become a lawyer to counter blokes like him,' Tom says, his tone shifting from laughing at whatever was about to be flicked to something more serious.

'And yet all you seem to do is argue to make millionaires billionaires,' I tease him. 'But that's what I need from you, I need ruthless Tom, I need you to tell me what to say, to get what I want.'

'Okay, well, let's start by deciding what you do want,' he tells me, snapping into professional mode. 'I take it you don't want to write flicking and sucking and whatever a duck buster is?'

'I think you might have misread that last one but, no, that's not what I want to do,' I tell him. 'I want to write funny, twisty murder mysteries with romance arcs running through them.'

'Okay, so what you need to do is march back in there, keep your head high, and remind yourself that you're hot shit, you're the professional, you've been successful before and you'll be successful again because you know what you're doing. And then you sit your editor down and you tell her that you believe in your idea, that you'll do a good job, and that you would really appreciate it if she would read what you had written so far so that the two of you can find a way to make it work for both of you.'

God, that sounds good.

'But what if she still says no?' I ask, because obviously I'm already thinking about what I'll do when it all goes wrong, before it's even happened.

'Then you tell her, right, okay, then I think perhaps I need to take a step back, to take a break, and think about what I'm doing, and what I want to do moving forward,' he replies.

'Yeah?' I say, unsure I can pull that off.

'Yeah, make her sweat,' he says. 'You have more power than you realise. If she thinks you're backing off then she'll panic. She needs you to write this book too, you know?'

'I'm in contract, obviously, so I can't not do it,' I remind him.

'But what you're forgetting is that it's a contract that goes two ways,' he says. 'Do you think your editor can afford to humour you indefinitely? She has other authors to read the work of, meet, email with and so on. You don't make the publisher a penny until you give them a book they can sell. It doesn't make her look good, to be wasting time with an author who isn't being productive.'

'Okay, I see what you're saying,' I reply, draining the last of my latte. 'So, basically, if I make it seem like I'm going to be a pain in her arse, who isn't making the publisher any money, she'll try harder to meet me in the middle, to create something we can both be happy with?'

'That's the plan,' Tom replies. 'But, Amber, listen to me, you have to believe in yourself. I don't mean this in a corny way, it's business. Anything that can be interpreted as any kind of weakness puts people off, and it doesn't make them want to give you what you want. Go in there with confidence, and be clear about what you want, but at the same time try to say as few words as possible.'

'Wait, you want me to be confident, but quiet?' I check.

'People who are nervous, anxious, scared – things that aren't viewed as positive traits – tend to talk more,' he explains. 'They say too much, they show their hand, and that weakens their position. So say only what you have to, but mean it.'

I puff air from my cheeks.

'Wow, okay, I get what you mean, and I definitely do all of that stuff, so that's good to know,' I reply.

'I know you do,' he chuckles. 'That's why you never got away with anything as a kid. It's probably why you have a chronic apologising problem too.'

'Something which I am tempted to apologise for, but I'll start as I mean to go on,' I say with a smile. 'Okay, I'll let you get back to work, and I'll go kill a little more time before I head back in to see Jen, and I'm leaving with the kind of reply I want this time.'

My confidence builds as my sentence goes on – of course, it's easy, when it's just me and Tom.

'That's what I'm talking about,' Tom says, wrapping an arm

around me, giving me a reassuring squeeze. 'You can tell me all about it later, at Mum and Dad's.'

'They just had to tell us they were getting pre-divorced before Dad's birthday,' I say with a sigh.

'And before Christmas,' he adds. 'It's going to be so awkward. But, hey, at least we're in it together.'

'Yeah, there is that,' I reply with a smile.

'And if all else fails, bring your mucky books, and we'll get them reading pages,' he suggests. 'That ought to keep them quiet.'

I know that he's joking but that might work.

'Okay then, I'll see you later,' I reply. 'Thanks so much for your help.'

'Thanks for lunch,' he says.

'You paid for lunch,' I point out.

'But I would've eaten it over my desk if you hadn't called, so you've saved me a bit of indigestion.'

'Oh, okay, well, I guess we're even then,' I laugh. 'See you later.'

Tom heads out, back to his serious job, whereas I bundle my novels into my bag and wander aimlessly outside.

I'll saunter back towards my publisher – hopefully, the VIP is gone now, and my editor will have time to hear me out.

I just need to remember what Tom said and do my best. And I need to do it now, before I lose my nerve.

6

I stride back into the publisher's office with all the confidence of a catwalk model in sky-high stilettos – although, if I'm being honest, I'm probably more likely giving Bambi on the ice. But I'm doing it. My brother's pep talk is still ringing in my ears, like I'm listening to a motivational podcast, and it's driving me right now. Today is my day. Nothing can stop me now.

Except, apparently, the security guard.

He's the kind of bloke who looks like he moonlights as a bouncer – but probably for fun, rather than for the money – a towering figure with a buzz cut, a jawline you could (and I'm sure he does) sharpen knives on, and arms that strain the fabric of his black shirt. He's wearing an earpiece because I'm sure an office building (okay, fair enough, it's a big one, but still) needs a doorman. Great, just what I need right now.

'Erm, excuse me, stop right there, please. Who are you? Who are you here to see?' he asks, giving me a look that suggests I might be here to loot the place, rather than for a meeting with my editor.

'I'm an author, I'm here to see my editor, Jen Brooks,' I say, trying to maintain my composure – why do I always feel like I seem suspicious when anyone questions me? You should see me going through passport control. 'I was here earlier – only a couple of hours ago, actually. There was a different guy working. Jen told me to come back after lunch.'

'We don't have a guy called Jen,' he replies.

'No, there was a different guy working earlier, but it's my editor, Jen, who I'm here to see, again,' I try to explain, the more I say, the more suspicious of me he seems. Wow, Tom was right, less is more.

He narrows his eyes before practically patting me down with them. Bloody hell, he'd better not actually pat me down. I know it's been a minute since I had a man's hands on me but, as welcomings back to the physical world go, this wouldn't be it.

Hazel Tree Books, my publisher, is based in London, in the infamous Cactus building, and I get it, it is home to newspapers, magazines and even a TV studio, so it needs security, but do I really seem like a legitimate threat?

'We've got a high-profile client in today, so we're doing extra checks. There have been reports of females trying to sneak into the building,' he explains.

'Oh my gosh, not females,' I say with a sarcastic gasp, barely resisting the urge to roll my eyes.

'What's your name?' he asks, his suspicion deepening.

'Amber Page,' I reply, standing a little taller.

The security guard looks me up and down again, scepticism all over his face, like he's having some sort of visible reaction to my words.

'Is that a joke?' he asks.

'No,' I say, exasperated because I get that all the time. 'That's my real name.'

People always ask me if I decided that I wanted to be a writer because of my last name. I always reply that, no, it was because I wanted a job with no financial security. My jokes don't always land – and yet I crack them regardless.

He seems even more suspicious but picks up the phone and dials. As he waits for an answer, I can feel his eyes on me, like he's expecting me to do *something, anything*, any minute. My guy is ready, which I guess is what you want from a security guard, but while he's wasting his time with me, more threatening females could be scaling the building.

'Jen Brooks, please,' he says into the phone, glancing at me. 'I've got an Amber Page here. Says she's got a meeting with her, so I just need to check. Yes, I can wait.'

I wander over to the waiting area, trying not to let my encounter with Mr Jobsworth rattle me. I glance at the decorative shelves that flaunt books by some of their biggest authors. I scan the titles, feeling a pang of envy and a twinge of motivation with it. Obviously, there are none of my books here. In fact, there aren't really any romance novels here – unless you count that horny golf one.

As I find myself once again questioning how much of a market there is for golf-themed erotica, the security guard's voice snaps me from my thoughts.

'Okay, you can go up,' he says, waving me toward the lifts.

'Thanks,' I mutter – for nothing – as I head over.

I walk quickly and confidently, trying not to lose my new edge (because, let's be real, I suspect it might be temporary).

When I reach the lift, I'm the only one there, and thankfully it's already waiting on the ground floor so I step inside and press the button for Jen's floor.

As I wait for the doors to close, I turn around to check my make-up in the mirrored wall. My reflection looks back at me with slightly smudged eyeliner and lipstick that, thankfully, hasn't ventured into Joker territory – despite my best efforts over lunch, when I practically inhaled my bagel. I pop my glasses onto my head and use my index fingers to clean up my eyeliner a little. Well, if I go in there looking like I've been crying, it's not going to give off the confidence I'm trying to pretend I found at the bottom of my lunchtime coffee cup, is it?

Deciding that's the best I can do to sort it out, I move my glasses back to their usual home, only to feel a pair of hands snaking around my waist and a body pressing up against my back.

'Hey, beautiful,' a man's voice practically growls into my ear as he nuzzles into my neck. 'You came.'

I scream and quickly push the man away, but we're in a lift and the doors are closed now, so it's not like there's anywhere for me to run. My heart is pounding. I start frantically digging through my bag for something to use as a weapon, though I suspect it's probably just filled with rogue pairs of knickers, empty Kit Kat wrappers, and lip balms that have seen better days. I wonder which would serve me best in a fight. Probably the knickers; they certainly freaked Ray out.

As I glance up, I notice the man staring back at me, and the look on his face is as horrified as mine.

'I'm so sorry!' he exclaims, backing away with his hands raised, showing me that he isn't a threat. 'I thought you were someone else!'

Slightly relieved, but very annoyed, I narrow my eyes at him.

'Do you make a habit of accosting women in lifts? Because if you do, you'll fit right in with the men here.'

That's probably a joke that only I will get but, still, like I said, I don't let a little thing like that stop me from cracking them.

'Only if they're my girlfriend and they know I'm supposed to be here,' he says, still looking mortified. 'You just look exactly like her – from behind, at least. Same figure, same hair, same walk. It's quite freaky, actually.'

'Not as freaky as being humped in a lift when you're not expecting it,' I reply, giving him my best death stare.

He laughs and apologises again.

'I really am sorry. I didn't mean to scare you. It's just... you really do look just like her,' he continues. 'But you're right, I should've been more careful. Sorry – again.'

Ahh, apologising inside an apology – a man after my own heart.

'I was checking my make-up, so I didn't have my glasses on – I didn't even know there was anyone else in the lift with me,' I tell him.

'I was on my way out when I saw you from behind, mistook you for someone else, and thought you were here to see me, so I ran in after you,' he explains. 'It all happened in an instant.'

I huff, still irritated but starting to calm down.

'Well, next time, maybe wait until you see a girl's face before you start kissing her neck, yeah?' I suggest.

He nods vigorously. I kind of feel like he's stifling a smile. I guess it is funny, now that it's not scary.

'Absolutely. Lesson learned,' he assures me.

As we step out of the lift, I take a moment to look him up and down. He's tall – 6'2", maybe, so quite a bit taller than me (I'm 5'7") – and muscular, with broad shoulders that suggest he spends a lot of time at the gym, or attacking women in lifts. His blonde hair is artfully tousled, giving him that perfect balance of rugged but sophisticated. His chiselled jawline is the kind that makes you think of movie stars and superheroes, and his blue eyes are piercing, framed by lashes that are far too long and luscious for any human being, let alone a manly man. Why do men always get the best natural eyelashes?

All at once, it hits me where I recognise him from. I don't know him personally, but he's definitely a familiar face. He's Caleb

Carney, the guy from that reality dating show, *Welcome to Singledom*. Now he's a full-time influencer, his face plastered all over social media, with millions of adoring followers. Jeez, no wonder women were trying to break into the building; he's pretty much everyone's dream man. He's definitely having a moment in the public eye.

I try to act nonchalant as the realisation washes over me, but I can't help the faint blush creeping up my cheeks. Caleb Carney, in the flesh, and he just mistook me for his girlfriend, and he practically humped me in a lift. Well, that's one way to give a girl a confidence boost – so long as we ignore the part where he saw my face and freaked out, but that was probably more likely from the misunderstanding, rather than him just really hating girls who wear glasses. Then again, Ray did.

'So, what are you doing here?' I ask, trying to keep my voice casual.

'I'm writing a book,' he replies with a proud grin.

'Of course you are,' I mutter, because why wouldn't he be? He's gorgeous, famous, and now apparently an aspiring author. I suppose they let anyone have a stab at it these days, if they have enough followers.

'I just had a meeting with my editor, and my marketing team,' he adds.

Oh my God, he has his own marketing team? Sometimes I'm not even sure I get marketing.

'I have a meeting, so I've got to go,' I tell him as we hover outside the lift, because I can feel my confidence fading again. How am I supposed to compete with influencers?

'I was just leaving anyway,' he says, but there's a strange look in his eyes. It's not that he fancies me, because why would he, but it's definitely something. He gives me a cheeky smile and a wink as he steps back into the lift, letting the doors close, leaving me more flustered than I'd like to admit.

'Amber, there you are,' Jen calls out.

Oh, now she seems pleased to see me.

'Hello,' I say brightly.

'Did you take the stairs? You are bright red,' she blurts as she looks me in the eye.

'Oh, no, I'm fine, I just had a weird encounter with Caleb Carney in the lift,' I reply.

'Ah, say no more, he's got us all a bit like that today,' she replies. 'Isn't he a babe? He's doing a book for us, you know.'

'He mentioned that, briefly,' I reply. 'Like an autobiography, or…?'

'No, no, a novel,' she tells me. 'A series, actually. Think *Knives Out* meets *The Hangover* – it sounds like it's going to be a lot of fun.'

Is she serious right now?

'Right, come on, let's get sat down for that chat. Can I get you a coffee?' she asks.

Oh, now she's breaking out the hospitality.

'I'm fine, thanks, I had one with my lunch,' I tell her.

'Oh, how lovely,' she replies. 'Come on then, sit down.'

She leads me into one of the glass-walled meeting rooms – a different one to before – and smiles at me.

'So, have you had any thoughts since we spoke last?' she asks me. 'Did you read any of the books? Are you going to give it a go?'

'Some,' I tell her. 'They're great, they really are, it's just not really me. This new idea that I have, I really believe in it, I think I'd do a really good job with it, and there is definitely a hungry market for it right now. I promise you that, if you let me finish this, instead of the regular romcom I've been working on, you won't be disappointed with it. I can turn it around to our original deadline – before Christmas – and then we can still publish next year.'

I mean, it needs a lot more work than the romcom but trust me, when you're writing an idea you love, it just flows from your fingers. It's a pleasure to write and you find yourself doing it for fun, from morning until night, because you're loving the world you're creating and you don't want to leave.

'Hmm, okay, right,' she says as she takes in my words.

And now I just need to bring it home, to give her that ultimatum, to show her that I do have a say in this, and she can take it or leave it.

'Otherwise, I don't know, if you're not happy, and I'm not happy, then maybe something is just off here,' I say. 'I think what I need is some time – a break – to really stop and think about what we're doing here, and what we do next. I know that you have a bunch of authors, and you only want what's best for us, but this is my book and after all of the hard work I put into it, I want the finished product to be something I can be proud of. I want to write you a book that you love – but I want to love it too.'

'Amber, it's like you're reading my mind,' she says, all smiles.

Oh, thank God she's reacting this way, what a huge relief.

'Yeah?' I check, with a pathetic level of hopefulness.

'Absolutely,' she replies. 'I'm hearing what you're saying and there's a lot we agree on. We both see how important it is that you stick to the publishing schedule we agreed on, we both think that this book needs to be something we're both happy with, and we both think a break would do you the world of good.'

I almost smile until I overthink her words. It sounds like a threat, an impossibility, and a contradiction.

'Well, you're in luck, I have a surprise for you,' she begins, shifting to the edge of her seat. 'There is a ski resort, not too far from Chamonix in the French Alps, called La Coquelicot Blanche.'

'Say that again,' I ask quickly, because that was too fast and too French for me to take in.

'La Coquelicot Blanche,' she says again. 'Don't tell me you haven't heard of La Coquelicot Blanche?'

I mean, technically I've heard of it three times today.

'I'm not much of a skier,' I say with a shrug.

'Everyone has heard of La Coquelicot Blanche,' she insists. 'It's where all the celebs go. Anyway, it's like its own little village, almost, and they have a hotel, a spa, lodges and so on, and then they have this one old château in the grounds. It has been there forever, and a few of our authors hire it once a year, as a sort of pre-Christmas writers' retreat.'

'Sounds lovely,' I say politely.

'I'm glad you think so, because you're going,' she tells me.

'Huh?'

'You're going. There is a free space, it's all paid for – Dickie Woodrup was supposed to be going, but he's had to pull out, for personal reasons.' Jen pulls a don't-ask face. 'So the others kindly suggested I offered his place to someone else, seeing as though it's non-refundable. They're all romance writers, and you know them – Mandy Hess, Bette Hinton and Gina Knox – so not only will you fit right in but it will be the perfect environment for you to get this draft done. Just think, having the three of them on hand to mentor you, the advice they could give you. Gina especially writes a really steamy story.'

'It's Christmas in a couple of weeks,' I remind her.

'Exactly, your deadline is looming,' she points out.

'But it's so last-minute,' I add.

'Amber, you're always asking me to see if I can get you quotes, from the other authors,' she reminds me. 'And to get you into the networking events – and you once told me you would kill to get into one of these writers' retreat breaks.'

I'm always asking her to ask the other authors for quotes and they always say no – usually because they're too busy, but sometimes I suspect they're just too busy for me. This is also why I ask her to get me into networking events too, and to get me into the writers' retreats – not because I think writing would be any easier on what is essentially a holiday (surely it would be harder?) but because I know that what I really need in this industry is friends. What is it they say? Find your tribe? Well, I don't have one. Publishing is one hell of a cliquey industry, and I'm yet to find a group I fit into. Inside the groups you have a world of support, and authors give quotes for each other, and share each other's books on their social media. Then there's me, like a lost little lamb, struggling to make friends. It feels like school all over again, when we moved to a new town, and I suddenly found myself eating lunch alone. It's a lot less lonely than eating canapés, staring at an abstract artwork, trying to style out standing alone at your publisher's massive annual party. It's a seriously strange sensation, feeling alone, when you're in a room with so many people.

'Look, all of the plans are in place – I'll send you all the info – it's all booked, so you don't have a thing to worry about. So, go, take the time, and finish writing your romcom – your original idea, that is – in a way that we'll both love, and then you can have Christmas without work on your mind,' she says, adding extra emphasis to the words that are there to remind me to abandon my new idea.

'I'm not sure I fancy it,' I tell her honestly.

'I'm not sure you have much choice,' she replies. 'What's the alternative? Breach your contract? Pay back your advance? It all sounds so messy and unnecessary. Best to just take the free holiday, chat with the other authors, make peace with being a romance writer, and come back nice and refreshed, okay?'

I don't know what to say. Not least because I didn't actually receive an advance on my contract – but fun to know that other authors who are deemed more worthy still do.

'Okay?' she prompts me again, a little firmer this time, but it still comes with that dead-behind-the-eyes trademark smile of hers.

'Erm, yeah, okay,' I finally say.

God, I could really do without this, but I guess it's a free holiday, and I do need to write this book so, ahh, maybe it will inspire me, maybe the others will help me? This industry really is so cliquey and the big-name authors like Mandy, Bette and Gina are great examples of those who only seem to support each other. So, I suppose I would be crazy to turn an opportunity like this down, if it helps me network. Perhaps if I spend some time with them they will see that I'm one of them, and who knows, maybe we'll make friends?

'Okay, fab, well, you've got a couple of days to get ready, and you'll be back in time for Christmas,' she tells me. 'I'll buzz all the details to your inbox. But Amber, listen, I do need you to stick with your original draft, okay? And no sneaking any murders into this one.'

I sigh heavily. I'm not feeling it, at all, but it doesn't seem like I have much choice.

'Great,' I reply.

I must be the only person in history to feel down in the dumps about being given a holiday at a fancy resort. But I don't ski, I'm not close with the other writers – not like they are with each other – and, worst of all, I do not want to write this book.

But it seems like I don't have a choice so I guess France it is.

Super!

7

Tonight I feel like I'm at a wake – but a wake where the man of the moment isn't actually dead.

It's Dad's birthday, so we're gathered at the house. Everyone is in the lounge sitting around the coffee table. Apparently Dad went out with his friends earlier, so this is a family-only function. Thank God, because I'm not sure the house could handle much more rowdiness than this. Tom has a big armchair to himself so he's sitting with a beer in his hand, and his legs draped over the side of the chair, like he used to do when we were kids. Then, on the L-shaped sofa we have Mum, Dad, Auntie Kay and Amy, my cousin, the one who set me up with Ray. This is the first time I've seen her since and, unsurprisingly, I haven't brought her a thank you gift.

And then there's me, sitting on the floor, making the most of the underfloor heating, and watching while my dad opens his presents.

But, yeah, it definitely feels more like a wake than a celebration, and the thing that's dead is, of course, the concept of family functions that aren't awkward, thanks to my parents' pre-divorce status. Even the balloons look deflated, and the 'Happy Birthday' banner has been hung on a wonk, which makes me wonder if Mum might have done it on purpose, as a little sneaky 'fuck you', because that's about as controversial as Mum gets.

'Here's one from me,' I tell him, handing him a gift bag.

'Thanks, Amber,' he replies, his voice strained but trying to sound cheerful.

'You're welcome,' I reply.

It's nothing exciting, just stuff Mum told me he was after a while ago.

'Golf stuff,' he says, holding up a golf glove and some luminous green golf balls.

Tom practically sprays the sip of beer he just took across the room.

'Thomas,' Mum ticks him off.

'Sorry,' he says, wiping his mouth with the back of his hand. 'I was just thinking about a golf book I read earlier. Amber didn't give you a golf book, did she, Dad?'

I shoot Tom a look.

'No, give over,' Dad insists. 'I don't need a book to teach me how to do it.'

'I don't know, I learned a thing or two from this one,' Tom replies.

'So, come on, Amber, I'm dying to know,' Amy chimes in, attempting to lighten the mood. 'How did your date with Ray go?'

I pull a face.

'Kind of awful,' I say casually. 'I threw my knickers at him.'

Dad winces.

'I don't think I need to hear this,' he says, throwing up his hands.

'It's okay, you'll want to hear this one,' I reply. 'Before he arrived, I found a pair of worn knickers in my trouser leg. I must have left them in there the last time I wore the trousers. Anyway, I hid them in my bag, thinking they would be safe but the date wasn't going well so I reached into my bag, to get my purse to give him money for the bill, and I accidentally pulled them out and dropped them on the table in front of him.'

Tom bursts out laughing, nearly choking on his drink yet again.

'That's brilliant,' he blurts. 'Honestly, that might be my favourite story ever.'

Amy looks horrified but can't help giggling.

'So it wasn't very good otherwise?' she checks. 'Honestly, I really thought the two of you would have hit it off, with you both being writers.'

I shake my head.

'No, he was kind of hostile,' I tell her. 'And he made me feel like the last mouldy piece of fruit on the tree that no one wanted to pick.'

Mum, who's been rather quiet until now, stirs like she's about to say something.

'I'm sure that's not true, Amber,' she tells me, in her best mumsy reassuring tone.

'Oh, no, he couldn't have been clearer about it. He described dating in your thirties as being like Christmas shopping on Christmas Eve,' I say, still feeling the sting of his words. 'Having to settle for what's left.'

'Oh, Amber, I'm so sorry,' Amy insists. 'Ray is a friend of the guy I'm dating. I had no idea he was like that.'

'It's okay,' I say, shrugging it off. 'I'll put it in a book. Putting things in books is cheaper than therapy.'

It's nice to hear everyone laugh for a moment so I figure, if my own personal mortification is getting laughs, I may as well continue to act the clown. Anything to make this evening less awkward.

'You think that's bad, just wait until you hear what happened at my publisher's today,' I continue.

'I was wondering if you were going to tell us how it went,' Tom says curiously.

'Kind of shit,' I say candidly. 'But, before I even got back there, something strange happened. I met someone – someone you might know.'

'Okay, this sounds more like my kind of story,' Auntie Kay says. 'Who did you meet? A celebrity?'

'Yep,' I reply. 'But I didn't just bump into him – if anything he bumped into me.'

'Go on,' Kay says. 'I'm on the edge of my seat here. In fact, Jill, can you top my wine up, please? This sounds like it's going to be good.'

Mum grabs the bottle of white from the table and dutifully fills Auntie Kay's glass. Auntie Kay loves wine, you can never give her too much. She even collects 'wine o'clock' decorations, and proudly displays them all around her house. I think my personal favourite – and there are so many to choose from – is her 'wine, wine, wine' sign, in her dining room, with each word in a different font, like 'live, laugh, love'. Hilarious.

'Right, so, I got into the lift at my publisher's office, and this guy suddenly grabbed me from behind, held me close, and started trying to kiss my neck,' I begin.

'Again, I don't think I want to hear this,' Dad chimes in.

'Well, I do,' Auntie Kay says, as her eyes widen with excitement. 'Oh, my goodness! Tell me more!'

'I screamed – because of course I did, I'm not exactly used to men trying it on with me in public – and pushed him away,' I continue. 'But then he started freaking out too, apologising profusely, saying he thought I was his girlfriend. He said I looked exactly like her from behind.'

Tom snorts.

'Wait, some guy mistook you for his girlfriend? In a lift? Who is this guy, and does he have a death wish?' he jokes.

'He doesn't have a death wish,' I reply, grinning. 'He's Caleb Carney.'

Auntie Kay practically squeals.

'Caleb Carney? *The* Caleb Carney? Oh, I loved him on *Welcome to Singledom*! He's so hot!'

'The influencer?' Amy replies. 'You know, I follow him, and he has like three million followers.'

Tom looks at me in playful disbelief.

'I'm surprised someone like that is dating someone who looks like you,' he teases.

'Thanks, Tom,' I say dryly. 'Anyway, he was very apologetic once he realised I wasn't actually his girlfriend. It turns out he's there because he's writing a book for my publisher – but that's not public knowledge yet, so keep it to yourselves.'

Amy pulls out her phone, her fingers flying over the screen.

'Caleb Carney... He's dating Annabelle Harvey-Whitaker,' she tells us. 'She's one of those posh girls from that reality TV show about rich socialites in Kensington.'

She holds up her phone and shows everyone a photo of a stunning blonde with perfect make-up and a designer wardrobe. I see Annabelle and Caleb on social media all the time and quickly scroll past them because, honestly, their perfect-couple brand is enough to make a girl sick. Looking more closely, obviously we have different faces but I guess I do look like her, in a general way, just like... you know the story of the Prince and the Pauper? I'm like her pauper equivalent.

Mum takes Amy's phone for a moment and holds it out in front of her, squinting at the screen, looking at it in that way only mums seem to do.

'Amber looks nothing like this Annabelle,' she muses. 'Although I can see why he might have thought it was her, without seeing her face.'

'Hilarious,' Tom adds.

'It's a shame he's not single,' Mum adds with a sigh.

Oh, yeah, right, because if he were single he definitely would have tried it on with me in a lift. Absolutely. One hundred per cent.

'I agree,' Amy chimes in, staring at her phone again. 'Meeting in a lift is like the ultimate meet-cute. And you should know that, Amber, being a romcom writer.'

'That's a good point,' I reply, laughing and shaking my head. 'But sadly, real life is never like it is in romcoms. There are no perfect meet-cutes, just awkward encounters and misunderstandings, and all of them end with me single.'

'Is this why you want to ditch the rom, and focus on the com?' Tom asks. 'And why you want to throw murder into the mix? Are you going to go on a spree?'

'Don't tempt me,' I reply, shooting him a look.

'I'll get the nibbles,' Mum says, shaking her head.

'So, are you going to tell us what your editor said?' Tom asks.

'At least let me get some nibbles in me first,' I reply. 'And maybe some more wine.'

'You'll be lucky,' Auntie Kay jokes, draining the last drop from her glass.

'Here we go,' Mum says, placing the tray on the coffee table. 'Help yourselves.'

Wow, the food looks amazing. Mum has really gone all out. I'm not sure I would put so much effort into something for someone I was pre-divorcing. Then again, perhaps it's that immature mentality that's stopping me from meeting someone in the first place.

There are delicate smoked salmon blinis, beautifully decorated with sprigs of dill. Mini quiches, still warm, in a variety of flavours, each one so vivid in colour from the fillings. A selection of cheeses, arranged like a work of art, complete with grapes, figs and crackers – cheese is basically my dad's lifeblood, so his eyes light up when he notices them. That weird little curved knife, it isn't for cutting the cheese, it's so that my dad can stab anyone who tries to take any.

There are also some wooden skewers with mozzarella balls, cherry tomatoes, and basil leaves, drizzled with rich-looking balsamic glaze, a pile of sausage rolls (Tom's favourite), and a bowl of mixed olives.

'Wow, Mum, you've outdone yourself this time,' I say, reaching for a quiche.

'Oh, it's nothing,' she insists modestly. 'Just some snacky bits.'

Auntie Kay immediately grabs a blini, pops it in her mouth, and then proceeds to pour herself another glass of wine.

'These are divine, Jill,' she says to Mum. 'You always put on such a lovely spread. And the wine – ten out of ten. Johnny, you're a lu...'

Kay's voice trails off. I think she was about to tell my dad that he was a lucky man, before remembering that they're getting divorced, or pre-divorced, or *whatever*.

I'm yet to talk to my mum, one on one, about her and Dad's big announcement. Honestly, I'm hoping that she's just going to tell us that she doesn't mean it, that it's not really happening. But that's not happened yet so I guess I'll have to ask about it sooner or later, it's just difficult.

'Thanks,' Mum says simply, smiling.

Right, time for me to play the clown again, because we're in desperate need of a subject change. Anyway, I need to tell them about my trip to France, so they don't wonder why I'm disappearing between now and Christmas.

'Okay, so, my meeting with my editor,' I chime in. 'It didn't go great. Not only is she not willing to let me explore other genres but she's insisting I finish my first draft before Christmas, and not only that, but she's shipping me off to France to write it.'

'You're going to France?' Mum says, shocked.

'Yep,' I reply.

'But... but what about Christmas? It won't be right if you're not here,' she says, her voice wobbling.

'Don't worry, I'll be back for Christmas,' I insist.

'Yeah, we wouldn't want to make things weird at Christmas,' Tom quips.

'It's just there is a space on this writers' retreat, and I can have it for free, so I'm going to the Alps for a week,' I tell her. 'But it will be fine, I'll write my book, and then I can have Christmas off. It will be great.'

'You sound like you're protesting a little too much,' Dad says.

I turn to look at him, to see him eating an entire wedge of brie, like it's a slice of pizza.

'I mean, I'd rather not go,' I tell him. 'I'd rather stay home and write a murder mystery, but what can you do?'

'You've got a good job, don't blow it,' Dad insists through a mouthful of cheese. 'Mark McDonald's son is desperate to be published. He wrote a book, about these shagging aliens, and self-published it. Mark gave us all a copy. It was bloody awful.'

'See, even Mark McDonald's son is writing sexy stuff,' Tom jokes.

'Amber writes stories that make people smile,' Mum says proudly.

'It sounds like she wants to write stories that make them scared for their life,' Auntie Kay adds with a laugh.

'I still want to write comedy, and romance, just, you know, a romantic comedy with a murder here and there,' I tell them.

'Murder mysteries are all the rage at my book club,' Amy adds.

'Can you go to my publisher and tell my editor that, please?' I reply.

'I will, if I get touched up by Caleb Carney on the way in,' Auntie Kay adds.

Everyone needs a randy, wine-loving auntie. It sure does make the family parties more entertaining.

'That wine bottle is empty,' Kay points out, right on cue.

'I'll grab another,' Mum says.

'I'll help you,' I reply, pulling myself to my feet.

I follow Mum into the kitchen where she grabs me and gives me a big squeeze.

'Oh, Amber, thanks for coming tonight,' she says. 'Things are so uncomfortable here. You and your brother have really lightened the mood.'

'Hey, what do people have kids for?' I joke. 'Mum, are you okay? This news, it's a big shock, and it's not like you.'

'Let's not talk about it now,' she says, fighting back the tears. 'All I know is that something needs to change and this is all I can think of. But tonight is about celebrating your dad's birthday, so let's not ruin it.'

I smile and give her another squeeze. You can tell she still loves him but, if she isn't happy, I can't force them to stay together, can I? *Can I?*

'Okay then, let's get back out there,' I tell her. 'Auntie Kay will start rioting, if she doesn't get her Pinot Grigio.'

'Honestly, if she drinks any more I'm going to have to open an eighteen-year-old bottle of Lambrini your dad found in his shed,' she replies.

'She'll love it,' I joke. 'Especially if time has made it more potent.'

'Come on, let's join the others,' she says. 'Hurry home, won't you, darling? I just want us to spend Christmas together, and be happy, one last time.'

'Mum, we'll have plenty of Christmases together in the future, no matter what our circumstances are, so don't worry,' I reassure her. 'But I will hurry back – mostly because I don't really want to be there.'

'Well, I'm proud of you for going,' she tells me. 'And it really is a shame that Caleb isn't single. I saw him on Amy's phone – phwoar.'

I don't think I've ever heard my mum say phwoar before.

I hook my arm with my mum's as we head back to the lounge.

I just need to get to France, get my book finished, and get back here to my family.

Well, whatever is left of it.

8

Have you ever had a dream so vivid that when you wake up you briefly forget what's real and what isn't? Like, one minute you're trying to write your Academy Award acceptance speech with Ryan Gosling kissing your neck, and the next, you're face down on your pillow, drooling. That's me right now. I can't even remember what I was dreaming about last night, not really, but as I stir awake, the fog lifts and the reality of my life sets in. Shit. I'm going to France. Actual France, the country, tomorrow, with barely a couple of weeks to go until Christmas. If it were any other time, under any other circumstances, I'd be buzzing. I mean, who wouldn't want to jet off to France and sip champagne by the Seine (I know that's not what I'm doing, but I'm a writer, and that sounds better for the purposes of my rant)? But everything about this trip just feels wrong.

Still lying face down on my pillow, I fumble around on my bedside table, slapping it with the flat of my hand until I manage to grab my phone. I roll over and hold it up in front of my tired eyes, squinting at the screen. Unsurprisingly, there's the usual stack of notifications from various apps that I wake up to every morning. But when I check my emails (which, admittedly, is probably not the healthiest way to start the day, and yet I always do it), there's nothing from my editor about the trip. Supposedly, Jen was sending my flight and hotel information through, but nope, nothing, nada – I wish I knew the French word for 'nothing' so I could say that too. Oh, imagine if she's changed her mind! If she's had a rethink, or better yet, she's read my new manuscript and decided that yes, she does like it, and it does work, and I can save myself the stress of heading off on a trip when what I really want to be doing is getting into the festive spirit, and getting a head start on my 'season's eatings'. Any other time I would be jazzed to have this opportunity, but not at Christmastime, not when I have a book to write with a gun to my head.

I drag myself out of bed and fire up my coffee machine. Yes, I know that it's a cliché to say I'm powered by coffee, but I really am. I feel like my brain doesn't even start to function until I've had at least one cup, and I need at least two before I can do anything. I always turn on my coffee machine before I even turn on my laptop, it's that important to the process. My laptop, which is on my sofa, can wait a few more minutes.

I really like living in the city in my apartment but it's oh-so tiny. I rent a one-bed aimed at young professionals – although, hilariously, I feel like neither of those things. I live in Canary Wharf, which often makes people jump to the conclusion that I'm doing very well for myself and living in a swanky pad. The reality is, I'm not exactly in the heart of it (although I can see it from my window, and it's a stunning view), so it does feel more like I'm on the outside, looking in. Instead, I'm in the equivalent of the cheap seats, in a building with as many apartments squashed into it as possible.

The place is sleek and modern, all right angles and neutral tones, with big windows that let in lots of light, but my tiny kitchen seamlessly blends into a little living area. You know those small IKEA showrooms, where they have compact living spaces that showcase a bit of everything? I live in one of those. I don't even have any separation between the spaces because it's not even a real one-bed apartment; it's a glorified studio, except they've put the sleeping area around a corner, so at least it feels like it's in a different room.

It's a cosy nook pretending to be a bedroom, with barely enough space for my double bed and bedside tables, but I make it work. The living area (sarcastically) boasts a two-seater sofa bed that doubles as my guest bed (not that I have many guests) and a coffee table that's perpetually covered in a mess of books, notes, and the occasional forgotten mug of coffee (or two).

My brother, Tom, on the other hand, lives in the posh bit of the Wharf, in a genuinely swanky place, with a bedroom door and everything. Not only does he have an actual bedroom, but he has a walk-in wardrobe and an en-suite bathroom. His kitchen isn't an afterthought squeezed into the corner; it's a proper kitchen with an island and every appliance you can think of. I mean, if you needed any stronger sign that he's 'made it', the man has a built-in air fryer, for crying out loud. A girl can only dream.

That's where I aspire to be, but the reality of moving there isn't as close as it looks from my window.

Seeing the twinkling lights of the financial district and the shiny, sleek, luxurious buildings while I'm hanging out here in my (seriously) small corner of the world can be either inspiring or depressing, depending on my mood.

As I grab the milk from the fridge, I hear my apartment buzzer.

'Hello?' I say, my voice croaky, probably because it's the first time I've used it today.

'Morning, Miss Page. It's Paul from reception,' Paul – our building's concierge – says, his voice coming through the tinny speaker, sounding almost as crackly as my own. 'There are some flowers here for you.'

Flowers? For me? My heart skips a beat.

'I'll be right down,' I reply, trying to keep a lid on my excitement.

I throw on a tracksuit in record time, nearly tripping over my own feet in the process, and pull my hair into a messy bun (messy because I did it quickly, I don't mean the stylish kind). Flowers! I can't remember the last time someone sent me flowers. Actually, has anyone ever sent me flowers?

I race down to the lobby, my mind buzzing with possibilities. Maybe it's an apology bouquet from Ray? Maybe Amy had a word with him? Then again, even after only spending a short amount of time with him, I can tell you that he doesn't seem the type. Perhaps they're from a secret admirer? Imagine that! Although that seems even less likely, doesn't it?

As I step into the reception area, I see Paul standing there, holding the biggest bouquet of flowers I've ever seen. The arrangement is so enormous I can't even see Paul, just his legs poking out from behind an armful of summery flowers in every colour of the rainbow.

'Wow,' I blurt.

'Whoever he is, marry him,' Paul jokes, peeking around the edge of the bouquet.

I laugh, my cheeks flushing a little as I notice a few residents passing through the lobby giving me curious smiles. I'm not used to being the centre of attention – well, not for positive reasons, at least.

'Thanks, Paul,' I say, taking the flowers from him. They're surprisingly heavy, and I'm almost afraid I might drop them. 'These are beautiful.'

'Enjoy them,' he says with a smile.

I make my way to the lift, trying to suppress the grin spreading across my face.

Once inside my apartment (my flowers take up about 75 per cent of my free space) I set the enormous bouquet on my kitchen worktop, the vibrant flowers instantly brightening up the tiny space, but then I can't wait a second longer to tear open the tiny envelope, to see who they're from.

I rummage through the petals to find the card. My fingers finally grasp it, and I pull it out.

The card reads:

Cactus. Midday. Let's work together.

Oh, I could explode with tears of joy. Instead I let out a huge sigh of relief. These must be from Jen! She must have read my manuscript, realised it's great, and decided that I don't need to go to some silly writers' retreat in France. My heart does a happy little jig. My body soon follows. Finally, something good for once.

But then it occurs to me – midday is not that far away! I glance at the clock and see that I have less than half an hour to get ready, if I'm going to make it there on time. I'm still in my tracksuit, my hair is a mess, and if I smell nice at all then it's simply because the flowers rubbed off on me.

I dash to the shower with a spring in my step, my mind racing. This is it! Jen loves my book – thank fuck for that! Maybe I won't have to endure a lonely run-up to Christmas in France after all. As the warm water cascades over me, I smile to myself. It's not that I don't love writing romance, or comedy, it's just that this itch I have, to write a murder mystery, needs scratching. It's all I can think about. It's the only thing I can muster up any genuine creativity for.

Rinsing off quickly, I hop out of the shower and wrap myself in a towel. Keeping my hair dry means that I can let a cloud of dry shampoo work its magic – I did that yesterday, so here's hoping it works again.

I dart around my apartment, gathering clothes, and mentally planning what I'll say to Jen. I feel like everything is finally falling into place.

So long as I'm not late, of course.

9

I feel good. I probably don't look it, with my unwashed hair and my quickly thrown-together outfit, but better to be a bit scruffy than late, surely?

It's freezing out today, so I'm wearing a super-thick pair of black tights underneath my shirt dress, along with a thigh-high pair of black boots and my black coat with the faux-fur collar – something Tom hilariously (hilarious to him, at least) calls my Jon Snow coat.

My make-up is carrying me today. I've gone heavy on the eyes, heavy on the lips – something I often do when I'm overcompensating. Well, if you have either really good hair or really good make-up, they will pick up the slack.

The streets of London are festively frantic. It's taking all of my effort to navigate the pavement, dodging frantic shoppers as I hurry along to make my meeting on time. I often wonder why it is that everyone loses their marbles at Christmastime?

My mum is the worst for it and now, if these flowers from Jen really do mean I'm no longer being forced to France, then the only downside is that I'll have to help her with the

Christmas food shop, as promised. It's not that I don't want to help, it's just that Mum is as guilty as anyone when it comes to overdoing it. It's not like it used to be, when the shops would close, so you needed to make sure you were stocked up. These days they're only really closed on Christmas Day, so there's no need to panickingly stock up on absolutely everything. Mum is the kind of person who will buy things that no one eats the rest of the year. Things like nuts in their shells, bags and bags of oranges, and enough cheese to make at least twenty cheeseboards. But this is the special Christmas cheese, so no one is allowed to eat it until the main event (or the days that follow). Honestly, one year Dad broke into the cranberry Wensleydale to make a sandwich on 21 December, and I'm surprised Mum didn't divorce him then.

As I arrive at the Cactus, I notice the same security guard from yesterday. Great, just great. This could go either way. On one hand, he should recognise me and know I'm not a threat. On the other hand, he might hold a grudge and be more likely to give me a hard time.

Deciding to kill him with kindness, I flash him my friendliest smile – as though we're old friends, bumping into one another in the street – and walk up to him.

'Hello, you!' I start – perhaps I need to tone it down a bit. 'I'm back – again. Here to see Jen Brooks – again.'

Lord, I'm being so awkward. Even I'm suspicious of me.

He squints at me, clearly either trying to remember who I am or pretending he doesn't recognise me at all. Who could blame him either way?

After a moment, he picks up the phone and dials. He exchanges a few words with someone, in suspiciously hushed tones, before turning back to me.

'They say Jen isn't in today,' he announces with a hint of satisfaction, happy he gets to turn me away, smirking like he's just won a small battle.

'She must be,' I insist, my smile starting to strain. 'I have a meeting with her.'

'There's nothing I can do,' he says, already looking bored of me, clearly ready to move on to the next person whose day he can ruin.

'Can I maybe pop up and check?' I plead, my voice edging into desperation. 'I really do have a meeting with her – and she only invited me to it today, so it's not like she's forgotten already. It's only bloody midday.'

'No can do,' he says, crossing his arms and looking like he's enjoying this a little too much. His biceps twitch, almost like they're powering up, as though he's gearing up to forcibly remove me. I think he's just waiting for me to give him probable cause.

'Please,' I start to beg him, feeling utterly defeated, but sticking with a tone that doesn't incite violence.

'It's okay, she's with me,' a male voice interrupts us.

I turn around to see none other than Caleb Carney standing there, looking handsome and confident – and it works.

'Mr Carney, of course, I didn't realise she was with you,' the security guard babbles, practically falling over himself to open the security gate for us.

'No problem,' Caleb tells him. 'Have a great day.'

'Thanks,' I mutter, feeling my cheeks flush. Caleb is the last person I expected to be my knight in shining armour – well, in black jeans and a Valentino T-shirt, but you take my point.

'You're welcome,' Caleb says with a grin as we head for the lift. 'Can I buy you a drink?'

Yesterday he was feeling me up, and today he's offering to buy me a drink. What's next? I don't know what he's up to, but it's something, and it's weird.

'I'm okay, thanks,' I say plainly.

'Ah, come on,' he replies.

'Look, I don't know what your game is, but I didn't appreciate you touching me yesterday, I didn't need you to save me today, and I don't need you to buy me a drink, okay? You're not the main character here, not everything is about you, is it?'

I cringe – inwardly, so he can't see – at my out-of-character outburst. It reminds me of when I was in Year 6, at a school disco, and a boy that I really fancied asked me to dance with him, and in my panic, I told him to piss off... only for it to turn out that he was asking my friend, not me. I clearly have no idea how to act around seriously attractive men (or boys in my class who, looking back, were awful creatures).

Caleb just laughs at me, his eyes dancing with genuine amusement. I feel like there's a joke I'm not in on here.

'I know not everything is about me, but today it is,' he says, his grin widening. 'It was me who sent you the flowers, calling you in for a meeting. A meeting with me.'

I'm stunned into silence for a moment. It's him who wants to see me? Surely not.

'You sent me the flowers?' I check – not that it isn't totally fucking obvious, but I don't know what else to say.

'Yes,' he replies. 'Sorry if I wasn't clear when, er, I just said that I did.'

'How did you find out my address?' I ask, frowning.

'I asked around upstairs,' he explains. 'My editor asked your editor, I think.'

'Don't you think that's kind of creepy?' I clap back.

'Oh, absolutely,' he replies with a grin. 'And kind of sexy.'

I'm not sure about it. It's a GDPR nightmare, if it's anything.

'So, why did you send them?' I ask, cutting to the chase.

'To meet you,' he says simply. 'So, can I buy you that drink?'

I might be rushing to the point but Caleb is still taking a leisurely stroll.

'They have a really nice café here – I think it's only supposed to be for people who work in the building, but they let me use it,' he explains. 'Everyone here is working, so they tend to be professional, and leave me to my lunch in peace.'

'Erm, okay, yeah, why not,' I reply, bemused. I'd be lying if I said my curiosity wasn't getting the better of me. What on earth could Caleb Carney want with me?

Caleb and I step into the lift together. I can't believe I just said that. Caleb Carney, and me, getting into a lift, together. What the fuck?

'I promise I won't get handsy today,' he jokes, raising his hands in mock surrender.

'Thanks,' I reply dryly, trying to hide a smile.

It's not that I'm opposed to it, in concept, because I'm only human, but something strange is going on here.

The Cactus cafeteria is far from your average work canteen. It's more like an upmarket café with prices to match – bloody hell, imagine working somewhere like this. Even the pastries look like they have great pensions.

The pièce de résistance, though, has to be the gorgeous roof terrace attached, which must be like a dream in the summer. Unfortunately, it's too cold to venture out there today (although I am tempted), but through the big windows, I can see practically every notable landmark in London, from the Shard to the London Eye.

Caleb turns to me with that infuriatingly charming smile.

'What would you like to drink?' he asks.

'Coffee, please,' I say, trying to sound as nonchalant as possible. 'A caramel latte, if they do them, if not then just anything sweet.'

'Anything to eat?' he asks, eyeing the pastry counter.

I hesitate for a split second before saying, 'No, I'm good.'

He smiles knowingly.

'I'll bring something, just in case you fancy it,' he tells me. 'Back in a sec.'

I sit at a table, watching him as he goes to order our drinks. It's like watching a celebrity on the red carpet. Everyone in here is staring at him because everyone knows who he is, whether they watched *Welcome to Singledom* or not. The crowd parts around him as he strolls by, casually throwing charming smiles at the ladies and nods at the fellas, making sure that every single one of them feels seen and acknowledged by him. That's nice, I guess, because there is nothing worse than meeting a celebrity you like, only to find out they're a dick who doesn't care about their fans. It's cute, that he gives them that special encounter, one that they can go and tell their friends and family about. Cynically, I suppose it's good for business too.

At the counter, the female barista looks like she's about to faint, her eyes turning into love hearts as she practically drools into the cups. Yum!

Watching their body language, their movements, and their expressions, I can't help but imagine their dialogue:

'Oh my God, you're Caleb Carney!' she squeals.

'Guilty as charged,' Caleb replies with a wink – or something to that effect.

'This is on the house,' she insists – I can see that she's refusing to take his money.

Caleb thanks her, picking up the tray and carrying it over to our table.

Oh, now I'm really intrigued. What on earth could this man want with me?

He sets down my coffee and a selection of sweet treats.

'I wasn't sure what you'd like the most, so I got a few options,' he tells me. 'A brownie, a blueberry muffin, and a big cookie.'

My God, look at that big cookie – it's the size of a dinner plate and I want to take it down whole.

'Wow. How much did all this cost?' I ask, slowly moving the plate with the cookie in my direction. I'm curious what a selection like this would have set him back. Caleb smiles as he notices.

'Nothing – they gave it to me,' he says, shrugging like it's no big deal.

'Why would they do that?' I can't help but ask.

'Since I was on TV, this sort of thing just happens,' he explains casually.

I try to act unimpressed, but inside I'm seething with jealousy. Free cookies? Imagine.

'So, it was you who sent me the flowers?' I say, getting the conversation back on track.

'Yes, it was,' Caleb admits. 'We've definitely established that. Did you like them?'

'Obviously, I liked them. Anyone would,' I reply. 'They probably cost as much as my rent.'

'I'm glad,' he replies. 'That you like them. Not the rent thing.'

I pull a face at him, bemused.

'What's wrong?' he asks. 'Don't you like your cookie?'

'It's the best fucking cookie I've ever had in my life,' I reply instantly. 'I'm just wondering what's going on, why I'm here, what you want from me. Because right now this seems really weird.'

'Well, that's probably because it is weird,' Caleb admits. 'I have a job offer for you.'

I recall the card that came with the flowers:

Let's work together.

'You want me to work with you?' I ask. 'How on earth can I do that? Oh, God, don't tell me you want me to ghostwrite your book because no way, not a chance, I've got my own to write, thanks.'

'Oh, no, it's nothing like that,' Caleb replies quickly, and I'm slightly offended that he doesn't want me to be his ghostwriter – even though I don't want to do it anyway. 'Yesterday, when I grabbed you in the lift, I really did think you were my girlfriend – my ex-girlfriend, to be more specific,' he explains.

I blink at him, on the edge of my seat, waiting to hear more. Even my cookie has lost my attention briefly.

'Annabelle and I have broken up, but it isn't public knowledge yet,' he continues. 'She dumped me, seemingly out of nowhere, so it was a bit of a shock.'

I hate to admit it but, before I fell asleep last night, I had a look at Annabelle Harvey-Whitaker's Instagram, and there were no signs that she and Caleb had broken up, although she hasn't posted anything about him recently.

'I told Annabelle that I would be here yesterday, and I asked her to meet me – to resolve our unfinished business – so when I saw you in the lift I just assumed that you were here, that she had turned up, and that she wanted to get back together. It's so strange, how alike the two of you look. Your figure, your body language – even your hands are the same.'

Caleb takes my hand in his, examining it, holding it like a specimen as he marvels at the fact I'm apparently his ex-girlfriend's hand twin. I never thought a man would only want me for my body but, if he did, this is definitely not what I had in mind. I can't help but glance around, feeling a few pairs of eyes on us.

'Facially you look nothing like her, though,' he's quick to add. 'You definitely have your own face.'

I frown. Annabelle is absolutely stunning so, if I were in that sort of mood, I could definitely interpret that as a reminder that I'm not as attractive. Maybe I'm reaching, though.

'Okay, I get it, I don't actually look anything like her,' I say, taking my hand back. But then I soften because it's not nice when a relationship comes to an end. 'I'm sorry to hear that you broke up.'

'I'm sorry too,' he replies. 'Because it's going to cost me a fortune.'

'Eh?' I blurt, confused.

'I make most of my money from brand collaborations – we both do – and I have all these products that I need to post on my socials, so the plan was that the two of us would go on a trip, take a bunch of photos, and then the money would come rolling in,' he explains. 'The plan was to take all of the products on a romantic trip away, because it's the two of us as an "it" couple or whatever that makes us more valuable to brands. I don't get paid until I post the content they want, and I can't post the content they want without Annabelle,' he explains.

'You can't take them without her?' I reply.

'A lot of them are for couples, or just for women,' he tells me. 'So, I can't do it without her, or without someone who looks just like her, so I was thinking, why don't you come with me?'

I fall about laughing – but then I quickly realise that he isn't joking.

'Is this like a *Pretty Woman* kind of deal?' I blurt.

'No, no, nothing like that,' he quickly insists. 'I'm thinking because you look like Annabelle, from the right angles, that you could come with me, and be strategically placed in the photos, and that way I can get paid – and I would pay you, of course, fifty-fifty.'

'You want to pay me half of what you're getting just to be a prop in your photos?' I ask, raising an eyebrow. 'How much are we talking?'

'*Thousands*,' he admits, widening his eyes for effect. 'Plus, you get a free holiday – anywhere you want, really. Annabelle booked the place we were headed, so I need to arrange somewhere.'

'But if it's supposed to be you and Annabelle in the photos, you can't just have someone pretend to be her, surely she'll expect the money?' I point out.

'I won't get into it, about how we have different managers, and accountants, and the tax reasons behind it, but basically we make deals individually, and separately,' he explains. 'Some are mine, some are hers, but my contracts are mine alone, and they don't specify that it has to be Annabelle in the photos, it's just assumed it will be, as she's my girlfriend. I can have any girl I want, in the photos, but with our break-up not being public knowledge yet, and me needing to get these photos online ASAP, it wouldn't look good, to have some new, random girl with me, it would look like I was cheating, or moving on too quickly, and brands don't want associating with that.'

I guess that makes sense, as bleak as it is.

'This is the money I live on, and it's thousands, Amber, and I can't afford to lose it, not until my author career takes off,' he explains. 'Do you think I would ask you, if I wasn't desperate?'

Hopefully he doesn't mean that the way it sounds. But I see where he's coming from, he hasn't just lost his relationship, he's lost his income, and when you look at it like that, who wouldn't approach a random girl who could be the answer to all of their problems?

I'm tempted, for a moment, but then I remember that with the flowers being from Caleb and not Jen, it means I'm still going to France.

'I'd love to,' I say, which isn't strictly true, but I'm letting him down anyway. 'But I've already got a free holiday lined up. I'm going tomorrow.'

'Where to?' he asks, looking genuinely interested.

'A ski resort in France,' I say. 'La Coq... Coq... Coq...'

Lord have mercy, why can't I stop stuttering the word cock at this man?

'La Coquelicot Blanche?' Caleb says, letting me off the hook. 'That place is super exclusive. I've been invited before, but I've never been. Do you know how impossible it is to book in there? It books up so far in advance, it takes money, and influence – anyway, that would be a great place to do it, so I could meet you there?'

'You could meet me there?' I reply plainly. After everything he just said? Is he serious? 'I'm staying in a château, in the grounds, with some other authors.'

'I could create my content there, for sure,' he says, as though that answers my question.

Wow, he really is desperate.

'Yeah, sure, I'll just meet you there,' I say sarcastically.

If it's impossible to get in, he won't meet me there at this short notice, will he?

Before Caleb can reply, my phone starts ringing. It's Jen, my editor. I hold up a finger to Caleb, mouthing: 'I need to take this.'

'Of course,' he says, leaning back in his chair. 'I'll eat this muffin while you're gone.'

I answer the call as I wander towards the exit.

'Hey, Jen!' I say brightly.

'Amber! Someone at the office mentioned you turned up to see me,' Jen says. 'I'm not in today.'

I scramble for a believable excuse.

'Oh, yes, I was just checking the details about the France trip,' I lie. 'You said you were going to send things through...'

'Great to see you're so keen!' Jen chirps. 'Everything you need for the trip has been emailed to you – it should be in your inbox now. Just bring your passport, your laptop, and pack your bag.'

'Great,' I say, trying to sound enthusiastic. It feels far from great, though. I force a smile, even though she can't see me. 'Thanks, Jen. I'm looking forward to it.'

'And I'm looking forward to hearing all about it! Safe travels, Amber,' she says before hanging up.

I stand there for a moment, my phone still pressed to my ear, processing what this means. When I turn back to look at Caleb, he's surrounded by a group of women, because of course he is. They're giggling and fluttering around him like moths around the big light.

Ohhh, suddenly it makes sense, the *real* reason he's brought me up here for a drink, and not taken me to a nearby bar or café – he doesn't want to be seen with me. If he was, and we were photographed together, then it would be instantly obvious that I wasn't Annabelle, as soon as someone saw my face. That must be why he wants me to go away to take photos with him too – somewhere he's less likely to be chased by paparazzi, so that he could keep my identity a secret.

Imagine if I could accept his offer – getting paid thousands of pounds just to hold a bottle here, wear a necklace there, or whatever it is influencers flog. It sounds like a dream. But dreams don't pay the bills forever, do they? Whatever I would make from this one-time secret influencer gig wouldn't last a lifetime, and it certainly wouldn't help build the career I've worked so hard on for years. I can't give up on it now. I have to go to France, and I have to make something work that Jen will accept. And, whether I can live with it, well, that would be nice, but it might not be possible.

I take a deep breath and decide not to return to Caleb. He looks busy anyway, and I have a bag to pack. Me? Avoiding an awkward conversation? Oh, you bet. Well, I'm not exactly used to rejecting men (in any format) so I can't imagine I'm all that good at it.

As I walk away, I can't help but feel a pang of regret. It would have been nice to live like an influencer, even it was just for a holiday, but I need to think about my future, and how I can make sure it's a good one.

I'm sure future Amber will thank me later.

10

I'm in my apartment, in my bedroom nook, and it looks like there has been a small explosion in my wardrobe, because it's currently empty and every item of clothing that I own is *everywhere*. Jumpers are draped over the chair, jeans are strewn across the bed, and I don't know how I managed to tangle so many bras together but I'm the proud owner of a ball of them apparently. It looks like I'm preparing for an Arctic expedition, but in reality, I'm trying to pack for a forced trip to a ski resort in France. Oh, and when I say it looks like I'm preparing for an Arctic expedition, make no mistake about it, I mean because I'm taking so much stuff, not that I'm remotely prepared for winter.

I have my Jon Snow coat, which is warm, but the fur isn't really practical. My Ugg boots, which keep my feet toasty and are fashionable, but aren't really for doing anything physical in. And I've packed various pairs of jeans and big jumpers, but I'm realising that I'm not exactly equipped for actual winter weather. I have cosy clothes, sure, but practical winter gear? Nope. I mean, I've got enough fluffy socks to open a shop, but no thermal layers. No waterproof gloves. Nothing that would hold up in a blizzard. I suppose I could always stuff my clothes with socks, to try to keep warm, because that will work. Not.

'This is ridiculous,' I mutter to myself, tossing another pair of socks into my suitcase.

The rest of my clothes are going to stay exactly where they are until I get back. I'll just sleep on top of them tonight, if I have to. Tidying up can wait. It's not like I'm going to have visitors before I go, while I'm away, or when I get back, is it?

Future Amber won't thank me for it, she'll be annoyed, but Amber right now can't be arsed. It was hard enough dragging it all out.

My phone rings, and it's a FaceTime call from Tom, so I grab my laptop to answer it on there, rather than balance my phone against a pile of clothes – not that I don't have enough piles on offer to do it.

'Hey, sis,' he greets me, his face filling the screen. 'Are you all ready for your trip?'

'Oh, who wouldn't enjoy being forced to fly to France right before Christmas to write a book they don't want to write, staying with people who don't really like them?' I reply sarcastically, folding a scarf and shoving it into the corner of my suitcase.

'You're not flying to France, Amber. You're flying to Switzerland,' Tom points out.

I roll my eyes at him, staring into the camera above my laptop screen.

'You know what I mean,' I reply. 'Anyway, you said you'd call me to tell me all about ski resorts, not to be a sarcastic arse. Come on, what am I getting myself into?'

Obviously I've looked up photos of the resort – and it does look beautiful – but I need the lowdown on these sorts of places from someone who has been (even if said person has only been a couple of times).

Tom leans back, thinking.

'I actually think you'll really like the place,' he tells me. 'Ski resorts are like these cute little villages, tucked away in the mountains, with cosy wooden chalets, snow-covered roofs, fairy lights everywhere, hot chocolate, plenty of alcohol – sort of like a Christmas card.'

'I mean, plenty of alcohol just sounds like Christmas,' I joke. 'Tell me about skiing, because seeing as though you've been twice – and that's two more times than I have – you're technically the family expert.'

'There are different slopes, ranging from beginner to expert,' he explains. 'Green slopes are for people who've never seen snow before, blue is for intermediates, red is for advanced skiers, and black is for the people who think they're invincible.'

'So I should stick to...?'

'The lodge,' Tom says with a laugh. 'I don't think skiing is going to be your cup of tea. But besides the slopes, there are the ski lifts and gondolas that take you up the mountain. They can be a bit intimidating if you're not used to dangling from a cable high above the ground, but that could be how you thrill-seek. Better still, and definitely more your cup of tea, there's the après-ski scene. It's basically what everyone does after skiing. Sitting by the fire, live music, people drinking and laughing, and lots of socialising. Some places even have night skiing, where the slopes are lit up and you can ski under the stars. But don't do that either. Absolutely no skiing at all, promise me?'

'Why not?' I ask, genuinely curious.

'Because,' Tom says with a smirk, 'you're not exactly known for your coordination. You're the queen of hurting yourself on thin air.'

'Name three occasions,' I challenge him, half-smiling.

Tom takes a theatrical deep breath.

'You closed the fridge on your hand, kicked your own shoe, and fell up the stairs running to the bathroom – and all of these happened last night, at Mum and Dad's,' he reminds me.

Yep, he's got me there.

I laugh, shaking my head.

'Fine, point taken. Maybe I'll just stick to the lodge and the hot chocolate,' I give in.

'It's for the best,' Tom agrees. 'But seriously, Amber, even without the skiing, it's going to be great. Just soak in the atmosphere, relax, and maybe take some inspiration for your book.'

'I'll try,' I promise. 'Speaking of our parents, how are things?'

Tom's smile fades a bit.

'How can you leave me to deal with their post-pre-divorce announcement fallout on my own?' he replies, half-joking, I'm sure.

'Oh, I would love to be there if I could,' I joke.

'I was there for dinner earlier, and it's not great,' Tom admits, serious for a moment. 'They're sniping at each other, finding fault in everything the other person does. I actually get why they're divorcing, if this is what it's like. I couldn't live like that.'

'It's sad, accepting it,' I reply. 'You think your parents will be together forever. Do you think they're serious?'

'I seriously think they will kill each other if they stay together much longer,' Tom claps back.

'I still think something must have happened,' I muse. 'They were ticking along just fine before. I'm not giving up hope yet.'

'Easy for you to say when you're pissing off to France to write porn,' Tom retorts with a grin.

I laugh.

'I'll be back as soon as I can, and we'll get through Christmas together,' I reassure him.

'Jokes aside, try to get your work done, and try to enjoy your-self,' Tom says, his tone softening. 'And keep in touch. But if you need more books reading for inspiration, ask someone else.'

I laugh again.

'Will do. See you soon, Tom.'

'Fly safe,' he replies.

With my case finally packed, I flop into bed, to try to get some sleep so I'm not totally knackered when I get up in the morning. Tomorrow, I'm heading to France. Well, Switzerland first – I'm flying to Geneva – but then I'm heading to France, to the resort.

Lying in my bed, I can't help but think about how ridiculous this whole situation is. I'm being shipped off to a ski resort to write a book I have zero interest in, surrounded by people who I'm sure would rather I wasn't there with them, despite what Jen says.

And as though everything isn't messy enough, I can't believe I'm saying this, but Caleb has got under my skin. I can't seem to stop thinking about him – well, about his offer, more specifically. I googled it earlier and people with his level of followers can get tens of thousands of pounds per post, depending on what it's for. Sure, I wouldn't have made enough to retire on, but it could have paid my bills while I figured this book out. Then again, in publishing it's all about momentum, and if I took time off then not only would I have probably never got back into it, but my readers would have forgotten all about me while I was taking my extended break.

Turning him down was the right thing to do – I think – not that I formally turned him down, more that I just ran away. I do feel sorry for him, though, and perhaps I would have helped him out, if I didn't have to put myself first.

Nothing is ever easy, is it? Nothing can ever just be straight-forward.

I close my eyes and try to shut off my brain. Sleep is something that has never really come easy to me. My mum always used to say that it was my creative brain, struggling to shut off. That's a nice thought. Perhaps that's why I relive arguments I had years ago, editing them as I go, thinking about how they could have gone better, or imagining future scenarios, and what I could do, what I could say – knowing full well I'll never do what I 'plan' though. I'm all ideas and no action, not in real life anyway.

Okay, time to get this over with. I just need to get to sleep, and then get tomorrow over with, and then sleep again, and then just do that a few more times until eventually it's time to come home for Christmas. When you look at it like that, it's not so bad.

Somehow I don't think it will go all that quickly, though, do you?

11

I don't know if this is just a sign of me getting older, or if I've always felt this way, but the thought of a day of travelling always fills me with dread, and today, when I woke up, I felt no different.

I have so much respect for people who want to – and do – see the world, because simply thinking about the logistics of it makes me feel stressed and exhausted.

Looking at my itinerary for today, even though I wasn't set to be travelling all that far in the grand scheme of things, I still couldn't muster up the enthusiasm for it. Catching trains, planes, and then a leg in an automobile (well, technically a bus) all take time, and that time adds up when you throw in the waiting around in between.

However, it has flown by so far – no pun intended – because I have a new addiction.

I'm currently on the plane, squished into a seat that feels like it was designed for a small child rather than a grown adult. It's not a long flight, just under two hours, but it's given me more time to spend with my new guilty pleasure: watching *Welcome to Singledom* – specifically, the series Caleb was a contestant on.

Honestly, I feel like I'm living my best life right now, watching the show, drinking cheap plane wine – and you know it's cheap when even I can identify it as being so. It doesn't taste like it came from France, and given that I'm heading there I would say I'm looking forward to better drinks, but I'm actually enjoying this. It's the perfect pairing for my new favourite TV show.

I'd never watched *Welcome to Singledom* before, so I had no idea what to expect. My hopes weren't high, though. Reality TV isn't exactly known for its high-brow content, and I wouldn't call myself a high-brow customer, but for some reason it's never appealed to me. Honestly, I've been missing out though, because it's so good, and so addictive. Of course, I'm enjoying it more than most, seeing as I know someone on it – if you can count two encounters with Caleb as knowing him – but I'm absolutely fascinated.

The show is like a cross between *Love Island*, *I'm a Celebrity... Get Me Out of Here!*, and *Married at First Sight* – with just a dash of *Naked and Afraid* thrown in for good measure. Sexy singles all live together in a made-for-TV compound on an alleged desert island for eight weeks – if they stay from the start until the end, because people are voted out a few times a week, and new people are dropped in now and then. The sexy singles have to couple up with an 'island partner' and then work together to survive. It's not as wild as it sounds; they have luxury areas they can stay in by completing challenges, while others have to fend for themselves on the beach. But even then, sleeping under the stars looks lovely, and romantic, even if the man they're cuddled up with turns out to be a total dog (so many of them are on this show, but the women can be just as bad, I'm finding out). The twist is that the couples are subject to change, with contestants able to choose new partners if they want to, or steal partners from other people, so the couples are constantly changing, with people scrapping over the 'island hotties' – the man and woman voted to be most popular.

So, I put on the first episode, just to see what it was like, just to see Caleb in action, and I haven't been able to turn it off since. Caleb is undeniably the star of the series. In the first episode, the boys all wait on the beach, and the girls turn up one at a time in speedboats, because of course they do, and choose the boy they want to be their island partner. Naturally, the first girl chose Caleb, but then the second girl turned up and stole him, then the third did the same – this happened six times. Before the show had even properly started, Caleb had been in a couple with every single girl on the island.

It seems like most of the contestants were small-scale influencers before they went on the show (they've all got huge followings now), with jobs like model and footballer appearing to be the most popular among island residents. But Caleb seemed to be one of the few normal people there – to the point where the other boys were kind of snobbish, putting down the fact that he had a regular job – although no one mentioned what it was. But as the show started, and the couples had to build shelters for their first night together, it quickly became clear that Caleb was the only one who had any sort of skills. He had a shelter and a fire knocked up in no time – that, coupled with the fact that he's smoking hot and charming, meant that all the girls fell even harder for him. As the series has continued, it's becoming clear that the prize money doesn't seem as important as the real prize: Caleb. The girls are practically tearing each other's hair out to get him, the boys are all so jealous of him – and no one can understand why he has so many useful survival skills, and he's not telling anyone, so the speculation is wild. One of the girls thinks he must be friends with Bear Grylls, a few of the boys reckon he's ex-SAS, but no one knows for sure.

And, of course, all the while Caleb takes it all in his stride. He's so charming to everyone, such an everyman, boy-next-door type – which only makes everyone want him more.

The island looks beautiful, with pristine white beaches and crystal-clear waters, and every single contestant is just as stunning and flawless too. I wonder if you have to be a ten out of ten to take part, or if only truly beautiful people have the confidence to do it. There's no way I could take part, if only because everyone wears swimwear the entire time, and I'd be worried about my bikini falling off, never mind trying to get one of the island studs to choose me over any of the other girls.

There's no one taking part in glasses, I can tell you that. Imagine if you took the best features from a selection of people and used them to make one perfect person – everyone on this show is one of those people, and Caleb has to be the ultimate Frankenstein's influencer, because he's got it all. Pumped but chiselled muscles, flawless white teeth, dimpled cheeks, great hair, clear skin. He has no distinct accent, no controversial views, his presence creates drama on the show but he isn't causing it. He really is the dream contestant.

The seat-belt light comes on, signalling that we're landing soon – ah, yes, real life, I forgot about that, so I have to stop watching, but I'll definitely be binge-watching more later. I'm excited to see what happens next. It will be something to do when I'm hiding in my room, putting off writing my book, and when I think about it like that, it doesn't sound like it's going to be much different from being at home, really.

I throw back the last of my wine and pack away my iPad as the plane descends.

Now it's time for my adventure to begin – and there's no way it's going to be as exciting as *Welcome to Singledom*.

12

After two butt-numbing hours on a bus that did not smell great at all, and a few more episodes of *Welcome to Singledom* to keep me sane, I have finally arrived at the resort. It's only afternoon still but I'm exhausted from getting up early, and travelling is just so draining. I'm doing okay, though, just knackered, and my bum feels like it's fused to the bus seat.

As for Caleb (well, TV Caleb, from the past) he's currently coupled up with Sunshine Greene – who has just been voted island hottie. All the guys are consumed with the self-imposed task of seeing who can steal her from Caleb, and are starting to turn on each other to get what they want. Naturally the other girls are fuming that Sunshine Greene is getting all of the attention now. Yep, I'm talking about *the* Sunshine Greene, who has only gone from strength to strength since the show finished. If I remember right, she's getting married next year, but not to someone she met on the show. As far as I can tell from googling on the bus (thank you, free Wi-Fi), no couple from *Welcome to Singledom* has ever stayed together for long after the show ended. Cynically, some people think the contestants just use the show as a vehicle to fame, rather than to find true love. Honestly, what has the world come to when people in swimwear on reality TV shows living on a desert island aren't in it for love?

Tom was right, La Coquelicot Blanche (yes, I have practised saying it in my best French accent) really is like its own little village. The higher you climb to get there, the more picturesque it becomes. The vibrant green fields gradually disappear in favour of a regular winter wonderland. The bus winds its way up narrow roads, the scenery transitioning from lush valleys to snow-kissed mountains – I feel like I've just wandered into a Christmas romcom movie because, seeing as though 'tis the season, the place is wrapped up in fairy lights.

Finally, we pull up outside the main hotel. The air is crisp and cold, the kind of cold that makes your nose run and makes you wish you'd packed more thermal underwear – or booked to go to Hawaii instead. There's snow gathered at the sides of the paths – does that mean it's going or that more is coming? – but looking up at the mountains confirms that there's plenty more where that came from. It's almost a shame that I can't ski, and that I promised Tom I wouldn't even try, because I bet the view from up there is unreal.

The hotel is a stunning, postcard-worthy building. It looks modern and fancy, while still looking like it's been here forever, like it's a part of the landscape.

Looking around the other areas, I feel like I'm inside a snow globe, complete with gently falling tiny snowflakes that have just started dancing around in the air. The crisp, cold air smells of pine trees and snow, and the faint aroma of woodsmoke wafting from the chimneys of the cute little chalets scattered around the grounds. Each chalet is adorned with festive lights and wreaths. I kind of wish I was staying in one of those.

As beautiful as it is, though, it's bloody freezing. I need to get inside and get warm ASAP. As I walk further into the resort, towards the hotel entrance, there is something to admire in every direction. Icicles hang from the eaves of the buildings, glistening like crystal Christmas tree ornaments. The paths are meticulously cleared, with just enough snow left behind at the sides to make you feel like it's a winter wonderland. There are small clusters of people gathered around outdoor firepits, bundled up in big coats and cosy blankets and sipping steaming mugs of hot chocolate or mulled wine – I just caught a whiff of the latter – their laughter and chat filling the air with a friendly, festive vibe.

I spot a hotel employee standing at a wooden desk just inside the doorway of the hotel entrance. He's wearing a uniform – but one that looks more comfortable and warm than I've ever seen a hotel receptionist wear anywhere else.

'Hello,' I say, trying to sound more cheerful than I feel. 'I'm Amber Page. I've booked in for the writers' retreat.'

The man smiles warmly as he checks the system.

'Ah, you are staying in the château,' he tells me. 'I will call someone to escort you there.'

I thank him and stand with my case, feeling a bit like a lost puppy, waiting for someone to appear. Soon enough, a small winter-friendly buggy-type thing pulls up alongside me.

'Madame, I will be taking you to the château,' the driver says, his French accent making everything sound all the more glamorous.

'*Merci*,' I reply, breaking out one of the few French words I know.

The man places my case in the back while I climb into the passenger seat – which I'm delighted to report is a heated one.

'How was your journey?' he asks as we drive along the snowy path.

'It was good, but I'm knackered,' I tell him.

The man, who is clearly French, doesn't seem to know the word 'knackered' because he gives me a funny look before taking that as his cue to drop the small talk.

It's only a short drive – a matter of minutes – along a tree-lined road that looks almost suspiciously picturesque. Snow-covered branches arch overhead, and twinkling lights are strung up along the path, leading the way for us. Finally the château comes into view, and... wow.

The château is stunning. A shady driveway leads to a large gravel parking area next to the main building. It continues towards a courtyard, where the woods give way to a large clearing that is crying out to be explored. A second path, followed by a flight of steps, leads to an elevated outdoor socialising area overlooking the forest. On the other side, a small old chapel is tucked away beneath the trees. The château itself is big – much bigger than I expected – with creamy-coloured walls and an ornate slate roof, like something out of a fairy tale. The dormer windows, the two large turrets – it's exactly what you imagine when you think of a classic French château.

'Your room is number four,' the driver tells me as we come to a stop. 'Would you like me to carry your baggage inside?'

I don't think anyone could carry my baggage for me – oh, he means my case.

'No, that's okay, *merci* again,' I say, my sentence a mess of English and French, but he just smiles and nods.

Standing outside, I take a moment to admire *everything*. It's the kind of place you see on Instagram, where influencers pose in perfectly curated outfits, looking like they're having the time of their lives, making everyone else wish they were there. The gravel crunches under my boots as I make my way to the entrance, the cold air sinking into my bones now that I'm no longer snuggling into the heated seat.

I step inside the large, wooden front door and already I can hear the sound of women laughing and, yep, glasses clinking. It's a welcoming sound, for sure, I just hope that I can fit in. The hallway is grand, with high ceilings and a massive chandelier that looks like it's made of ice crystals – a nice nod to the weather outside. There's a roaring fire in the hearth, which starts thawing me out right away. So long as I can sit in this room, with this fire, at least I know I'll be okay. I'm such a baby when it comes to the cold.

I know I should probably pop in and say hello to my new (temporary) housemates, but I think I'll find my room first, put my case there, and throw on another jumper because I'm freezing.

Then I'll go find the others, say hi, and get a glass of wine of my own. Something tells me that I'm going to need it.

13

My room in the château is positively charming. The walls are painted a soft, warm cream, with dark wooden beams crossing the ceiling. There's a large, plush bed with an intricately carved headboard, piled high with fluffy pillows and a thick, cosy duvet topped with layers and layers of extra blankets.

A small sitting area by the window has a couple of overstuffed armchairs and a tiny wooden table, perfect for curling up with a good book or, more realistically, writing one on my laptop. The view from the window is breathtaking, looking out over the snow-covered grounds and down the road back towards the resort. There's a fireplace, too – my own fireplace! – and it's already lit, casting a warm, golden glow around the room and making it feel like I'm in a dreamy, snuggly cocoon.

If it were as simple as spending time here in my room, occasionally popping to the resort for a hot chocolate and a little bit of fresh air, then maybe, just maybe I could vibe with it. But it's not that simple, is it? I can't hide in my room for the whole trip, can I? *Can I?* No, no, I can't. It's time to go and greet the others.

I head down the long, winding staircase, following the sound of laughter, until I find myself in a lounge. In there, sitting around the fire, nursing glasses of wine, are three familiar faces. Mandy Hess, Bette Hinton, and Gina Knox. It's Gina, who is currently tucking into a generously sliced piece of cheese, who notices me first.

'Amber, darling, hello,' she says brightly. 'Jen said you would be joining us.'

Oh, so at least they knew that I was coming. I was worried, when I didn't hear from any of them, that they might not know.

Gina is the younger of the three – but she's still at least ten years older than me. I'm on the young side for an author, I guess, which makes me feel like a bit of a baby sometimes. I know, deep down, that I have as much right to be here (in this job) as everyone else, but I don't always feel like everyone takes me seriously. Everyone else in the industry – in my genre, especially – seems to be older, more established, with families and comfortable lives. I sometimes feel a bit like the odd one out, but I know I'll get there eventually... hopefully. Some days it's easier to believe than others.

Gina is very glamorous – you can somehow tell she writes steamy romance, but only if you know to look for it. There's a cheeky flirtiness behind her eyes, but otherwise, she doesn't look the type. She has glossy dark hair that falls in perfect waves around her shoulders, a figure that could give a swimsuit model a run for her money, and a wardrobe that looks like it's made of money.

Then there's Bette Hinton, who gives me a big smile and a wave. She writes cute titles, usually set at the seaside, with feel-good, life-affirming storylines. She's the older of the three, in her late sixties, and has that warm, bubbly, mumsy vibe about her. Bette is holding two glasses of wine – one red, one white. Her hair is a soft grey, styled in a neat bob, and she's wearing a colourful, slightly eccentric outfit that looks like it was chosen specifically to brighten up the cold winter weather here. Her face is lined with laughter, and she has the kind of smile that makes you feel instantly at ease. You just know she's going to be friendly with you, even if she doesn't mean it.

And finally, there is Mandy Hess, very much the main one, the boss-level author. I was a big fan of Mandy's work growing up, so naturally I was jazzed to meet her, and Mandy was nice to me at first... until my first book did well and people started describing me as 'the new Mandy Hess', which I'm guessing she wasn't very happy about because she's been hostile towards me ever since. Mandy is the last one to turn around, like the last judge on *The Voice*. She's in her fifties, with sharp, chiselled features, short, stylishly cut blonde hair, and it's hard to explain but she just seems to give off the underlying authority of a head teacher – something about her demeanour makes you want to stand up a little straighter, and watch your Ps and Qs. She's dressed in a tailored, sophisticated two-piece, and here I am, in jeans, and my oversized jumper with thumb holes – thumb holes that I made myself, by poking holes in my long sleeves.

'Amber, hello, dear,' Mandy says, her tone polite but cool. 'We were taking bets on whether you would turn up.'

'Well, here I am,' I reply, trying to keep my voice light, because if she's making fun of me, I need to make it seem like I'm in on the joke.

'How are you doing, and how was your journey?' Bette asks.

'It was fine, thanks,' I reply. 'This is a beautiful place – thanks so much for inviting me.'

I know, that's not technically true, and they would probably prefer it if Dickie Woodrup was here (he's very nice and charming to his friends/people he believes are his equals) but I'm what they've got.

Bette smiles. She's nice enough, but I will never forget the time when I asked her if she would read my book and maybe give me a quote that I could use to promote it. She told me she hated reading romance and that it was bad enough she had to write the stuff. I guess decades in the industry will do that to you, but even so, it was disappointing, like finding out the person who sings your favourite love song is a serial adulterer.

'Jen mentioned you were struggling with your book,' Mandy says, her pouty smile patronising. 'It's not as easy as it seems, is it?'

I force a smile.

'It's just my latest, and creative differences with my editor,' I explain, standing up for myself. 'Is this a good place to get work done?'

The three women laugh.

'Oh, no, no, no,' Mandy insists. 'No one actually comes here to write, do they, ladies? We do it to avoid our families in the run-up to Christmas.'

I settle into an armchair next to the fire. It's nice in here – a good spot to get cosy. The room is spacious yet cosy, with a high, timber-beamed ceiling that adds a touch of rustic charm. The walls are adorned with vintage paintings and tapestries – artworks that feel very much on theme in a château. Soft, ambient lighting from a combination of antique chandeliers and wall sconces bathes the room in a gentle, golden glow – which is much needed, because not much daylight comes in from outside, through the small windows.

The lounge's centrepiece is definitely the grand stone fireplace. It's massive, with a huge fire roaring inside, that not only gives off an almost overwhelming amount of heat, but also ASMR levels of crackles and pops. It's so relaxing.

Above the mantelpiece, an ornate mirror reflects the warm light around, upping the cosy ambience. Plush armchairs and sofas, upholstered in rich, deep shades of burgundy and forest green, are arranged in a semicircle, setting the scene for the conversation. The only part of the room that is imperfect is the coffee table in front of us, that is littered with wine bottles, glasses and snacks. It's messy, but not out of place. It's a very French spread.

Bette chuckles, taking a sip from her glass of red wine.

'My husband takes care of everything back home,' she explains. 'He's got Christmas down to a fine art now, and I get to relax here. It's the only way to do it.'

I think about Bette's social media accounts, where she routinely roasts her husband for laughs. All she seems to do is make fun of him for his quirky little ways and grumpy old man energy. It's a bit of a surprise to hear she actually relies on him so much.

'I spend the big day with siblings and their families,' Gina explains. 'They all have kids, so they're used to doing everything, and I get to simply turn up and be the cool auntie without any of the stress.'

I smile, imagining Gina doling out extravagant presents – bought with the money she makes writing spicy books – and sipping wine before slipping away when things get too hectic.

Mandy leans back in her chair, her posture relaxed but still somehow perfect.

'My children are grown up now, so the burden is on them to make the big day happen. I've done my time,' she explains.

Mandy lost her husband a few years ago. It must be so difficult having someone with you every day, for decades, and then suddenly finding yourself without them. Things like Christmas and birthdays must be so hard, feeling like someone is missing, having that empty seat at the table. Even when she's being a bit snooty, she'll always have my sympathy, because that's rough.

'Sounds like you've all got a good system,' I say, thinking about

the endless lists and last-minute shopping trips that seem to domi-
nate my Decembers. Hopefully doing all of my shopping online,
and having it delivered directly to my parents' house, works out. By
the time I get home, and check that it has all arrived, it will probably be too late to do anything about it. I suppose I can always
dash out on Christmas Eve, to grab some last-minute bits – a (not
at all) wise man once described it as being like dating in your thirties, I believe.

'It is,' Mandy replies with a hint of a smile. 'And it means I can
come here and focus on… avoiding work.'

Gina laughs, and Bette joins in, so I chuckle too. Anything to
fit in.

It's interesting that they don't really want to be around their
families in the run-up to the big day. The last thing I want is to
avoid my family, and my parents are divorcing.

'We understand you need to work and we will happily give you
advice if you need it,' Gina says kindly.

Bette smiles and nods in a way that is polite but non-
committal.

'Yes, of course,' Mandy agrees – not that she sounds like she
means it. 'We're having dinner in a couple of hours, by the way.'

Swift subject change. Expertly deployed.

'I might go lie down until it's dinner time,' I say.

Honestly, I'm exhausted already. It's probably from the travelling but a small part of me feels like I'm standing on ceremony
when I'm around this lot.

'We have staff who cook for us and clean up after us – it's a
dream,' Bette explains. 'And it's just us, staying here in the château,
so they're at our disposal.'

That does sound lovely, and it will be nice to be spoiled. This
room is so cosy, with the roaring fire, and the thought that I could

just curl up here and have people bring me anything I want sounds glorious.

'Speaking of delicious, have you seen the Frenchman who takes care of the château?' Gina asks me. 'I don't know if he's just the caretaker here, or of the whole resort, but he lives here in the château.'

'I haven't seen anyone yet,' I admit.

'Keep an eye out,' Gina tells me with a wink. 'There are other men working here, obviously, but you'll know him when you see him.'

'Okay, sure,' I say with a giggle, as I pull myself to my feet. 'I'll go rest up before dinner.'

'Don't worry,' Bette calls after me. 'We'll save you some wine.'

It's hard to imagine this lot saving wine, instead of just drinking it. Then again, we are in France, so presumably, there's plenty more where that came from.

14

I wake up in my room at the château, groggy and confused. My first thought is that I must have slept for hours, but a quick glance at my phone tells me otherwise. Thirty minutes. Thirty flipping minutes! That doesn't even count as a nap, does it? Not a good one anyway.

It feels like hours since I was downstairs with the ladies, but apparently not – the seat I was sitting in is probably still warm.

My brief nap has done nothing for me. I still feel exhausted – in fact, if anything, I feel even more tired – but sleeping isn't going to happen, not if I'm going to join the others for dinner. I guess late afternoon isn't the best time for a snooze, and dinner is soon, so I may as well try and tough through it.

Maybe I need to wake up instead. A shower, brushing my teeth, a cup of coffee – anything to shake off this grogginess. Perhaps if I go through the motions of morning, it might trick my body into thinking it's time to be awake.

I sit up and stretch, taking in my surroundings once more. This room is like a scene from a fairy tale, and the four-poster bed, with its soft, creamy linen curtains and all its pillows and blankets, looks like something out of a fantasy novel.

The room has a very distinctive smell, although it's one that I can't quite put my finger on. I can smell the fire, obviously, as you can throughout the château, but it has this whiff of... church? More specifically like the incense they use in Catholic churches. It's a sort of mixture of old wooden furniture and incense. It's a nice scent, I promise. I wonder if it is the natural smell of the place or if it's something they pump in on purpose.

Right, time to make a move.

I tear myself out of the bed with a sigh – I miss it already.

I open my suitcase, looking for my toiletries. The bathrooms must be shared here because my room doesn't have an en suite. It's an old building, after all, not a Travelling Inn chain hotel, and – shit, where is my toothbrush? I rummage through my things, mentally retracing my steps as I packed my bag. I distinctly remember packing it last night... then unpacking it to use this morning... then forgetting to pack it again. Oh, for God's sake.

This place is fancy – surely they have complimentary toiletries for forgetful guests, and if they don't, well, perhaps one of the other authors brought a spare. Yes, I know that's rich of me, wondering if anyone brought a second toothbrush, when I didn't even bring one.

We're staying here in the private château, so it's not like there is a reception or anything, and it's a little walk back to the main part of the resort, so perhaps bits like that are already in the bathrooms.

I grab my make-up bag – thank goodness I didn't forget that because, in a way, that probably would have been worse – and leave my room in search of a bathroom. Who knows, maybe I'll get lucky for once? And if I don't, well, I could do with freshening up before dinner anyway.

Walking along the corridor, I pass numbered doors until I find one marked with a small bathroom sign. And it's occupied. Brilliant.

I keep moving, my eyes scanning for another likely door. This is such a big place, it must have more than one bathroom.

I spot a plain door, but one with a lock, which is a pretty good sign that it's at least a loo, right? My heart is in my mouth, as I dare to open it.

Oh, thank goodness, it is a bathroom. Just imagine, if I'd walked into someone else's room. Now that feels more like my brand of luck.

I lock the door behind me, take off my baggy jumper and start to unbutton my jeans when another door on the opposite side of the room – not the one I just came in through – swings open. I freeze, my hands halfway down my hips.

A man – who I'd guess is in his late thirties – steps in, wearing nothing but a towel slung low around his hips. His tanned skin glistens with water, his dark, wavy hair dripping wet and skimming his shoulders. He's good-looking in that effortlessly sexy, French kind of way. As he smiles, his cheeks dimple, and the skin around his eyes crinkles. This must be the 'delicious Frenchman' the others mentioned.

'Oh, hello,' I say, trying to sound casual despite the fact that I'm standing here half-dressed.

'*Bonjour*,' he replies with a charming smile and in an accent that makes my knees weak. 'Are you lost?'

'No, um, well, maybe,' I say, cool as ever. 'I'm Amber. I'm one of the writers staying here.'

'Henri,' he introduces himself. 'I take care of the place. You look too young to be a writer.'

I blush.

'Oh, thanks,' I say, like he's just paid me the world's biggest compliment – it's the accent, I swear. 'I was just looking for a bathroom.'

'This is my private bathroom,' Henri explains. 'It connects to my bedroom. But you are welcome to use it – I will just remember to lock the hallway door next time, if I'm in here.'

'You don't have to do that,' I say quickly, then realise how that sounds. 'I mean, you don't have to share your bathroom with me.'

'It's okay,' he says with a shrug. 'I don't mind.'

I can't help but smile at his easy-going attitude.

'Well, thank you,' I reply. '*Merci*. That's very kind of you.'

'If you need anything, just ask me,' he says, his gaze lingering on me for a moment longer than necessary.

'Actually, now that you mention it, I forgot my toothbrush. Do you have any spares here?' I ask hopefully.

Henri smiles.

'No spares, sorry,' he tells me. 'But there is a shop in the resort that sells things like that. I can take you – once I am dressed, of course.'

'Oh, you don't have to do that,' I tell him and, again, it sounds like I'm telling him not to get dressed, rather than saying I don't need his help. 'I appreciate the offer, but I need to get ready for dinner,' I explain.

At the mention of dinner, I'm suddenly very aware that I'm still standing here in my bra. I quickly fold my arms over my chest, trying to cover up.

Henri laughs again, a deep, warm chuckle that makes the little hairs on my arms stand on end, like someone just rubbed my entire body with a giant balloon.

'I am learning that romance writers are very flirty,' he tells me.

'Flirty?' I reply.

'The other ladies, they like their flirty jokes,' he says. 'And you,

Amber, do you always barge into strangers' private bathrooms, or am I just lucky?'

I laugh, trying to play along.

'Oh, only when the strangers are as charming as you,' I tell him. 'We romance writers are flirty, but incredibly fussy.'

He grins, leaning casually against the door frame.

'Ah, so I am special?' he replies. 'Good to know.'

'But, yeah, you might want to lock your door next time,' I say, feeling my cheeks heat up. 'You never know who might walk in. I'm very understanding but the others, well, who knows how they would react?'

Henri shrugs, his dimples deepening.

'Maybe I like to live dangerously,' he tells me. 'It keeps life interesting when you don't lock the door.'

Is it hot in this bathroom, or is it me? Or is it Henri because, oh my God, he's so unrealistically charming?

'Well, I definitely didn't expect to find you here,' I tell him. 'But you don't seem dangerous.'

'Nor did I expect to find a beautiful woman in my bathroom,' he replies smoothly. 'But, I don't know, maybe you do seem like trouble.'

I bite my lip, trying to suppress a giggle. I need to change the subject, ASAP – basically quit while I'm ahead.

'So, you're the caretaker here? What does that entail?' I ask.

I let my arms go loose, to try to look less awkward, styling out standing here in my bra. Well, he certainly doesn't look uncomfortable, chilling in his towel.

'A bit of everything, really,' he replies. 'Maintenance, guest services, ensuring beautiful women find the bathroom...'

Oh, he's not giving up, is he?

I laugh again, shaking my head.

'You must have a lot of stories,' I reply.

'Oh, many,' he tells me. 'Perhaps a writer like yourself would appreciate hearing them.'

'So long as they're romantic,' I reply.

I'm not quite sure if I'm flirting or just desperate for inspiration. With Jen wanting me to writer spicier scenes, I can imagine Henri's stories being more than inspiring, if they're that kind of story.

'So, you're an expert in matters of the heart?' he asks curiously.

'I wouldn't say expert,' I laugh. 'But I do enjoy a good love story.'

'And are you living one?' he asks, his voice dropping to a more serious tone.

I blink, caught off guard by the question. Is he asking if I'm single?

'Well, no, not exactly,' I confess. 'Not right now. I'm focusing on my book so, if I'm getting intimate with anything, it's that.'

Oh, I was doing so well, until just then. I was cool, flirty, and kind of mysterious. Now I sound like I, what, shag my own book? That's probably the least awkward explanation.

'So, no leading man in your life?' he teases.

'Not at the moment,' I say, feeling a bit self-conscious.

'Pity,' he says softly. 'A beautiful woman like you deserves a grand romance.'

'What about you?' I ask, shifting the focus back to him.

'No, nothing for me,' he replies. Henri's smile returns, bright and charming. 'But, still, if I can help you with your book, you know where to find me – just knock.'

He says all of this like he's joking but, bloody hell, he's inspired me enough to write another series.

'I do,' I say, feeling a mix of excitement and nervousness.

Henri gives me one last lingering look before he nods.

'Okay, I'll let you get ready,' he tells me. 'It was nice to meet you, Amber.'

'It was nice to meet you too,' I echo, my heart racing as he finally leaves the bathroom.

As I stand there, topless, trying to process what just happened, I can't help but smile.

I plonk myself down on the toilet seat – just for the seat. Henri was the last thing I was expecting to find behind this door, but Gina was right. He is kind of delicious.

Maybe this retreat won't be so bad after all.

15

It was worth coming on this trip for the food alone, it turns out.

I'm in the dining room – which weirdly reminds me of the one from *Saltburn*, thanks to its grandeur and the fact I watched the movie recently, and otherwise have basically no points of reference for such fancy dining spaces – with Mandy, Bette, and Gina. We're tucking into a delicious French dish – Coq au Vin – prepared for us by the château chef, served to us by the château waitstaff. Yes, I feel fancy as hell right now.

God, it's good. The tender chicken, slow-cooked in red wine with mushrooms, onions, and bacon, only seems to get better with each bite. I'm getting to the point where I'm starting to feel full, but it seems like a shame to waste a bite of it – which is probably why I'm wiping my plate clean with the freshly baked bread, smothered in herb butter.

'Oh, and I've really got into pottery,' Mandy continues – she's currently listing all of the activities she fills her days with, when she's between books. 'There's something so therapeutic about moulding clay with your hands. I've made a few decent vases but that's not why I do it – crafts are good for the soul.'

Bette nods enthusiastically.

'I love knitting,' she adds. 'There's nothing like curling up with your needles and a whisky on a chilly evening.'

I stifle a smile, because that sounds funnier than Bette intended, I'm sure.

'I've made scarves, sweaters, and such, but I'm obsessed with knitting dog jumpers at the moment,' she continues, confirming that it's definitely knitting needles she's on about.

'I'm with you both,' Gina says, finally retiring her cutlery. 'I dabble in a bit of everything – painting, cross-stitching, even some jewellery making. It's nice to take a break from writing and just create something for the love of creating.'

'The earrings you gave me are just fabulous,' Mandy tells her. 'You should sell your jewellery.'

'I'm happy to give them as gifts,' Gina insists. 'But I suppose if the writing thing doesn't pan out...'

She laughs, as though the idea is ludicrous. I wish I had that confidence in my work.

'Never going to happen,' Mandy reassures her. 'Which is why I treasure my earrings.'

'How lovely – do you have them with you?' Bette asks.

Mandy's face falls.

'No, not with me,' Mandy replies. 'I keep them safely in my jewellery box.'

I get such a phoney, disingenuous vibe from Mandy. It's almost like she will kiss your arse, if it serves her, but otherwise she doesn't have time for you. She's the kind of person who would pretend to love a gift if she wanted to keep you on side, but tell you that it sucked if she wasn't bothered.

Gina smiles and bats her hand to let Mandy know she isn't offended.

'Hobbies are so important,' she concludes. 'I'm sure I'll be obsessing over something else next week.'

I listen quietly, feeling a pang of envy as they chat about what they do for fun. I wish I had time for arts and crafts. If I have any free time, I spend it tidying my apartment or washing my hair. I'd love to be like them, enjoying long breaks between books, but I always seem to find myself stumbling sleepily from one project to the next. Any downtime I do have, like a true millennial, I spend it staring at screens – something that feels a bit too much like work sometimes. I mean, they said we'd grow up to have square eyes, and I guess I do wear glasses!

At first, I liked my fast-paced way of working. I loved being busy, doing a job I love – I felt so lucky – but this new book is kicking my arse. I just can't get excited about writing another romance novel, and I get that my editor wants me to write more of what worked before, but that doesn't feel authentic to me. I'm a writer, a creative, with ideas that I want to bring to life. What I need is to find that balance between doing something I enjoy and something I can make a living from. Right now, it feels like it can only be one way or the other.

'Amber, you seem quiet,' Gina says, pulling me out of my thoughts. 'This is a space where we can talk freely, you know.'

'You have just as much right to be here as us,' Mandy adds, somewhat patronisingly. 'You shouldn't feel like you don't fit in.'

I haven't mentioned feeling like I don't fit in, so Mandy's comment only makes things feel more uncomfortable. I decide to change the conversation.

'I met Henri, before I came down,' I tell them.

'Oh, isn't he gorgeous?' Gina says, bouncing her eyebrows up and down.

'He's single,' Bette points out, practically singing the words. 'I asked.'

'I get the impression he's on the lookout,' Mandy chimes in. 'For a mature woman, though, someone refined and experienced.'

Gina nods thoughtfully.

'He's clearly a very flirty man,' she points out. 'Relentless, really.'

If Henri was flirting with me earlier then I shouldn't read too much into it, because Gina makes it sound like he's that way with everyone. Well, if I were a ten out of ten, I would probably flirt with everything with a pulse too, just to flex that I could.

'I do genuinely think he's interested, though,' Mandy points out again. 'I think one of us could have him, if we wanted.'

'How could he choose between us?' Bette asks.

Yeah, because that's going to happen.

Okay, sure, I'll play along for a second. Well, surely Bette is out, because she's married. The rest of us may be single, which is surely the minimum requirement, but that still doesn't mean he's actually interested in any of us.

'I fancy my chances,' Gina says with a confident smile. 'Seeing as though I have youthful maturity on my side.'

'Are you calling me old?' Mandy snaps, semi-playfully, but I suspect she is genuinely a little offended.

'No, I'm calling Bette old,' Gina jokes.

Thankfully, Bette laughs, so I do too.

'I suppose you think you're in with the best chance, being the youngest?' Mandy says to me, still ticked off.

'We're all romance writers,' I point out. 'We're all familiar with the tropes, which surely means any of us would be in with a shot equally – we're all experts in falling in love.'

Hopefully that's the best thing to say, to defuse the situation.

Mandy narrows her eyes at me as a smile slowly creeps across her face. Oh, I don't like the look of that.

'How about a wager?' she suggests. 'The four of us compete,

using the tropes, to see which one of us can woo the foxy Frenchman first.'

I laugh but then I realise Mandy is serious. I mean, obviously using the tropes in our books makes sense, because they're the themes of romance, and it's easy to do a storyline like 'brother's best friend' on the page, because you're making it all up, but you can't exactly force that one in real life, can you? At least not with a man you've just met.

'Oh, I love it,' Gina says excitedly. 'Let's do it!'

'I'm in,' Bette says – then she must notice the look on my face. 'Oh, Bernie won't mind. You know what they say, what happens in France stays in France.'

No one says that.

'So, Amber, are you in?' Mandy asks. 'Or are you scared that you'll be beaten by one of us oldies?'

'I don't know,' I start, laughing it off.

'I thought you were here to enjoy this retreat with us,' Mandy says. 'That you were one of us. And this is what we do for fun...'

'This and drink wine,' Bette adds.

That bit I'm already good at. I pick up my drink and drain the last of the wine from my glass.

'Okay, sure,' I say. 'Why not? Count me in.'

I'm not actually in, and have no intention of playing this seriously silly, incredibly weird game, but I want to keep the ladies on side. Well, I might actually need to take Gina up on her offer of giving me advice with my work, if I'm going to try to make things spicy, like Jen wants me to. Oh boy, I just threw up in my mouth at the thought. I'm just not a sexy person, at all, I have zero game, and a goofy giggle. I've never even been able to talk dirty in the bedroom, because I always feel – and probably sound – so silly.

'We're all starting at square one,' Mandy says. 'And we all have an equal chance.'

'Not quite,' I chime in. 'I've forgotten my toothbrush, so I can't brush my teeth. Does anyone have a spare?'

'No, Amber, no one has a spare toothbrush,' Mandy answers for everyone, narrowing her eyes at me like I just suggested I hadn't ever owned one, rather than that I forgot mine.

'That's okay, Henri told me where I could get one,' I say. 'He offered to take me.'

I don't mean anything by it, I'm not rubbing it in, but I notice a flicker of recognition on each of their faces.

'Oh, so you've been flirting with him?' Bette says, raising an eyebrow.

'No, no, no, I just asked him if he has a spare toothbrush in his bathroom,' I clarify.

'In his bathroom, hey?' Gina persists.

'It was just a friendly question,' I add, trying to put the issue to bed.

'She's doing "friends to lovers",' Bette says knowingly. 'Well, that's given me an even better idea. Game on.'

I just laugh. Are these three really, seriously going to compete for Henri? There's no way I'm going to actually join in with this game, not a chance, but at least it will be fun to spectate.

This writers' retreat is definitely not what I expected.

16

Waking up... wow... I'm in heaven. I feel like I'm lying on a cloud, wrapped in the fluffiest blankets, floating through the sky. It's like I've been sleeping in a hug. No aches, no pains, just pure, blissful rest. I can't feel a hint of pressure anywhere – I swear, I feel weightless, which I am surely not after the amount of food I put in my body last night.

You know, I don't even remember the last time I felt this good – when I woke up, or generally. It's not even 8 a.m. yet and I'm never normally awake at this time – but I'm so energised that the thought of going back to sleep doesn't even feel like an option. Of course, there's a difference between not wanting to go back to sleep and not planning on getting out of bed.

There's only one problem, though. Well, one immediate problem, shall we say – let's conveniently ignore that my parents are breaking up and I'm supposed to be writing a book that I don't love. The immediate problem is that I really, really need to brush my teeth. I couldn't do it after dinner last night because the resort shop was already closed and now I really do feel gross.

Even though I don't want to leave my cosy little cocoon, I do have an early-morning energy I am in no way used to, so now is probably the best time to go and pick up a toothbrush from the resort shop.

I roll out of bed, throw on some jeans, and pull out a fresh, oversized jumper from my bag. Not just any jumper, one of my fancier ones today. The thought of Henri being in the château, and potentially bumping into him, makes me want to try a little harder – is that weird? I'm not exactly going all out but I'm applying plenty of make-up, brushing my hair, and spritzing myself with perfume. Normally, this early in the morning, I don't even bother with my glasses, let alone wrangle myself into a bra.

After using Henri's bathroom – without any awkward run-ins or embarrassing mishaps – I wander around the château. I spot a couple of staff members, but Henri is nowhere to be seen. Not that I'm stalking him or anything; he did say he'd take me to the shop. There's no sign of him though, so I guess I'll make my own way there, on foot – well, it's not like it's far, just that it's cold, and I guess the company would have been nice.

So, bundled up in my Ugg boots and faux-fur coat, I head outside. The morning air is crisp and fresh, feeling like a thousand tiny knives when I breathe it in, and creating foggy bursts in front of my face as I breathe out. The sky is that perfect pale blue that usually hints at a clear, bright day ahead – so maybe I won't see any snow actually falling today. There's still some on the ground though, still fresh enough to make that really satisfying crunching noise when I go out of my way to step on it. The road is clear otherwise, which makes general walking from A to B much easier. The air smells so fresh, with hints of pine, and burning wood – even the fires smell fresh, which is weird. Everything just seems so natural and clean and reminds you that you're alive.

I'm relieved that the walk to the resort isn't long – even if it was quicker in the buggy. Wow, I can't believe how busy it is for 8 a.m. I guess skiing enthusiasts like to hit the slopes early, before the dark winter evening sets in. That or ski holidays are like stag dos, where you start drinking at breakfast.

You know, skiing may not be my thing (and I may have promised Tom that I wouldn't go near the slopes), but I have to admit, the fashion is on point. Everyone looks so funky, warm, and cosy. Maybe I can just wear the clothes, without actually getting involved in any of the action. Not that I'm all fur coat and no knickers (yep, I remembered to put them on, rather than just storing them in my trouser leg today) but I definitely think a nice thermal pair of ski trousers will make these walks back and forth to the resort go a lot smoother. Even if I fall on my arse, at least my arse will be warm.

As I wander into the resort, it's like stepping into a scene from a movie, or the set-up to shoot an advert at least. It's just so picture-perfect, so busy with people, but in such a peaceful way.

The large open reception area is just stunning, blending new and traditional styles seamlessly. I can't tell if this place is brand spanking new or if it's been here for a hundred years. I suspect the truth is a mixture of the two.

Massive wooden beams criss-cross the high ceiling, adding a rustic charm, as do the cosy fireplaces dotted around. But then the furniture is so modern. Plush, comfortable seats in rich, warm colours, strategically placed, making the whole space look contemporary but still with super-inviting snuggly vibes. It looks like if you allowed yourself to sink into one of those armchairs that you would never get up again – both because you couldn't, and because you wouldn't want to.

The fact that it's Christmastime gives the place an extra magical, festive air about it. Twinkling fairy lights are strung along the beams – although I don't think they would look out of place all year round – and there are festive decorations everywhere. Everything is tasteful though, and natural, with green garlands and wreaths (ones that look like they're made from real trees) and subtle ornaments. The tree itself is huge, like someone chopped down one of the big ones from outside and dragged it in, although I can't begin to imagine how they managed to get it through the doors.

Over to the side, there's a coffee bar that's calling my name – I smell it before I see it – serving up hot drinks and fresh pastries. The smell of coffee and freshly baked croissants wafts through the air, wrapping itself around my body like a lasso, pulling me in, and I'm so tempted to grab something, even though I told the ladies I'd join them for breakfast. I don't suppose there's any reason why I couldn't grab a pre-breakfast snack, right? I'm basically a hobbit when it comes to meals. Second breakfast is a thing in my world too. Plus, it's not like I need to mention breakfast number one, when I turn up for breakfast number two, is it?

The coffee bar itself is like an art installation. It's got this sleek, modern design with a dark wooden counter, with the most beautiful detail carved into it, contrasted beautifully by the shiny chrome fixtures of the coffee machines. Behind the counter, there's a display case filled with an array of mouth-watering pastries – croissants, muffins, cookies, and some decadent-looking cakes that are probably, in theory, way too rich for this early in the morning, but I know in my heart that I could absolutely take one down right now.

The barista, a friendly looking guy with a green Santa hat, is busy making a cappuccino, the machine hissing and steaming, and it should be an unpleasant noise but really it only adds to the atmosphere.

Everything about this place makes me feel like I've walked into a dream. The combination of the elegant décor, the festive touches, the inviting warmth from the fireplaces, and the delicious smells wafting from the coffee bar – it's all so perfect that I have to remind myself it's real. And to think, I didn't want to come here. Now that I'm here, I'm not sure I want to leave.

Out of the corner of my eye, I spot the shop and head over to grab a toothbrush first. This place is like a mini department store, with everything you could possibly need – so, really, when you think about it, I don't actually need to leave. I mean, other than me not being able to afford a place like this if I weren't filling someone else's spot, I feel like I could be quite happy here.

I want to check out the souvenirs – because I'm a sucker for a good snow globe – but I should crack on with what I came here for. There will be plenty of time for shopping, and picking up some last-minute Christmas gifts before I head home.

I head to the toiletries section, scanning the shelves for toothbrushes. Wow, they've got everything, from hair dye to haemorrhoid cream, and everything for the bits in between. They've even got a massive make-up counter, and signs up saying there's an on-site salon and spa. Really, truly, what else could I need from anywhere else? If it turns out there's a McDonald's, around the other side of the mountain, and assuming my family could visit, I really can't think of what more I could want.

Here we are. Toothbrushes. As I stretch my arm out to grab one, another hand lunges for the same item. I look up, and lo and behold, it's none other than Caleb. Okay, wow, this place really does have everything.

'What are you doing here?' I blurt out, genuinely surprised, trying to keep my potential morning breath to myself.

'We arranged it,' he says with a casual shrug. 'Remember? You told me to meet you here...'

My jaw practically hits the floor.

'I was being sarcastic!' I reply. 'I didn't actually think you'd show up, especially not at such short notice – you told me this place was impossible to book in to.'

Caleb just chuckles.

'I made a few calls,' he tells me, as if it's the most natural thing in the world. 'I thought I was going to have to find your château, to meet up with you, but here you are.'

I just stare at him for a moment.

'Looks like you forgot your toothbrush too,' he says through an amused grin.

'Um, yeah,' I reply, really, truly not knowing what else to say.

Caleb takes the toothbrush from my hand.

'Let me get that for you,' he insists.

'Erm, I can buy my own toothbrush, thanks,' I reply, teetering on the edge of snapping but managing to keep a lid on it.

Does he think I'm that hard up, that I can't afford a toothbrush? Because, technically, this will be my second toothbrush, yep, two toothbrushes, I'm doing well, thanks.

Caleb laughs, as though he can tell that I'm ranting at myself, inside my brain.

'I know, but humour me,' he says, already heading for the checkout.

Curiosity getting the better of me – one of the curses of being a writer – I follow him, wondering why I would need to humour him.

At the counter, the cashier practically lights up at the sight of Caleb approaching him.

'Hello, Monsieur Carney!' he exclaims, swiftly taking the tooth-brushes from him, placing them in a bag. 'Do you need some toothpaste too?'

Caleb glances at me, and I realise I actually do need toothpaste. What a fantastic adult I am.

'Yes,' I practically confess.

'Yes, please,' Caleb tells the cashier, flashing a grin. 'Or should I say "*oui*"?'

The cashier – who I've just noticed from his name badge is called Pascal – laughs. 'Don't worry, sir, all our staff speak perfect English,' Pascal reassures him. 'Many of our guests are from the UK and the USA.'

'Good to know,' Caleb replies, chuckling. 'My French isn't great. I was one of the kids in my school who chose to study German, instead of French.'

'Oh, *sprichst du Deutsch*?' Pascal replies.

'I studied it, but I don't remember a word of it,' Caleb admits with a laugh.

'That's quite all right,' Pascal says with a smile. 'One moment, please.'

Pascal calls over another employee and says something to him in French.

I wonder if Caleb is well known here, in France, or if the staff have been told to expect him, because they know he's a big deal in the UK. I guess a place like this could really benefit from his endorsement, especially if they have lots of guests from the UK.

'Have you checked in yet?' Pascal asks Caleb.

'Nah, not yet, my bags are over there, in the lobby,' he replies. 'I thought I'd grab the essentials I forgot first.'

'I'll have someone come to check you in, and show you to your room,' Pascal insists.

'I'm in a chalet, I think it's called Mon Chou?' Caleb replies.

Pascal nods knowingly.

'Ah, the honeymoon suite,' he replies. 'Here for a romantic getaway?'

'Something like that,' Caleb replies with a dorky chuckle.

The other employee returns with the toothpaste, only for

Pascal to give him more instructions, again in French, before turning back to Caleb.

'There's no charge for these essentials,' Pascal insists, handing the bag to Caleb.

Caleb just smiles sweetly.

'Are you sure?' he checks.

'Absolutely,' Pascal replies, before another thought seems to strike him. 'Ah, one more thing...'

The other employee reappears, this time with two small hampers.

'Your welcome baskets, for a romantic stay,' Pascal explains, handing them over to Caleb. 'On the house.'

'Oh, thanks,' Caleb says, looking genuinely pleased. 'They look great.'

'Just wait by your baggage, and we'll send someone right over,' Pascal instructs him.

Caleb looks at me and nods in the direction of his bags, indicating for me to follow him, so I do. And now it's just the two of us again. Just me, him, and enough suitcases for a family of five. Wow, he does not pack light.

Caleb takes out one of the toothbrushes and shoves it in his pocket before handing the paper bag to me.

'Here you go,' he says. 'You can have the toothpaste. And it looks like there is a his and hers basket, so you can take the hers, if you like.'

I can't help but laugh.

'Do people always just throw free stuff at you?' I ask curiously.

'Sometimes they just hand it to me instead,' Caleb jokes, before turning serious. 'Look, I think we might have got our wires crossed, and maybe me being here is a surprise. Why don't you come and see me later when you've had time to think about it? I'm here, you're here, I've got cases full of crap, and a big chunk of change that could be headed your way...'

Pursing my lips in thought, I consider his offer. He's right. I am here, he's here, and I could help him out. And the money would be good.

'All right, sure,' I reply. 'Do you want to put your number in my phone? I'll buzz you when I'm free.'

Caleb nods, taking my phone and punching in his digits.

'I gave myself a missed call, so now I've got your number too,' he replies. 'Just in case you were planning on not calling and then hiding in the mountains to avoid me until I left.'

I laugh, shaking my head.

'You know that this whole thing is so bizarre, right?' I check.

'Oh, yeah, definitely,' Caleb agrees with a grin. 'See you later.'

Completely weirded out (but still vaguely amused) by the whole situation, I take my things and head for the door. No, wait, screw it, I am going to get that coffee, and a pastry – I think I need it now.

I can't believe Caleb bloody Carney has actually turned up here. I mean, to be fair to him, he did say that he was going to come, and I did tell him he could – but I was joking. But he's here now, and the least I can do is hear him out. It might be the easiest money I've ever made – well, easier than writing a book, anyway.

Armed with my latte and my croissant, and with my dental essentials and my random hamper, I step outside. Oof, the cold air hits different now, after being in the cosy hotel for so long, but feeling the cold is way down the list. I feel bemused, surprised, and excited if I'm being honest.

This trip just keeps getting weirder and weirder. I'm almost terrified of what might happen next – but I'm excited too because, trust me, stuff like this doesn't usually happen to me, and I doubt it ever will again. So maybe I will make the most of it. Let's see what Caleb says later. I've got a breakfast to get to first – and one to eat before I get there.

17

As I push open the grand double doors of the château, I can't help but admire how the morning sun warms up the tone of the creamy-coloured walls.

I just love that feeling of walking in and out through the doors, and the way the temperature shifts all of a sudden. When you walk in it's like stepping into a big, warm hug – sort of like when you step off the plane when you fly to a hot country, and you step through the door and it instantly feels like you're walking into a wall of heat. It's just like that, except it smells delicious, and helps the feeling come back to your fingers.

I stroll through the fancy hallway, my footsteps echoing on the hard floor, letting my nose lead me in the direction of breakfast. Not that I don't know where the dining room is, but if I didn't the smell of freshly baked *something* would give it away. I can't wait to find out what it is.

Walking into the dining room, I find Mandy, Bette, and Gina already parked at the long, elegant breakfast table. They're surrounded by the breakfast buffet of my dreams – no wine this time, although I wouldn't be shocked if I found out Bette's coffee was Irish instead of French. Either they've hardly touched a thing, or I've arrived just in time, because everything is still picture-perfect.

It's the fanciest continental breakfast spread I've ever seen. Usually I'm a scrambled-eggs kind of girl if I'm going for savoury, or American-style pancakes if I fancy something sweet. Silver trays are loaded with golden, flaky croissants, pain au chocolat, and other delicious-looking pastries that would serve as a delicious chaser to the one I ate on the walk here. Then there is the savoury stuff – meats, cheeses – and various jars with different spreads and conserves in. Back home I would laugh if anyone suggested I eat cheese for breakfast but here it just feels right. There is freshly baked bread, which must have been what I could smell walking in here, as well as a large glass bowl full of fresh fruits. Again, I'm not really one for fruit on a morning (unless it's in a pancake or a Danish) but this looks too good to resist – I'm sure I'll feel healthy when I eat it, even if it is part of my second breakfast.

My stomach growls as I look over it all, longingly, which only helps to conceal the fact I've already eaten.

A young woman in a crisp white uniform moves gracefully around the table, pouring coffee into dainty china cups. She looks up as I approach and flashes me a smile.

'Good morning! Would you like a cup of coffee?' she asks.

'Yes, please,' I say, smiling back. Even though I can still taste the coffee I just had, but you can never have too much coffee, can you?

This tips the ladies off to the fact that I'm here, so we all exchange polite good mornings.

Taking my seat at the table, as the waitress fills up my cup, I take a look around the dining room. The high ceilings are decked out with fancy mouldings, and huge windows draped with heavy ruby-red velvet curtains let in beams of morning sunlight that make the polished wood floor gleam. You couldn't get away without dusting this room, that's for sure. There's a massive antique sideboard against one wall, piled high with even more dishes, ready to refill the table – although I suspect these are the ornamental plates, not the ones we use.

'Amber, up and at 'em already?' Mandy says, her voice as chipper as a salesperson on commission. 'You look like you've been out in the cold. Are you having breakfast with us?'

'I just popped to the resort shops for a few bits and bobs,' I explain, trying to sound nonchalant. 'And yes to breakfast.'

'Goodness – you really were unprepared for this trip, weren't you?' she says, nodding towards my bag. Mandy's tone drips with condescension, her words delivered in that patronising baby voice she seems to only use with me. 'If we had known, we would've had a whip-round, wouldn't we, ladies?'

It takes all my strength and focus not to roll my eyes at her, because you just know she's trying to make me feel bad.

'I was just spoiling myself,' I insist, lifting my chin slightly.

'The day I spoil myself with a toothbrush, shoot me,' Mandy laughs, and the others join in. Everyone has to laugh at Mandy's jokes, even when she isn't funny, it turns out.

'Actually, I bought myself a hamper,' I lie smoothly, hoping to put a stop to her smugness.

'Oh, what did you get?' Gina asks, her curiosity piqued. 'Let's see.'

I know, I didn't actually buy myself this hamper, but I'll bet it's full of fancy, luxury products, and when this lot see it, it's going to wipe the smiles off their faces. They'll never know I didn't actually pay for them. I know, I shouldn't have to resort to little scams like this to save face, but it will make the week go a lot faster. I need a little win, especially when it feels like it's me vs. Mandy.

But just as I step closer to the table, placing the hamper down where everyone can see it, Mandy's eyes zero in on me, her nose twitching like a bloodhound's.

'Amber, you're... you're covered in something. It looks like pastry flakes. Have you already eaten?' she asks accusingly.

See, this is why I was worried, about having pre-breakfast breakfast, because Mandy clearly has a tone.

Ah, shit. I forgot to dust myself off after my croissant. Honestly, pastries, Greggs sausage rolls – it's always the same deal. I always have to do that awkward dance to shake off the crumbs.

'Oh, you know what, it was the weirdest thing,' I start, hoping inspiration will strike. I am a storyteller, after all. 'This bird flew over me, a big one, and it was carrying something in its mouth – it looked like a croissant – and it just sort of rained bits of pastry down above me, like snow. Wow, I thought I'd dodged it. Thanks for letting me know.'

I brush myself down, trying to look as dignified as possible, hoping that they believe my frankly ridiculous story. Mandy narrows her eyes, clearly unconvinced.

'A bird?' Mandy repeats in disbelief.

'What sort of bird?' Bette chimes in, her brow furrowed in confusion.

Honestly, I couldn't even guess at what kind of birds they have here. We're in the mountains, surrounded by snow. If we were in London, I'd say it was a pigeon and no one would bat an eye, because everyone knows pigeons have the audacity, but here... do they even have pigeons?

'It was just so fast, I didn't get a chance to see what kind of bird it was,' I reply, hoping that will put an end to the interrogation.

'And yet you saw what kind of pastry it was,' Mandy points out, her tone as sharp and knowing as ever.

'Well, it did land on me, it turns out,' I say with a shrug, trying to sound casual.

I mean, it sort of did land on me, just, you know, in my mouth.

Mandy purses her lips but doesn't press further. I can see the gears turning in her head, like she knows I'm lying, she just isn't sure why.

'Anyway, come on, show us this hamper,' Gina says, leaning in with eager curiosity. 'Get you, spoiling yourself.'

'I know, it's naughty of me, but sometimes you need little treats to make you feel good on the inside,' I say, trying to sound like I do this sort of thing all the time, as I open the hamper.

I throw the lid back, and I can feel every pair of eyes in the room zeroing in on it.

'Bloody hell, that will make you feel good on the inside,' Gina says through a snort, clearly trying to suppress a laugh.

All I can do is stare at the contents. Right on top is a big purple dildo. And not just any dildo – it's huge, and detailed, and flecked with sparkles for some reason. It's giving Edward Cullen from *Twilight*... I'd imagine.

And that's not all. There are random bottles of body oils, flavoured lubes, nipple tassels, and more types of condoms than I even knew existed before today.

I finally muster the strength to flip the lid shut, my cheeks burning. Bloody hell, France, is this what a romance kit includes here? What happened to a massage and a cuddle?

'Okay, wow, I must have picked up the wrong hamper, or been given the wrong one because, yeah, no, that's not what I wanted,' I babble, hoping they believe me. It's hard to sound like you're telling the truth about one thing, when you're lying about something else.

'There's no shame in it,' Gina insists, patting my hand. 'If you've read one of my books, you'll know I'm all about the self-love.'

'What did you think you were going to do with the condoms,

alone?' Mandy asks, eyes narrowing with faux innocence. 'Unless... no! Is this all to woo Henri? Wow, you are taking this competition seriously.'

She lowers her voice as she says this. Even though there are no staff members currently in the room, she is in touch with reality enough to know that, to other people, there's something very weird about her 'race to shag the caretaker' wager.

'No, God, no, nothing like that, it was supposed to be bath stuff,' I insist, trying to salvage what's left of my dignity.

'Oh, you can use those in the bath,' Gina informs me earnestly.

I place the box on the floor – out of sight, out of mind – and take my seat. I pick up my coffee and take a big sip. Right now I wish mine was Irish, it might help me feel less mortified.

'You're a dark horse, aren't you?' Bette teases, waggling her eyebrows, refusing to let it go.

'No. No, I'm not,' I insist, shaking my head so vigorously it gives me a headache. 'In fact, I was hoping I could speak to you ladies about it.'

'About your sex life?' Mandy exclaims, her fork hovering in front of her mouth like she's suspended in time.

'No, about my book,' I reply quickly, feeling my cheeks flush – or flush more, I guess, because I'm still bright red from showcasing a dildo on the breakfast table.

'What are you having trouble with?' Gina asks.

'Jen wants me to write spicy scenes,' I tell them. 'I've never done it before. In fact, I always tend to favour the com over the rom. But Jen thinks it's important, and she wants me to try, but I just don't know where to begin.'

'Do you have anything I can read?' Gina asks. 'I could give you some pointers?'

'I can't even get anything on the page,' I confess. 'Or, if I do, I delete it. Everything I write is just so cringey. It feels like spice for the sake of it, I don't know how to do it authentically. Does that make sense?'

'Well, you've come to the right place,' Gina says with a confident smile. 'Spice is my thing. First, you need to connect with the feelings yourself. If you can't feel the love, neither can your characters.'

'So, what do you suggest?' I ask, feeling a bit desperate. Presumably she isn't going to tell me to get a boyfriend because, believe me, sis, I would if I could.

'Take one of my books upstairs and woo yourself,' Gina says, her eyes twinkling with mischief. 'Get in touch with your own feelings, and your own body. If you can't turn on yourself, how are you going to turn on your readers?'

I wince. I think that pretty much sums up the problem I'm having. How am I going to turn anyone on?

'So your homework is to turn yourself on,' Gina tells me.

I blink at her, unsure if I've heard correctly.

'You mean...?'

'Yes, exactly,' Gina says, completely unfazed. 'Take this box of goodies up to your room, light some candles, run a bath, read some steamy scenes, and just let yourself go. Woo yourself.'

Sorry, it's just that it sounds a bit like she's telling me to go upstairs and have a wank. She's not telling me to do that, is she? Oh, she is. Oh, boy, I feel awkward. I'd rather go back to looking at the dildo together.

'Trust me,' Gina insists.

'You won't know until you try,' Bette chimes in. 'It's all in the name of research. Gina's advice worked wonderfully for me.'

Bette has Gina levels of spice in her *Summer at the Seaside* books? I've read Gina's spicy scenes, and it's hard to imagine any of Bette's characters getting their back blown out behind a beach hut.

'Right,' I say slowly. 'Research.'

'Just spare us the details,' Mandy insists, which is funny, because that's the opposite of what I'm supposed to do in the book.

'Maybe I'll give it a go,' I tell them, almost certain that I won't. I mean, I guess I could set the scene, and hope that it inspires me, but... oh, I don't know.

'That's the spirit,' Gina says, clapping her hands. 'Trust me, if you can tap into those naughty thoughts, your writing will be so much stronger. And who knows, you might even learn a bit more about yourself along the way.'

Bette leans in, a mischievous twinkle in her eye.

'So, guess who I saw on my way to bed last night,' she starts, her voice low and breathy.

'Go on,' Mandy prompts her.

'Henri,' she announces triumphantly. 'And I decided to conduct a little experiment.'

'Oh, do tell,' Mandy says, her interest piqued.

Bette grins, clearly relishing the opportunity to share her story.

'Well, I may have... pretended to trip and fall, to see if he would rush to my aid,' she tells us. 'I thought that, if he likes to be a knight in shining armour, then I would throw myself at his mercy.'

'And did he?' I ask, unable to contain my curiosity.

Bette's grin fades slightly.

'Not exactly,' she admits. 'There I am, sprawled out on the floor, waiting for Henri to come rushing over with his charming smile to gallantly offer his big strong arms in assistance. But instead, he looks down at me and says, "Oh, my grandmother falls all the time. I'll get a couple of the female staff to help you" – his grandmother, can you believe that?'

I can't help but laugh at the image of Bette sprawled on the ground, only for Henri to be kind and caring, rather than taking advantage of her while she's on the floor. She's old enough to be his mum, at least. Did she really think that would work? He was probably just worried she had broken her hip, rather than instantly horny.

'So I suppose I'm going to have to change strategy again,' Bette concludes.

'Do you think he's grumpy or sunshine?' Mandy wonders out loud. 'I can't tell, because he's French, I think, but if I can work out which, I'll play the other. That's what I'm going to try first.'

'I'm going for a combination of holiday romance and forbidden love,' Gina announces with a sly smile. 'I'm going to make him think he can't have me, then that he can't have me for long...'

'And Amber is going for seduction, it turns out,' Mandy adds.

I laugh, shaking my head.

'No, no, no seduction,' I protest. 'The only person I'm planning on seducing here is myself, it turns out.'

Right on cue, a server walks into the room to check on us, over-hearing what I just said. Her cheeks flush bright red, and she quickly mumbles an apology before darting out of the room again.

Awkward. So awkward.

Gosh, this whole thing has put me right off my second break-fast. Don't get me wrong, I'll still eat it, but it won't taste the same.

Is Gina right? Will setting the scene for seduction really work? Is the only way to find out to give it a go? I suppose it is, but how?

Wow, I guess I really am out of practice, if I don't even know how to seduce myself.

18

I can't quite believe I'm saying this but I'm in my room, with the contents of my romance hamper spread out in front of me, and I'm taking Gina's advice.

Well, I'm taking part of her advice. I've set a romantic scene for myself, but the only thing I'll be doing with my hands is writing – well, hopefully. So far it's not so good.

I'm in my room, perched on the edge of my bed, wearing the ridiculously lacy, barely there lingerie from the hamper. I feel like I look like I'm about to shoot a low-budget porno, or the person on an Only Fans-type site who can't even get people to subscribe to her free stuff.

With a glass of wine in one hand (yep, apparently I need to get drunk even just to woo myself, and yes, I know it's not even lunchtime but cut me some slack, I'm trying to create a mood here) and my laptop balanced precariously on my knees, I'm trying my best to think spicy thoughts but really I'm thinking about everything else – did I turn off everything I needed to turn off in my flat, an argument I had in 2009, what time lunch is, who played the male lead in the movie *Jeepers Creepers*...

Blah. No, stop it, think sexy thoughts, think sexy thoughts. I really can't imagine this working for me but maybe that's why it isn't working. I just need to believe.

I'm doing my best. The room is dimly lit, with candles flickering softly on the bedside table. I have some romantic music playing quietly. The ambience is perfect, or at least it should be. The only thing I'm missing is a man – which is nothing new – but to be honest I'm not even sure that would help.

Oh, come on, Amber, you can do this. I take a big sip of wine – yes, I know it's only lunchtime, but it's *for my art*.

I flick (poor choice of words) to a point in my manuscript where the main character and the love interest finally get together. This should be the perfect place for a spicy scene, right? I take a deep breath and try to channel my sex goddess.

He leaned in, his breath warm against my ear as he whispered…

Nope, too romantic, too soft, right? I delete the line and try again.

Our lips met in a passionate kiss, his hands roaming down to my…

No.

I grab his…

No! Ergh. I'm starting to think half the battle with this is knowing what to call things. Penis is too formal, willy is too silly, dick feels a little aggressive – I could just go for an absolute wild-card word, like, I don't know… dong?

He whipped out his dong.

Okay, now I just sound like I'm taking the piss. I let out a frustrated sigh and take another swig of wine. This is hopeless.

Determined to give it another go, I start typing again. I'm not going to stop, even if I think what I'm writing is shit, because you know what they say: you can't edit an empty page.

As our lips meet, I feel a shiver run down my spine. His hands find their way to my ~~chest~~ ~~tits~~ ~~boobies~~ hips, and he pulls me close. He runs them up my body, slowly, eventually settling on my neck. His grip tightens and it takes my breath away. Actually, I can't breathe. The look in his eyes changes, from wanting to needing – needing to kill me!

Nope, I need to stop it, I'm not allowed to write about murders. I just can't help it, my creativity wants me to kill people and crack jokes. I can't explain it. Perhaps it's because my love life isn't exactly popping, so I'm just not feeling inspired to go down that route, instead I have some sort of literary bloodlust that I need to satisfy.

Jen doesn't want people choking each other – actually, if it was a sex thing, she probably would – so I need to focus, to get back on track.

Hmm, what else can I do? What else can I do?

I'm bombarding my senses with all things romantic – candles, wine, lingerie – but it's just not enough. Maybe I need to kick it up a notch. Perhaps if I could smell something romantic, it might jump-start my brain. Aromatherapy is a thing, right? I rummage through the hamper and grab a bottle of scented massage oil. It's made with lavender and jasmine, and according to the label it promises pure relaxation and romance. Perfect, because I feel neither of those things right now. I'll take either at this point.

As I unscrew the cap it's hard to imagine this doing the trick, but I can smell it already and it does smell nice at least. The bottle has one of those little nozzles designed to dispense just a few drops at a time. Standing in front of the full-length mirror, I aim it at my chest and give it a gentle squeeze. I figure like you rub menthol there when you have a cold, perhaps this could work in a similar way?

Of course, because it's me in this scenario, instead of a few delicate drops hitting my skin, the entire nozzle pops off. Oil gushes out like a burst water main, drenching me from my collarbone down. I stare down in horror as the slick, floral-scented liquid pools on my skin, and it's heading for the floor.

Oh, for God's sake. I look like I've been gunged. No, I look like I've doused myself in lube. There's spicy and there's... whatever the hell this is.

Panicking, I glance around the room. If I don't clean this up fast, I'm going to destroy the antique furniture or the pristine probably original wood floors. My mind races, and there's only one solution: I need to get to a bathroom, ASAP, without getting this oil on anything.

I'm a slippery mess, and it's only getting worse, and unsurprisingly holding my hands on my body isn't doing much to hold the oil in place, because of course it isn't.

I make a bolt for the bathroom, slipping and sliding on the polished wooden floor – possibly aided by rogue drips of massage oil. But as luck (specifically my luck) would have it, someone's in there. Seriously? Again?

I have no choice. I'm going to have to use Henri's bathroom. I race down the hallway, still holding my hands to my chest, as though that's going to stop the massage oil from dripping everywhere. My feet slap against the floor, leaving a shiny trail of evidence in my wake.

I'm turning the place into one big slip-and-slide.

Please be free, please be free.

I reach Henri's door, twist the handle, and – oh, hallelujah – it swings open. I barrel through, only to slam head first into something solid.

Not just solid. Warm, wet, and almost entirely naked. And my also warm, wet, almost entirely naked body has just clapped with theirs. I know who it is before I even fully understand what the hell just happened.

I stumble back, my eyes wide, my breath held. Henri stands there, fresh from the shower, a towel wrapped around his hips. His eyes are just as wide as mine, and now he's covered in oil too.

I let out a scream, a mix of shock, collision, and sheer embarrassment.

'Oh my God, I'm so sorry,' I babble, trying to find something, anything to cover myself with. A towel is the best I can do, and it's probably ruined now. 'I can explain.'

'Can you?' Henri's smile is cheeky, his eyes dancing with amusement. 'I think this is a story I would love to hear.'

Before I can say something, anything, to make this better, Mandy bursts into the room, her eyes darting from Henri's towel-clad body to my oil-slicked, lingerie-wearing one. Her mouth drops open, and her face goes through a range of emotions: confusion, realisation, and finally, horror.

'Oh,' Mandy says, her voice flat. Then, more horrified, 'Ohhh.'

'It's not what it looks like,' I insist.

I mean, it is exactly what it looks like, but it's not what she thinks it looks like.

'No, that's okay,' Mandy says, backing out of the room. 'I shall leave you to it.'

Henri just laughs and his laugh is so warm and charming, this whole thing is almost worth it... but not quite.

'And to think, I thought a group of romance writers could be boring,' he jokes. 'Do I need to wash this off?'

He nods down at his bizarrely well-oiled, toned (can't help but notice) body. I want to crawl under a rock.

'It's just massage oil,' I explain weakly.

Henri's eyes gleam mischievously.

'Oh, do I need someone to rub it in?' he asks, with a wink.

I'm so red I'm doing everything I can to avoid catching my reflection in the steamy mirror, because I probably look so embarrassed, and realising that will probably only make me feel worse.

I glance down at my feet awkwardly, only to realise that my lingerie is absolutely saturated in oil, in a way that only washing it can fix.

'Do you have a washing machine here?' I ask, trying to move this shitshow along.

'We have a laundry room,' Henri replies, still smiling. 'We have someone who does the washing twice a week. She's not here today, but guests are welcome to use the facilities.'

'I'll do that, thanks,' I mumble. 'Actually, I'll go do it now and leave you to clean up.'

Before Henri can say anything else, I dash out of his bathroom and back down the hallway, praying no one else sees me in this state. Thankfully, the other bathroom is now free – I'm guessing Mandy was in there before, which is how she heard me scream, and the reason I'm going to need to do some damage control later.

I rush into the bathroom, shut the door behind me, lock it, and start cleaning myself up, dropping my oil-soaked lingerie into the bath where it can hopefully do no more damage.

I mean, I was just then the most intimate I've been with a man for a long time, wearing lingerie, covered in massage oil. But is this what Jen wants? Somehow, I don't think so.

19

I'm starting to settle a little now but I've been letting my imagination play tricks on me, down here in the laundry room.

I made my way down the narrow steps, after asking a member of the kitchen staff for directions, and with each creaky step I took I started to paint a picture of what I might find down here. It's dimly lit, with exposed pipes running along the low ceiling and walls painted a drab grey that looks even more dismal under the flickering fluorescent light – not very château-y at all. Then again, it's too cold to be outside with a washboard, as my brain is imagining it back in the day.

The whole place reminds me of that scene in *Home Alone* where Kevin is scared of the basement – dark, slightly musty, and eerily quiet apart from the hum of the washing machine churning away in the corner.

I stare at my underwear, through the little washing machine door, trying not to dwell on what just happened. I think that's why I'm letting my imagination run away with me, because it's easier to entertain the idea of a ghost stuffing me into the tumble dryer than it is replaying my most recent bathroom interaction with Henri.

Because of effing course there is more than one bathroom interaction to choose from.

Trying to scare myself out of an existential crisis is all well and good, until the door swings open and Henri walks in.

I jump about a foot in the air.

'Henri! You scared me!' I blurt.

'Did I?' he asks, clearly unable to think of a logical reason why.

Probably best I keep my imagination to myself.

'I didn't recognise you,' I tell him with a smile. 'I've never seen you not soaking wet.'

'That's because you keep looking for me in the bathroom,' he teases. 'Which reminds me, thank you for the moisturiser. My skin has never felt softer.'

I laugh, because if you can't laugh...

'You're welcome,' I reply. 'It was technically massage oil, so hopefully the essential oils calmed you enough to take the edge off the shock. I can explain what happened, all of it, by the way. There's a perfec— erm, a logical explanation.'

I have to walk that back a little, because it's definitely not a perfectly logical explanation, but I can explain it.

Henri waves a hand dismissively.

'No need to explain. Though I am a bit disappointed,' he says. 'I thought all the sneaking around was in aid of me.'

Don't blush, don't blush.

'Do guests often barge into your room, in their underwear, and throw themselves at you?' I ask.

'It's what you English call an occupational hazard,' he tells me cheekily.

Fair enough.

Henri smiles as he glances around the room, stopping when his eyes home in on the washing machine behind me. I follow his gaze and feel my cheeks heat up as I realise he's looking at my underwear, spinning around in there. I don't know why but it feels more embarrassing than it did when he saw it on my body.

'Oh la la,' he says, raising an eyebrow and giving me a teasing grin. 'Those were a good choice. Very beautiful.'

'Are you seriously hitting on my underwear?' I joke.

He laughs, holding up his hands in mock surrender.

'Only in the most respectful way possible. I promise,' he insists.

I shake my head as the mood lightens.

'I'm not usually the kind of girl to air my dirty laundry in front of people,' I tell him. 'You've got to let me explain, so that you don't think I'm a pervert.'

'I don't mind thinking you're a pervert but, okay,' he replies.

I take a deep breath, leaning back against the wall behind me.

'It's just... I'm having trouble writing romantic scenes at the moment,' I begin. 'The other authors suggested that if I set a romantic scene to write in, that it might inspire me to write romantic stuff.'

'Like method acting,' Henri says, nodding.

'Yes, exactly,' I reply, almost excitedly, because he gets it. 'But I was zero method and all madness. Everything just seemed to go wrong, and I didn't find myself feeling inspired to write anything but slapstick.'

Henri's smile softens.

'Well, perhaps I can help you out,' he suggests. 'This is a very inspiring and romantic place, after all. I can recommend some locations that might spark that romantic creativity.'

I perk up at that.

'Really? That would be great!' I reply.

Henri nods.

'Sure. I have some work to do now, but later I can give you the grand tour. Ideally somewhere other than the bathroom.'

I laugh, and practically melt at his cheeky grin.

'I'll hold you to that,' I tell him. 'Thanks, Henri.'

He gives me a playful salute and heads for the door.

'I'll see you later, Amber,' he says.

'Bye, Henri,' I say, feeling a rush of relief to have smoothed everything over. Of course, I still have to try to explain things to Mandy. I can't imagine her being so understanding.

Okay, I've messed around long enough. Time to get on with what I'm actually supposed to be doing today, that might actually benefit me in some way. Meeting Caleb.

I take my phone from my pocket and message him, telling him I want to meet, and that I'm willing to work with him. Well, it's something to do, and if things go south with my career, well, it's some money. How long it will last me though, I have no idea.

20

I generally consider myself to be quite a boring person, and anything that makes me interesting never really seems to impress anyone. For starters, telling people I live in Canary Wharf usually earns me a few raised eyebrows and impressed nods. But that all changes when they actually see my shoebox of an apartment. They would be more impressed if I lived, I don't know, literally anywhere else. Living in what people regard as a small home, in a nice area, seems to give some people the ick, almost like they find something offensively inauthentic about it, like they feel like they've been mis-sold someone well-to-do, who they imagined in a penthouse.

And then there's my job. You'd think people would be impressed by the fact that I write books for a living, right? Wrong. Telling people I'm a writer mostly results in them looking at me like I just said I'm an aspiring wizard or I'm trying to manifest an income with the phases of the moon. It's like they instantly imagine me as some penniless, self-published writer, typing away on an old computer in a messy bedroom (hey, my laptop is relatively new!). Which is hilarious, because the self-published writers I know are the ones raking in the big bucks, while I'm sitting here with my traditional publishing deal, struggling on, with no real freedom over what I get to write, or when (or where, it turns out) I get to write it.

Honestly, when people find out I write books, they just assume it's a silly little hobby, not a real job. A self-indulgent act of creative whimsy. It's only when they find out that my series did pretty well that they start to take me seriously. Not that I find it easy to tell people about my success; I tend to let them think I'm just another struggling writer instead. Ironically, I am struggling right now, but for completely different reasons.

Generally speaking, my day-to-day life is peaceful to the point of dull. I mean, sure, I manage to embarrass myself on a regular basis, and I keep myself entertained with a steady stream of ill-timed jokes, but nothing really exciting happens to me. Until this week, that is. This week has been like stepping into an alternate universe where everything that can go wrong will go wrong, in the most spectacular fashion, and with a healthy dose of massage oil over the lot of it.

I've been bouncing from one ridiculous situation to the next, constantly thinking to myself, I can't believe this is happening or I can't believe I'm doing this. It's like living in a sitcom, only without the laugh track to make me feel good about my jokes or better about my life choices.

Take right now, for instance. Here I am, standing at Caleb's door, at the chalet he's staying in, knocking and waiting for him to let me in. I can't believe I'm here, or that this is happening, because this sort of thing never happens to me – and yet I feel like I'm uttering that phrase every few minutes.

'Hello,' he says, greeting me warmly as he opens the door. 'Come in, it feels freezing out there.'

'Thanks,' I say, stepping inside and immediately feeling the warmth of the place.

This chalet – the honeymoon chalet, no less – is gorgeous. It's got this large open-plan living space with a roaring fire that is practically insisting on romance. The décor is what you'd expect (or dream about, even) from a contemporary chalet in the Alps: lots of wood, plush furnishings, and views from every window, from every angle, each like a different postcard from the same stand. Looking out over the trees, and the snow, and the sky – nothing is moving. It really is like gazing at a work of art.

'Wow, this place is really nice,' I tell Caleb, trying not to sound too envious of how the other half live. 'I'm staying in the old château, in the grounds. It's nice, but it can be cold, and the hallways are a bit creepy. This is way more my scene.'

Well, if I could afford this scene, it would be.

Caleb smiles.

'Yeah, it's not like that here,' he says. 'Not lonely at all – even though I am on my own. I feel like I'm in the heart of the resort, living in luxury, but still with plenty of privacy. This place guarantees it for its guests, so that's a bonus.'

I nod thoughtfully. Imagine having to worry about your privacy like that. As a writer, even if some people have heard of me, no one spots me in the street. I don't have to worry about being stopped for a chat or a photo, being hassled, either in a well-meaning way or worse. Caleb must get mobbed wherever he goes, so places like this must be a nice break from real life for him. I guess, for all the good stuff he's got going on, I have to feel a bit of sympathy on that count.

'Well, as fun as it is here, there are still less distractions at the château than there are back home, which is good seeing as though I'm supposed to be here to finish my book before Christmas,' I tell him – still not all that confident I'll be able to do it.

'How's it going?' he asks me.

'Don't ask,' I reply.

Caleb opens his mouth, as if he's going to say something, but something suddenly pops into my head and I just have to ask...

'Hey, what was in your hamper?' I ask curiously.

'Erm, just romantic stuff,' he says casually.

'Like what though?' I reply.

'Oh, nothing special,' he says. 'Chocolate, rose petals, bubble bath.'

'What?' I squeak. 'Are you serious? You got chocolate!'

'I already ate it, obviously,' he says. 'Sorry. Didn't you get any in yours?'

'The closest thing I got to chocolate was flavoured lube,' I tell him in disbelief.

'What flavour?' he asks with a curious smile.

'Oi, I'm serious,' I reply, stifling a laugh. 'Mine was full of sex stuff. I opened it in front of people, it was so embarrassing.'

'Ah, come on, there's nothing embarrassing about a bottle of lube, it probably just looked like lotion or something,' he reassures me.

'Yeah, yeah, I'm sure you're right,' I reply, but then I shift my tone. 'And the big purple dildo that I flashed to everyone at the dinner table, I'm sure that probably looked like something else too – an effing penis!'

Caleb cracks up.

'I don't know what's funnier,' he says. 'You whipping out a wanger at the dinner table, or the fact you say "effing" – I do know, it's the dildo, but it's all hilarious.'

'It's a force of habit,' I tell him. 'I use it in my books a lot of the time, because some people don't like too much swearing.'

'Really?' he replies. 'I love a good fuck.'

I flash him a smile.

'And using the word too,' he adds cheekily.

'People say that swearing isn't very creative, or it's for people with a limited vocabulary, but just think about how versatile that one word really is. Fuck you – angry. Fuck me – shocked.'

'Let's fuck – horny. Fuck it – resignation,' Caleb adds. 'Hey, this is fun.'

I laugh, because it really is.

'Let's fuck with him – mischievous,' I add. 'Let's fuck him up – violent.'

'You're so fucking awesome – compliment,' Caleb says.

'But you can substitute them for "eff",' I point out. 'Don't eff with me – threat.'

'Oh, but the real thing just sounds much more impactful,' he points out.

'Well, I hope you enjoyed your free fucking chocolate,' I joke.

'Well, I'm not saying anything about what you got,' he adds with a laugh.

'I suppose you got this place for free too,' I muse as I glance around the chalet.

'Actually, no, I'm paying for my stay,' Caleb replies. 'I'm sure dropping my name helped me bag a last-minute booking, and they did offer me the chalet for free, but the catch with freebies is that you have to promote them. I don't want anyone to know I'm here – and they did, so I thought best to book it with no strings attached. I figured if you were helping me out, well, if any photographers managed to sneak in, they'd see you weren't Annabelle, and the jig would be up.'

'Does it really have to be Annabelle in your photos?' I ask curiously. 'If they just want you to plug products on a romantic break, surely you can do that with any girl?'

Caleb pulls a face, as though he's mulling things over again, but then he seems to land on the same conclusion.

'I think because I made the deals while I was with Annabelle, and we were basically everyone's favourite couple on Instagram, brands might not want to see me peddling romance with someone new,' he points out. 'No one even knows we broke up, so it might seem like I've moved on really quickly, or like I'm cheating on her – the optics would be all wrong. The brands might pull their deals, and I'd lose out on a lot of money.'

I wonder just how important money is to Caleb. It seems like it's very important, although I guess money is important to everyone. Living isn't getting any cheaper. And money is the reason I'm here, so I really can't judge him, can I?

I was never a fan but I certainly saw a lot of Caleb and Annabelle online. They were Instagram's sweethearts. Everyone loved them – except for me. Personally, I was always sick of seeing their smug, loved-up faces everywhere (although, thinking about it, that's probably something that goes hand in hand with being so single for so long). If I hadn't met Caleb, I probably would have felt a weird relief at their break-up, to not have to see their seemingly unrealistic, blissfully happy life, but I did always view their relationship cynically, like it was one big marketing ploy. Sitting here now, hearing what Caleb wants me to do, doesn't exactly change that, but I do get the sense that he actually liked her. Plus, any break-up sucks, right?

'Okay, so, what's the plan?' I ask, ready to get down to business.

Caleb motions for me to sit down on the sofa by the roaring fire. I oblige, sinking into the softness, while he retrieves a suitcase from the other side of the room. He drags it over with a grunt, unzips it, and starts pulling out items like a magician pulling endless random items out of a hat.

'So, here's the deal,' Caleb begins, spreading out a collection of clothes, accessories, and random gadgets on the coffee table. 'I have bags full of products and whenever I fulfil my end of the deal and share something on my socials, I get paid. Each product pays a different amount. For example...' He rummages through one of the bags and pulls out a pair of handcuffs. 'I have a selection of items from a well-known trendy adult store, and products like these tend to pay higher.'

I blink at him, unable to hide my surprise. Not that you make more money from stuff like that, just at the sight of him dangling handcuffs in my direction.

He quickly waves his free hand, as he stuffs the handcuffs back in the case.

'We don't have to do anything like that, I'm just saying,' he adds.

I let out a sigh of relief. Well, I've seen my fair share of things in the romance hamper, but if I couldn't even bring myself to wear nipple tassels in my own company, I'm not sure playing sexy dress-up with Caleb is going to feel like a casual walk in the park.

'So, do you think we can really pull this off?' I ask him, changing the subject, although probably not choosing the best words. It's ironic that, even though I'm a writer, I always seem to put my foot in it with my choice of words.

'So long as we don't get your face in the shot, no one is going to be able to tell the difference,' Caleb insists. 'Unless you have any secret tattoos – you don't, do you?'

'Only the one of Vincent van Gogh's *Starry Night* that covers most of my back,' I reply with a completely straight face. 'But don't worry, it won't be a copyright issue, because in mine all of the stars are replaced with breasts.'

Caleb stares at me, wide-eyed.

'I'm joking!' I quickly insist. 'No, no tattoos. I'm too indecisive, and too much of a baby – at least I think I am.'

'Oh, you're cracking jokes?' Caleb teases with a grin. 'I forgot you make those. That's all good then. The gig is yours.'

I muster up some faux enthusiasm – although, if I'm being honest I'm actually incredibly curious about the process, and am oddly looking forward to playing at being an influencer, even if it's only for a few days.

'So, when do we start, boss?' I ask.

'When are you free?' he replies.

'Well, I'm having dinner with the other writers this evening,' I reply. 'So, tomorrow?'

'Tomorrow sounds great,' he says.

'What will you do tonight?' I ask, curious about his plans.

'Oh, I'll find something to amuse myself,' he replies with a shrug. 'Did you know they have a nightclub here?'

'Wow, really?' I say, genuinely surprised. 'I had no idea.'

'Yeah, they have all sorts,' he tells me. 'Maybe we can do some exploring together.'

'That would be great,' I say, wondering if they have anything else I should make the most of while I'm here, on my free trip, hanging out with the king of freebies.

'Yeah, I know how to treat my fake girlfriend,' he jokes.

'Oh, please,' I reply, playfully holding up my hand in a stop motion. 'I'm more like your prop girlfriend, if anything. Right, well, I'll get going. See you tomorrow.'

'See you tomorrow,' he replies with a smile. 'Maybe we can take you to get your nails done in the morning.'

'What's wrong with my nails?' I ask, offended for a split second, but as I glance down at my dark purple nails, now chipped and in need of some serious TLC, I can see where he's coming from.

'You're going to be holding lots of things in your hands,' he points out. 'The nails always have to be on point.'

'I bet they don't for the men,' I clap back, eyeing his hands.

Caleb holds out his hands, and okay, he does actually have really nice nails for a bloke. They don't look like they've been manicured, necessarily, but they're neat, with just enough shine to not be suspicious.

'Fair enough,' I say with a laugh as I head for the door. 'See you tomorrow.'

'See you tomorrow,' he replies, still grinning.

I head back out into the cold – boy, it always feels worse, when you've been warm for a while.

Okay, truthfully, I am actually really looking forward to this weird little project. It will be nice to have an interesting life for once, even if it is only for a few days – and it isn't technically my life.

21

I feel like a teenager, although, to be honest, not even my own parents held me accountable like this. I thought I was a grown woman – turns out I was wrong.

'Where have you been?' Mandy asks, her tone sharp and clearly annoyed.

'Down at the resort,' I say simply, my heart pounding. I have no idea what I've done wrong, but I fear the consequences anyway.

Mandy's eyes narrow, and I would guess that her blatant irritation isn't really about me being late at all. It's more likely about seeing me with Henri earlier, in his bathroom – something she has yet to bring up with me, and I can't say I'm looking forward to when she does.

'We thought you weren't going to show up for dinner,' Mandy adds, her voice dripping with disappointment – and, again, I'm not sure if she's annoyed I didn't turn up on time, or that I eventually did.

'Have I missed it?' I ask, glancing at the table that looks neatly set.

'No, but that's not the point,' Mandy replies, crossing her arms.

Then what is the point?

Bette, sensing the tension, jumps in.

'You're here now,' she says with a smile. 'That's what matters. Just in time to eat.'

'But the point is...' Mandy starts, but her voice trails off as Henri enters the room.

'Oh, Henri, *bonjour*,' she says, her tone shifting to something much more cheerful and bright. It's like she has been possessed by a ghost (one who is pretending to be French, because she's doing that cringe thing of talking with a bit of an accent, like a French person speaking English).

'Hello, ladies, I just thought I would see how you are finding your stay?' Henri says, his accent as dreamy as ever.

I can't say I'm not grateful that he's taken the heat off me.

'Oh, fabulous,' Mandy gushes, batting her eyelashes. Honestly, it's like she has morphed into a new species, all for Henri's benefit.

'Simply divine,' Gina adds, with a wide smile. She is able to play it a little cooler around him, but you can tell he has her on the hook too.

'Meh,' Bette says, shrugging her shoulders indifferently. 'It's all right.'

Henri looks taken aback by Bette's bluntness. I think we all are.

'Is there anything else you ladies need for your room, or anything that might make your stay better?' Henri asks, his smile back in place, not letting it rattle him for too long.

Mandy and Gina both shake their heads vigorously, insisting everything is perfect, while Bette remains nonchalant, verging on rude actually.

Henri turns to me, his eyes warm and interested.

'Amber, have you found anything inspiring today?' he asks me.

'I've explored the resort a little, but not much,' I admit, not telling anyone who I've been spending time with.

'I'll make a list of the best spots for you,' he offers kindly.

Before I can thank him, Bette interrupts us.

'We're about to eat dinner, Henri. Could you give us some space, please?' she says – again, so rudely.

This isn't like Bette at all. Usually, she's friendly and mumsy, but now she's practically pushing him out the door.

Henri, ever the gentleman, politely excuses himself and leaves us to our meal.

Once he's gone, Bette's demeanour shifts back to her usual warm self.

'Okay, what's going on with you, Bette?' Gina says, asking the question I think we all want to know the answer to.

Bette grins giddily.

'I'm trying to get an "enemies to lovers" thing going on with Henri,' she explains.

Mandy rolls her eyes.

'Bet, the wager is off. We're not playing any more,' she informs her. 'It was only supposed to be a bit of fun, but Amber took it too far by dressing up in lingerie and throwing herself at him. Offering it on a plate is not in the spirit of the competition.'

Embarrassment surges through every vein in my body.

'That's not what happened at all!' I quickly insist. 'I was trying what Gina suggested – to set the scene and get in the mindset to write spicy scenes – but everything just... went wrong.'

'Mishaps in the bedroom are common,' Gina says with a reassuring smile. 'Don't worry about it.'

'But, Gina, it doesn't usually happen when one is on their own,' Mandy points out.

'Dinner is served,' a server announces, entering with a trolley loaded with plates.

And, once again, the heat is off me. Bloody hell, this is exhausting, feeling like I'm under scrutiny every bloody second.

I'm also glad that the silly wager is off – not that I ever intended to compete.

As the conversation shifts to more mundane topics, I realise I need to try harder to fit in with these women... if I actually want to fit in, that is. It's hard to impress someone like Mandy, who seems to prefer when you don't interact with her but then gets offended when you don't.

I have absolutely no idea how I'm going to navigate this one but I'll have to figure something out, if I want to stick around.

22

I was settling into bed when my phone started buzzing with an incoming video call from Tom. I figured he was just calling to check in so I answered smiling brightly, happy to see his familiar face pop up on the screen. But then I noticed his strained expression and, now that we're through the small talk (when he asked how my trip was going, I decided I would tell him it was fine, and not get into too much detail about anything), he's starting to talk about things back home and it sounds like it's all getting worse.

He lets out a heavy sigh.

'Honestly, Amber, it's a mess,' he tells me. 'Mum and Dad are driving me insane. They're arguing constantly, and I'm stuck in the middle. They keep trying to get me to take sides.'

I frown, feeling a pang of guilt.

'What are they arguing about?' I ask. 'What is there to argue about, if they've already decided that they're separating?'

'Everything,' he tells me, rolling his eyes theatrically. 'Money, jobs about the house, what to have for dinner – you name it. It's like they can't agree on anything any more. And they both want me to back them up. Mum keeps saying Dad doesn't appreciate her, and Dad says Mum is always nagging. I'm tired of being their referee.'

'I bet,' I say, wishing I could be there to help. 'But it's not your job to referee. We're their kids, not their therapists.'

'But it's hard to ignore when you're here, and you love them both,' he replies. 'They're both saying things that are just... hurtful. Mum telling Dad he's useless around the house, and Dad saying all Mum is good at is shopping. They've never been this bad before. It's like since you left, things have taken a real turn for the worse.'

I bite my lip, feeling a wave of helplessness – and a huge dose of guilt, because Tom shouldn't be dealing with this on his own.

'I'm so sorry, Tom. I wish I could be there,' I tell him. 'You know the last place I want to be is here doing this shit.'

'I know,' he reassures me. 'I know you would be here if you could. It's just that I could really do with you here. If you were home, we could take a side each and try to get them to work things out. Right now, I feel like I'm fighting a losing battle on my own.'

'I'm so sorry,' I repeat, feeling a lump in my throat. 'I promise I'll be back soon, and we'll figure this out together. Just hang in there a little longer.'

Tom nods, though he doesn't look very reassured.

'Yeah, okay,' he says. 'Sorry for calling you while you're away.'

I think for a moment.

'Do you think I should come home?' I ask him. 'Would you feel better if I did? Because I'm sure if I explain to my editor she will understand.'

I'm absolutely certain she will not understand, or even care all that much, but Tom doesn't need to know that.

'No, no, don't do that,' he insists. 'I think I just needed a bit of a rant.'

'Well, you can call me to rant, any day, any time,' I tell him. 'I've been messaging with them, here and there, just letting them know I'm okay, and asking how they are, but they're not mentioning it. I'll try to call them, when I can, and see if I can get anything out of them. Otherwise, I'll be home soon, and we'll find a way to make it better. Just try to stay calm and don't let them drag you into their fights. Focus on your own stuff as much as you can.'

'I'll try,' he says again, looking a bit more resolute. 'Thanks, Amber. Just talking to you helps a bit.'

'Anytime, Tom,' I say, managing a small smile, but my God I feel so guilty, because if the roles were reversed and I was handling this alone I would be going crazy too. 'I'm always here for you, even if it's just over the phone.'

'Thanks,' he says, giving me a weak smile in return. 'Get some sleep, I know it's later there. Goodnight, Amber.'

'Goodnight,' I say, giving him a wave before I hang up.

I put my phone down and lie back on the pillow, staring at the ceiling.

I don't know how I'm supposed to help fix things at home when I can't even manage my own life.

Mum and Dad have always bickered but it's always been in that fun way that couples who have been married for a long time seem to almost enjoy. They're like a pop-up theatre group, doing a bit, making everyone around them laugh by taking the piss out of each other. Perhaps they're not always joking.

I feel the weight of my family's problems pressing down on me and, along with all of my own problems that I need to solve, for the first time in a long while, I'm not sure I'm up to it.

23

Waking up after another good night's sleep is a luxury I'm starting to get used to, even if my dreams were filled with a chaotic mix of my parents trying to kill each other, and me trying to write a book while a giant nipple tassel chases me down the street – no prizes for guessing what's on my mind.

And all of this happened only when I did eventually fall asleep, that is. Last night it wasn't easy. My call with Tom about my parents has left me feeling a bit on edge. Are things really that bad at home? Are they really over? Perhaps when I get back I can help, even if it's just to smooth things over and establish a new normal. But, God, I wish they would stay together. I'm sure Mum would be fine, but Dad? Who is going to take care of Dad? He isn't going to know how to look after himself, let alone find someone else to do it for him. Bloody hell, I certainly am not going to become the person who ends up cooking and cleaning for him – I'd end up killing him.

As I stretch out in the luxurious bed, I realise just how well rested I feel despite the late night. This bed is heavenly, and it's doing wonders for my sleep quality – I wonder if the same bed could work the same magic back home, but I doubt it, I think perhaps it only works in the Alps where everything is peaceful and the air is so clear. Maybe.

My stomach rumbles, reminding me that my body has already adapted to the two-breakfast way of living. I've slept in a little today, so my stomach is clearly demanding I put something in it already.

There's a knock on my bedroom door, interrupting my thoughts. I quickly throw a jumper on over the vest and shorts I slept in before I answer it. Today restarts the ticker on the number of days it has been since I last flashed my underwear at anyone. Let's start as we mean to go on.

'*Bonjour,*' a cheerful voice greets me as I open the door.

Oh, God, it's Henri. I bet I look like a mess – bed hair, sleep still in my eyes, the whole messy works.

'Oh, hello,' I reply brightly, trying to style it out. 'How's it going?'

I lean on the door frame, trying to look casual, but probably just looking weird.

'I'm very well, thank you. How are you?' he asks, his smile warm and genuine.

'Yeah, can't complain,' I say, mentally reminding myself to rein in the chipperness. No one is this chipper, this early – especially not me.

'I was wondering if you'd like to go for a walk around the resort with me,' Henri says. 'I can show you the sights, see if any of them inspire you to write. It would be nice to set a book here, no?'

I can't hide my smile. I'm not doing anything on purpose, not trying to play the tropes to my advantage, and yet he still wants to give little old me a tour of the place.

'I'd love to,' I reply. 'Just let me get dressed.'

Henri grins.

'Great! I'll treat you to breakfast while we're out,' he tells me. 'So we can leave right away.'

My smile widens even more.

'Okay, sure, I'll be ready in a few minutes,' I tell him.

'I'll wait downstairs,' Henri says. 'Feel free to use my bathroom, knowing it's safe.'

'Oh, I much prefer it when you're in it, keeps me on my toes,' I dare to joke.

Henri chuckles.

'I'll see you downstairs,' he replies.

I close the door and start excitedly rummaging through my suitcase for something to wear. After a few minutes of deliberation, I settle on a cosy yet stylish outfit – a pair of skinny jeans, a warm sweater, and my really big scarf to snuggle up behind. I quickly run a brush through my hair, slap on enough make-up to look somewhat presentable, and then head downstairs.

Henri is waiting by the fireplace in the hallway, looking effortlessly handsome in a casual yet well-put-together outfit. I wonder if I've seen him wearing clothes more times than I've seen him in a towel yet...

He smiles when he sees me, and my heart does a daft little flip, because I'm only human.

'Ready to go?' he asks.

'Ready,' I reply, trying to sound more confident than I feel.

We step out into the crisp morning air, the château looking as picturesque as ever in the daylight.

'I'll drive us,' Henri says, nodding towards his sleek black 4x4.

'Great,' I say, relieved to save myself a trip along the road. Imagine falling in front of him? I'd never live it down.

Henri opens my door for me, ever the gent, and when I sit down on the seat I realise that he has pre-warmed it for me.

'Okay, let's go,' Henri says, as he puts on his seat belt.

Did I mention things like this never usually happen to me?

24

As the chilly air rushes past me I pull my scarf tighter around my neck.

Henri looks like he's nice and toasty – and effortlessly handsome, of course – in a sleek black coat.

The snow crunches under our feet, courtesy of Jack Frost, who topped it up overnight. It isn't enough to bring the resort roads to a close or cause any problems, but it's more than enough to build a snowman or have a snowball fight – not that we're planning on doing either.

The grounds are beautiful and the blanket of snow only adds to the scene.

Henri leads me to a small gazebo overlooking a frozen pond.

'This is the place where an Italian couple got engaged recently,' he says, his breath visible in the cold air. 'The man wanted the whole place lit up with candles and sprinkled rose petals. We said we would get it set up for him, and it was all going well, but then we received a report that the bad weather would be arriving early. We had to get staff from all around the resort – even me – to get everything ready in time but we did it and it was beautiful.'

I can picture it in my mind, and it does sound incredibly romantic – and the fact that it almost went wrong, until everyone worked together, only makes it sound even more dreamy.

'Wow, that's amazing,' I tell him. 'You just know that they're never going to forget that.'

We walk a little further, closer to the heart of the resort, and yet we still feel out of the way.

'Over there is our outdoor hot tub area,' he tells me. 'Perfect for warming up after a day on the slopes. But here is my favourite part – the hot springs.'

It's hidden away from the main resort, so like most of the cool stuff this place has to offer I didn't know it was here, but the hot springs are showstopping.

There is a cluster of hot tubs, generously spaced out, with privacy screens between them so you can enjoy your soak, the view and your privacy. Then there are the hot springs – natural pools with dreamy-looking water that is just so inviting. You can tell that the water is hot, thanks to the steam, and the air around it smells amazing – like a spa, but in a really rich, natural, earthy way.

One of the springs is occupied by a couple, who look so into one another that they don't even notice us walking past. The steam rising from the pools creates an almost dreamy cloud around them.

'Wow, this is just... wow,' I blurt.

'We have tried to make the place as magic as possible, combining old and new, original features with modern additions and comforts,' he explains.

'It's really paid off,' I tell him. 'I'll definitely be coming back to this spot.'

'I rarely get time to enjoy it,' he replies. 'But, if I have the time, I will come with you.'

As he smiles at me I involuntarily glance away from him, smiling at my feet.

It's not every day a hot Frenchman says he'll essentially have a bath with you, is it?

Henri leads me to a charming little bridge that arches over a frozen stream, and then along a path that leads to a secluded garden. Even in winter, covered in snow, the garden is beautiful, with evergreen shrubs and white-dusted benches.

'This garden has a bit of history,' Henri says, gesturing around. 'If you like a good love story, you will love this. Old stories tell that a young prince and a commoner fell in love here, centuries ago. His family disapproved so they would meet in secret, here, in this garden. The prince is said to have planted those evergreen hedges as a symbol of their everlasting love. People who know the story come here, to touch the leaves, and some say that if you sit on one of these benches and make a wish, it will come true.'

I smile as I stroke the leaves, then sit on a bench, closing my eyes for a moment as I make my wish.

When I open them, Henri is watching me with a soft smile. A piece of hair has fallen in front of my face, which Henri gallantly reaches out for, tucking it behind my ear.

'Did you make a wish?' he asks.

'Maybe,' I reply, smiling back.

'I don't suppose you will tell me what it was?' he asks curiously.

I mean, I can't tell him that I wished for a little inspiration to write spicy book scenes. Henri thinks I need romantic scenes, not horny ones – to be honest, I think if I told him I needed spicy inspiration, it would only sound like a dodgy chat-up line anyway.

Next, he leads me to a quaint little chapel nestled among the trees. It's simple yet beautiful, with a bell tower and stained-glass windows.

'This is the resort chapel,' Henri tells me. 'It has seen countless weddings over the years. It was here long before the resort was. We are very fortunate to have our own chapel – if you ever want to get married. My sister married here, it was beautiful.'

I smile. I'm glad he only flirted with the idea of me getting married, rather than asking me my thoughts on it, because I don't even know what I'd say. Well, as the saying (sort of) goes, those who can, do. Those who can't write stories about it.

'That's so touching,' I say, feeling a lump in my throat.

'Let's move on, before you get ideas,' he teases.

Nearing the main hotel building again, Henri takes me towards the ice rink – which unsurprisingly is empty at this hour in the morning. The pristine-looking ice sparkles under the lights. I've never actually been ice skating but I suspect Tom would have made me promise not to do it, along with skiing, if he had known it was on offer.

'This ice rink has a special place in my heart,' Henri says, his eyes twinkling. 'My family has used it for years – for generations. Of course, we have modernised it, and made it safe, and family-friendly, but it still feels like the one I used to use, when I was a child.'

Interestingly, as well as working here, Henri seems to have a lot of history with the place.

'Do you like to ice-skate?' he asks.

'I, erm, I'm not sure I've ever tried,' I reply – well, I am actually sure that I haven't, but I feel like a dork admitting it, so I guess this is me playing it cool.

'Would you like to skate now?' he asks. 'Just me and you.'

Oh, God, what a spectacular opportunity to embarrass myself.

'I'm not sure I'm any good at it,' I say, my confidence fading fast.

'I could teach you,' he suggests. 'It will be like the movies. I'll hold your hands, keep you steady, if you fall I will catch you, dip you, make it seem like I'm going to kiss you – all for your book, and for inspiration, of course.'

Biting off his hand is just one of many physical things I could do with him that are springing to mind right now but – oh God, shit, crap. It's Caleb, he's coming this way. He looks like he's out for a run, and he's fussing with his headphones so he hasn't seen me yet, thank God, and I don't want him to. Well, how do I explain my relationship with Caleb to Henri? Obviously we don't want anyone to know what we're doing, because I'm trying to pass myself off as Annabelle, which means we'll have to say we're just friends, who arranged to be here at the same time, and because that's not true then I'm going to be all shifty about it – it's going to seem like something sus is going on. Best no one who knows me connects me with Caleb, just in case. Sometimes the harder you try to explain things, the worse they sound. Also, I really, really don't want the other writers finding out about this, because I think they already think I'm a weirdo, and this will only add to that.

I hook my arm with Henri's and pull him close, practically dragging him behind a tree until the two of us are tucked away in a clearing. I hold my finger to my lips, as if to say: shh.

My heart is beating so loud I can hear it in my ears. Henri steps closer to me, almost like he's leaning in, smiling.

'Amber?' he says softly.

I notice, over his shoulder, that Caleb has headed the other way. I think we're in the clear.

I step back from him, worried it seems like I was about to put the moves on him.

'Sorry, I thought I saw a moose,' I tell him. 'I must have imagined it. Do you have those here?'

'The dessert?' he asks, puzzled.

I can't help but snort.

'No, you know, a moose,' I say again, holding my open hands

up on the top of my head, trying to make them look like antlers. I'm still not sure he knows what I mean.

'Erm, no, no moose,' he replies. 'Sorry, perhaps my English isn't that good.'

'Are you kidding? Your English is perfect,' I insist. 'Where did you learn to speak it?'

'At school,' he tells me simply. 'We all learn English at school.'

'Right, but I learned French at school, and I barely remember a thing,' I tell him. 'I don't remember them teaching us anything really useful, like how to order a croissant, but randomly I can remember how to briefly describe my bedroom. Oh, and how to say goldfish, for some reason. But I'm not holding any conversations anytime soon.'

Henri just laughs.

'Then it is lucky for us I speak English,' he tells me. 'And that I can order your croissants for you.'

I feel like a genuine Brit abroad right now.

'Perfect,' I reply. 'Maybe we could do that now, actually, because I'm starving, and kind of dizzy, and don't they say you should never skate on an empty stomach?'

Henri laughs again – I assume all this laughing is with me and not at me.

'Okay, so, let me walk you to the resort village, and get you something to eat,' Henri says, ushering me back towards the path. 'Then I have to go for a meeting but perhaps we can visit the hot springs later, see if we can see the moose.'

I laugh because he still has no idea what that means.

'Okay, sounds great,' I tell him.

I actually have a meeting too, with Caleb – and I need to pop to get my nails done first, apparently – so it seems like I might have timed things just right.

Well, almost just right. I never thought I would be in my thirties and hiding behind a tree.

25

It's a big resort, so it makes sense, but it turns out there are more places to eat and drink than there are (exaggerating slightly) people. Restaurants, bars, cafés, stands – I don't know if there is anything you can't get here, which is wild because you would think being stuck up the Alps might limit what was available. Heck, there's even a sushi bar, which looks phenomenal, but it's not the first thing you think of eating when you're up a mountain.

I'm in one of the smaller, more intimate cafés with Caleb, our lunch laid out before us like something out of a glossy magazine about French living.

It really doesn't get more French than this. We've got a fresh baguette, a selection of cheeses, a plate of charcuterie, a *salade niçoise*, and a small pot of creamy pâté. Caleb looks a bit like a DJ as he spins the plates, making sure everything is just right.

Finally happy with the layout, he starts snapping flat-lay photos, some just of the food, others he strategically manages to work his watch into. We're also both wearing some kind of smart rings, the kind that monitor your heart rate and all sorts, so I need to try to work mine into some of my snaps. I'm also taking a bunch of food photos for my own Instagram because, even though I don't have many followers, I love to post food pics.

'Wow, this looks so good,' I say as I follow his lead, positioning my phone above the table.

Caleb, like the pro that he is, gently nudges a piece of cheese into place, making sure everything is arranged just right.

'Here's a tip,' he says, glancing up at me. 'Natural light is your best friend but these spotlights above us could ruin your shot. Make sure you're not casting any shadows over the food. And try different angles – overhead shots are great for flat lays, but sometimes a close-up can capture the texture and details better. Just watch for those shadows.'

'Ooh, thanks,' I reply. 'I never thought an actual influencer would be giving me tips on how to take my foodie pics.'

I adjust my position, taking a few overhead shots before moving in for some close-ups of my wine glass – while I hold the stem with my smart-ring-clad hand, of course.

'How's this?' I ask, showing him my screen.

'Not bad,' he says, studying my photos. 'Try angling the glass, just a little, but wait for the wine to stop swirling around in the glass before you take the photo. Oh, and someone told me this one, and I don't know how professional it is, as far as advice goes, but it has always helped me. When you go to take your photo, always do it while you're breathing out, and breathe out nice and slowly. That's the best way to get the steadiest photo.'

'Wow, okay,' I say, keen to give it a try.

I hold my glass, as instructed, my ring clearly on show. I wait for the contents of my glass to settle, take a deep breath in, then as I slowly breathe out I hit the button.

'How's that?' I say, showing him the new photo.

Caleb leans over to inspect my work, a smile spreading across his face.

'Look at that, it's perfect,' he tells me. 'See how you captured so much more detail?'

'It's the best photo I've ever taken in my life,' I say, semi-seriously. I was joking but the more I look at it, the more I think it actually might be. 'Boys can be dicks, when you take too many food pictures.'

Caleb laughs, I think because I said boys instead of men, almost like I'm chatting to him like we're teenage gal pals.

'Men, I mean,' I quickly correct myself. 'On dates and stuff. I think some of them see it as a red flag.'

'Do you know what I see as a red flag?' he replies. 'People who care about stuff like that. If someone wants to take a fucking picture of a slice of cake, let them take a fucking picture of a slice of cake.'

I laugh.

'Anyway, now for the easy part,' he continues. 'We get to eat it.'

I do not need telling twice.

'So, are you ready to talk about your book?' he asks as he digs in. 'You made it sound like you might be struggling. Plus, I figure if you've taken yourself up a mountain, you must really need to concentrate.'

'My editor sent me here, thinking it might help,' I reply. 'The problem is that my first books did really well, so my editor wants me to write more romcoms, but now she wants me to add in sex scenes. She doesn't think what I'm doing is spicy enough.'

'Oh,' he says simply. 'Do you not really get into the nitty-gritty with that stuff?'

'I don't,' I reply. 'Not because I'm opposed to it, because I'm just not a sexy human.'

He laughs.

'I think I get what you're saying,' he replies. 'So, what do you have so far?'

'I have the bones of it, I just need to up the word count, and that's where my editor wants me to add in the spicy scenes,' I reply. 'About 20k worth.'

'Twenty thousand words of shagging?' he replies. 'Is that normal?'

'Is any of this normal?' I reply with a shrug.

'Fair point,' he says, thankfully understanding what I meant. 'Perhaps I could help you?'

'Oh yeah?' I reply.

'Yeah, when we're done here, come back to my chalet,' he suggests. 'We can take some more photos – I've got more jewellery, clothes, face and body products, books, all sorts – and between shots maybe I can help you with your writing. Two heads are better than one, right?'

Of course, the first thought to pop into my cynical little brain is to wonder whether or not I really want to take writing advice from a celebrity who is publishing a ghostwritten book, but I guess two heads are better than one – the more head the better, as I'm sure my editor would say.

'Okay, sure, thanks,' I reply. 'Maybe if we bounce off each other...'

Caleb's eyebrows shoot up.

'Not like that,' I quickly add with a laugh.

'You never know, it might work,' he jokes. 'But, hey, look, you're talking dirty already. How hard can it be?'

'Now you're doing it,' I point out, sniggering at his choice of words.

'See, we make a great team,' he points out.

We do. We've got the fun, flirty banter down for sure, but I've always been great at that part. It's what happens next that I can never quite pull the trigger on.

26

I'm sitting in Caleb's romantic chalet, with Caleb (who is objectively gorgeous), by a lovely warm fire, eating chocolate, drinking wine, surrounded by a whirlwind of free products, clothes, accessories – all sorts of things. Oh, and I'm getting paid for it. A situation like this should, in theory, make any woman the horniest she has ever been, right? At least from the point of view of writing spicy scenes, but despite Caleb agreeing to help me try to get the ball rolling, nothing is happening.

'I hear it happens to everyone,' I joke.

Caleb smiles. He's lounging on the couch, looking every bit the cool-guy influencer he is, while I'm staring at the empty notebook he gave me, trying to figure out how to even begin writing a spicy scene.

'Tell me what the characters are doing,' Caleb suggests.

'Well, they've just found themselves trapped in a beach hut together, and it has forced them to talk about their feelings, and they can't resist each other any more so they end up kissing,' I tell him. 'And then it sort of fades to black.'

'So your editor wants you to actually write the sex scene,' he replies.

'Yeah, but I've seen the amount of detail these spicy writers go into, and it's a work of art,' I tell him. 'But it feels right. It doesn't feel right for my book – take this scene here for example. The two of them were chased into the hut by a giant crab carrying a broken bottle it picked up from the beach. It would be weird and jarring to suddenly launch into a graphic description of her riding him reverse cowgirl.'

Caleb snorts so hard his wine looks like it's about to come out through his nose. He coughs and splutters.

'You have to warn a man, before you say something like that,' he says with a laugh.

'I'll know for next time,' I reply with a smile.

At least he finds me entertaining.

'Honestly, Caleb,' I sigh, pushing the notebook to one side. 'These scenes are so much more difficult to write than you would think.'

'Really?' he says, disbelief edging into his voice. 'Isn't it just like... descriptive dirty talk?'

'Oh boy,' I say with an overly dramatic roll of my eyes. 'If I even dare to think that is true, and I try to write something, I am quickly reminded that it's basically a skill people either have or they don't. And I don't.'

'All right, let's give it a shot together,' he says, sitting up and grabbing a notebook. 'How about: "She gazed into his eyes, her heart pounding as he leaned in closer..."'

'"...and then the giant crab sideways walked in, and asked them if they wanted him to hold the camera",' I add.

We both burst out laughing.

'Go on then, what happens after she leans in?' I prompt.

'He takes off her bra?' he suggests.

'Does he take off her top first?' I ask.

'No, *she* does,' he continues, like he might be on to something.

'And then?' I press him.

'And then he... he... sucks her tit?'

My sharp intake of breath is louder than I intended it to be.

'Okay, even you don't sound convinced by that,' I tell him with a laugh. 'That sounds so blokey.'

'Well, how else do you say it?' he replies.

'*I don't know*, that's the problem,' I insist.

'If you were going to ask me to do it, how would you ask?' he says, trying a different route, but it's a route that makes me think of Caleb 'sucking my tit' and it takes all of my strength not to blush or babble.

'I wouldn't,' I reply. 'I would just sort of... have it exist near your face.'

'Have it exist by my face?' he repeats back to me. 'Okay, yeah, you're right, you're terrible at this.'

I can't deny that, as bleak as this situation is, it is very funny.

'See? This is what happens every time I try,' I say between giggles.

'Okay, okay, let me try again,' he says, still chuckling. '"He wrapped his arms around her, pulling her close, his lips brushing against her ear as he whispered... Do you want to see my... Pokémon card collection?"'

Now it's my turn to be unimpressed.

'Pokémon card collection?' I echo.

'Yeah, I panicked, I didn't know what word to use for...' He nods at his crotch. 'What word do women prefer?'

'Squirtle?' I suggest, smug that I have just enough knowledge of Pokémon to crack a joke. 'I have absolutely no idea. I even gave dong a go.'

Caleb smiles and cocks his head curiously. Lord have mercy, every word I utter is phallic.

'Amber, you're right,' he concludes. 'I can't think of a word to say that doesn't sound like I'm trying to parody something I heard in a porno.'

'I can write the part of the dialogue where he says he's here to fix the washing machine,' I offer up.

'Fix the washing machine?' Caleb replies with a snort. 'How old is the porn you watch? That's one from the archives.'

'What would you have said instead?' I reply. 'Bearing in mind this is going to tell me a lot about the kind of guy you are and what you're into.'

He looks at me with those cheeky eyes of his, narrowing them slightly, as he grins.

'Yeah, I'd stick to the influencing,' I tell him.

Honestly, I know I'm not one to talk, but this just reminds me that Caleb publishing a book, just because he's a big name, is so unfair. Still, we move. Technically, I'm muscling in on being an influencer, rather than staying in my own lane, so on this very rare occasion it's a two-way street at least.

'Let's just do some photos,' I suggest. 'At least we know that's worthwhile.'

'I've got some wellness books we can pretend to read by the fire and snap some pictures,' he says, pulling out a couple of books with colourful covers.

'Wellness books?' I reply, raising an eyebrow. 'Sounds... interesting.'

We arrange ourselves in front of the fireplace, trying to look all cosy and relaxed, like we're engrossed in our books, but all the while making sure my face isn't in any of the shots of me, and as intellectual as possible.

Unsurprisingly, it turns out that my face isn't the only part of me that gives away that I'm not actually Annabelle – my fashion does too. Thankfully in Caleb's bag of tricks he has all kinds of clothing for me to wear, and while none of it is my usual style, at least no one knows it's me.

The book I have is all about how to manifest your inner goddess – and I know that you shouldn't judge a book by its cover, but neither the cover nor the blurb gives any indication of how exactly it's going to teach people to do this.

'Let's see what pearls of wisdom this one has to offer,' I say, flipping open my book at a random page.

I clear my throat and read aloud: '"To truly connect with your inner goddess, you must first reset your aura by bathing in moonlight, on the third day of your menstrual cycle, while chanting the following words..." – Caleb, at best this is shit. Worst case it's kind of offensive and totally stupid.'

'I don't even know when the third day of my cycle is,' he jokes with a heavy sigh. 'I know, I know. Obviously I think that's a load of shit too.'

'I don't know if I want to read more or throw it into the fire,' I say.

'Isn't that the sign of a good book?' he replies.

'Just hurry up and take my photos, before I destroy it,' I insist.

He snaps a few photos of me, pretending to be deeply engrossed in the book. Then he takes a seat next to me, and we take a few more shots together, trying to look like the epitome of relaxation and enlightenment – still while hiding my face, of course. Holding up the book actually comes in really handy.

'Do you really agree with everything you plug?' I ask, setting the book down – on the table, I've managed to resist cremating it.

Caleb shakes his head.

'If anything goes against my morals, I obviously say no,' he says firmly. 'But for things like this, I just find a way to have a disclaimer. Like, I'll say, "Looking forward to reading these and seeing what they're all about" – showing that I haven't read it yet, but if anyone ever asks me if I recommend them, I'll be honest.'

'That's smart,' I say, nodding.

'Exactly,' he replies, snapping a few more candid shots of me – arty ones, with the fire in the background.

Just as we're finishing up our photo session, my stomach decides it's the perfect time to make its presence known with a loud rumble.

'Sorry about that,' I say, blushing slightly. 'My stomach knows it's on holiday, and all it wants to do is eat.'

Caleb laughs.

'I'm hungry too,' he replies. 'How about we go for pizza? There's a great place at the top of the mountain, you have to go up the gondola to get there.'

'Well, I've never said no to pizza but I've also never been on a gondola,' I reply, feeling ever so slightly apprehensive about trying something new.

'You'll be fine,' he assures me with a warm smile. 'And if you're not, well, the pizza will be worth it.'

I laugh, following his lead, grabbing my coat.

'Okay, let's do it,' I say, with a confidence I don't really have. I am excited though.

It's actually quite fun, being an influencer. Who knew?

27

I can now add a gondola ride up a mountain to the list of things I have done. Granted, it's not a long list, but this would definitely go near the top.

As the doors closed and the gondola began to climb, I watched the ground slowly pull away from us. The snowy landscape, with skiers and snowboarders carving graceful lines into the powder, looked more like a work of art the higher we climbed. The people below grew smaller and smaller, until they looked like tiny, colourful dots dancing around below us. Honestly, it was so beautiful, my nerves disappeared in an instant. It was almost too surreal to be scary, because it was a sight I had never seen before, it was like my brain didn't recognise the fact that we were dangling from a great height.

The air feels so much crisper, and so much colder up here. I feel like I'm up in the sky, like we're standing where the snow comes from – like, if it were to start snowing now, it would be something that happened beneath us, sort of like when you're in a plane high above the clouds.

And now here we are, at the pizza place, and it was definitely worth the climb.

It's so charming, and rustic, with wooden beams and traditional décor but then it has these huge windows with panoramic views of the surrounding mountains. A roaring fire crackles in a stone fireplace, casting a warm glow over the room, and then there's another fire – the real MVP – roaring in the wood-fired pizza oven. The smell of fresh dough, rich tomato sauce and melted cheese is filling the place and I'm breathing it in like I'm in a sauna.

Caleb and I found a table near the window, the view of the snow-covered peaks serving as the perfect backdrop for our meal (and background for our photos). We ordered a couple of pizzas: one classic margherita and one with prosciutto and brie, deciding to share them both. Now we're chatting while we wait and, as fun as Caleb is to chat to, my stomach is calling out for pizza.

'This place is incredible,' I say, looking out the window at the unreal view. 'I don't think I've ever eaten anywhere like this before.'

'It really is,' Caleb agrees. 'There's something about being up here, away from everything, that just clears your mind.'

'That's exactly what I need right now,' I say with a sigh.

'You don't need to clear your mind, you need to make it dirtier,' he jokes.

I laugh.

'If I'm being honest, it's not just the spice that is the problem,' I confess.

'Oh?' he replies curiously as he sips his Coke.

They serve them nice and cold, in glass bottles – why does Coke taste so much nicer from a glass bottle?

'The main problem with the book I'm writing is that it's not really what I want to be writing,' I tell him.

Caleb looks at me, tilting his head, his expression suddenly more curious than ever.

'Okay, so what do you want to be writing?' he asks.

'Funny murder mysteries,' I tell him. 'Basically, I want to write what you write, just with a bit more of a romantic comedy vibe. But my editor won't let me switch genres because my romcoms did so well.'

And apparently only celebrities get to write fun, trending books – or pretend to at least.

Caleb nods thoughtfully.

'That's tough,' he says. 'It's no fun when you're not feeling it. Have you talked to her about it?'

'I have,' I reply, frustration creeping into my voice. 'But she's not interested. Sex was all she really had to offer me.'

Caleb laughs at my choice of words as he leans back in his chair. He rubs his chin thoughtfully for a second or two.

'You know, if you're really not happy doing what you're doing, or what she's asking you to do, then you shouldn't do it,' he says.

I laugh – oh, to be a rich man in this world – shaking my head.

'I can't just breach my contract,' I tell him. 'As much as I would love to right now.'

'Who said anything about you breaching your contract?' he says with a mischievous glint in his eye that kind of excites me. 'Contracts work both ways – and yours probably favours your publisher anyway. You don't need to break it. You need your publisher to break it.'

I look at him, intrigued. He's definitely right about my contract favouring my publisher, and I wonder if his is the same because he's a big name. To be honest, it probably is. With these big publishing houses, I very much get the sense that the house always wins.

'What do you mean?' I ask.

'Write them a book so bad that your editor thinks you've lost your touch,' Caleb explains. 'Make it so unbelievably terrible that she couldn't possibly publish it, or want you to write another one like it. She'll either drop you or let you switch genres. Either way, you're free to do what you want.'

I'm laughing but the more I think about his idea, the bigger the smile on my face grows.

'That's... actually brilliant,' I tell him. 'Manipulative, kind of terrifying but, yeah, brilliant. But how easy is it to write a bad book on purpose?'

Caleb grins.

'It's probably easier than you think,' he replies. 'And I can help you.'

I can't help but laugh. Now that I can probably trust him to do, ghostwriter or not.

'You must know your genre inside and out,' he points out. 'So you'll know what not to do, what doesn't work, the things that your editor hates – just do all of that stuff.'

'And what about the spicy scenes, do I just not bother?' I say.

'I guess you could leave it out but, I suppose, if you want her to believe that you've really tried, just keep doing what you're doing – which doesn't sound good – and throw those in,' he says.

'I could put my dong back in,' I say excitedly, not realising how my choice of words sounds, as usual.

Caleb laughs.

'Yeah, exactly, put your dong back in,' he says with a snigger.

Oh, and right on cue, our pizza arrives. However, in a twist on the usual, it's Caleb who the server overhears saying something dodgy, not me. Usually in situations like this I curl up and die but Caleb just owns it.

'Ah, cheers, buddy,' he says. 'These look great.'

He's not wrong. Both pizzas look absolutely incredible, with just the right balance of toppings, cheese with the perfect level of pull, and basil that smells as fresh as it did when it was still on the plant.

'Dig in,' he says. 'Pizza first, book sabotage later.'

'Sounds good to me,' I say with a smile.

Oh, and it tastes good to me too. I would crawl up this mountain on my hands and knees to get another one of these – *that* good.

We chit-chat about anything and everything while we eat but, honestly, I cannot get Caleb's idea out of my head. I hadn't even thought about it – but why would I? Why would I think to write such a crappy book that no one will want to publish it? I've been so focused on working out how to do a good job that I hadn't even considered doing a bad one on purpose.

I've got my original draft still, but there's no harm in saving a copy, and adding in some awful scenes, right? It's something to think about.

28

I arrive back to the château to hear the muffled sounds of laughter and conversation drifting through the hallway. I follow the voices to the dining room, to say hi, and find Mandy, Bette, and Gina, sitting at a beautifully set table, glasses of wine in hand, chatting animatedly.

'Amber!' Mandy calls out, spotting me in the doorway. 'We've been waiting for you to eat. Where have you been?'

'I went for a walk,' I reply, hesitant to mention that I've already eaten. 'Sorry, I didn't know you would be waiting for me.'

'We always eat together,' she reminds me. 'So, unless we hear otherwise...'

I force a smile and take a seat at the table, feeling the pressure to join in.

'Great timing,' Bette says, uncovering a hot plate filled with... with... I'm not even sure what it is. Some kind of casserole. 'We were just about to dig in.'

It does smell nice, and even though I'm not hungry, I load a small portion onto my plate.

The chatter resumes around me, and I find myself gradually relaxing.

'So,' Mandy says, topping off everyone's wine glasses, 'we've been talking about setting our next books here at the resort. See whose story turns out the best.'

'I bet Bette's will be the most scenic,' Gina chimes in, nodding towards Bette.

'Oh, definitely,' Mandy agrees. 'The worlds you build and your descriptions are always so vivid.'

'And Mandy's will of course be the funniest,' Bette says with a smile.

'And Gina's book will be the spiciest,' Mandy adds, winking at Gina.

They laugh and toast each other, but no one mentions me. Well, I doubt any of this lot have ever even touched one of my books, still, it would be nice to be included in the conversation. Pointing out that they're kind of excluding me probably isn't the best way to fit in. Plus, they did wait for me for dinner, I guess.

After a few bites, I clear my throat, and dare to speak.

'I just wanted to let you know I'm planning to sleep in tomorrow, I'm feeling quite tired,' I tell them. 'So feel free to have breakfast without me.'

'Okay, but make sure you're in for dinner,' Bette says, her tone leaving no room for argument. 'I'm cooking dinner for us all tomorrow night.'

'And I'm pouring the wine,' Mandy jokes – topping up her glass for dramatic effect.

'Okay,' I reply, mentally acknowledging that this definitely doesn't sound optional. 'I'm really looking forward to it.'

As the evening ticks along I find more and more that, in all of their conversations, even the ones about writing, there isn't really much room for me. No mention of me, no one asks me questions, and it's impossible to get a word in.

I know, I shouldn't be complaining, because I've been asking Jen for months if she could get me a seat at the table, and now I have one but... I don't know. Just because you're sitting at a table, doesn't mean you have a seat at the table. I'm going to have to work on that one.

29

As I try to steady myself on my skis, my brother's warning echoes in my head. I did promise him that I would stay away from skis and yet here I am.

Caleb stands beside me, looking effortlessly cool in his ski gear.

'Are you sure you're okay?' he asks, concerned but amused.

'I've never skied before,' I admit, wobbling slightly.

'You still haven't,' he teases. 'You're just standing still.'

We're at the bottom of the slopes, standing on relatively flat land, in hired ski gear that does not look cool in my opinion. Around us, seasoned skiers glide by with ease, their colourful jackets creating a vibrant blur against the white snow. And then there's me, standing still, and just about upright – probably not looking cool at all.

When Caleb said that taking some pictures of some ski content might be good for him, to unlock future opportunities, I said that I was happy to help. It turns out I am neither happy nor helpful, though.

'In that ski mask you could pass for Annabelle from pretty

much any angle,' he jokes. 'It's a great time to take photos – in fact, it's a shame you can't wear it all the time.'

'We just need to do more masked activities then, I guess,' I say – obviously not serious. 'Fencing, perhaps?'

'Good idea,' he replies. 'Maybe a bit of bondage? That could be good for your book. Two birds.'

'Two birds, ay?' I tease him. 'We'll see if I survive this first.'

He moves closer, positioning himself behind me.

'Okay, here's what you need to do,' he says. 'Bend your knees slightly, lean forward just a bit, and keep your weight centred.'

Fuck, is this supposed to be so hot, or am I just sex-starved? I swear, his hands are warm through my jacket as he helps adjust my stance, like he's leaving a big, hot handprint wherever he touches me. It feels kind of nice having his hands on me, guiding me. Jeez, maybe it really has been too long since I had a boyfriend.

'Like this?' I ask, my voice wobbling, as I try to do what he's telling me.

'Perfect,' he says. 'Now, just pretend you know what you're doing. Smile for the camera.'

Caleb snaps a few photos, and I try to look as natural as possible, which is harder than it sounds when you're balancing on two thin planks of... wood? Plastic? Either way, they don't feel at all sturdy. Still, perhaps if I act confidently, I'll be more balanced, whereas if I'm timid and shaky I'll probably make a mistake.

It turns out trying to be confident in skis is the mistake.

I slip almost immediately, and as Caleb lunges to save me, he loses his balance too. We both go down in a heap of skis and limbs, landing on the soft (ish) snow below.

It feels like the world is spinning, and for a second I panic because I can't see out of one eye – only to realise that my goggles have got turned around a little.

Finally certain that we're okay, we both burst out laughing.

Caleb turns to me, snowflakes clinging to his face.

'Are you okay?' he asks.

'Yeah,' I giggle. 'I think so. Wow, skiing really is an adrenaline rush.'

'You still haven't skied,' he laughs as he grabs me, pulling me close.

True.

'How about we take a selfie?' he suggests, holding up his phone.

'Oh, go on then,' I reply. 'Cheese.'

We both grin at the camera, our faces close together – so presumably this photo is for personal use, rather than for his Instagram.

I'm surprised to admit it but I'm having a great time. It feels so nice, having someone to share this with. To be goofy with, to roll around on the floor with. Of course, Caleb isn't actually my boyfriend. He's just pretending. I need to remember that. Still, it really is nice.

30

I don't mean to sound like I'm exaggerating when I say this, but the food here at this resort restaurant (one of many) is nothing short of incredible, and this might be one of the best meals I've ever had in my life.

This place is the complete package. The vibes are great, the music is just the right level to be enjoyable when you listen, but ignorable when you want to chat. The cocktails are amazing and the company isn't bad either.

The second my eyes hit the menu I knew what I was going to have: a burger, with bacon, brie and caramelised onion relish, and a side of French fries. There is so much good stuff on this menu, and I tend to be the sort of person who always orders the same thing at the same restaurant, which I need to try not to do here... but if I did, I wouldn't regret it. This might be the best burger I have ever tasted – ever – and the French fries just feel all the more French for me, well, being in France right now. They don't get more legit than this, do they?

Caleb and I have been chatting for hours and I have to say, I'm surprised at how much it turns out we have in common – both now and when we were younger.

From pirates to Powerpuff Girls (yep, I had a phase where I was into both – my birthday parties took a jarring turn from one year to the next), our childhood obsessions have a lot of crossover, over the years. Even in our teens we both had the same phase, when we were obsessed with pop-punk (except he didn't go as far as to get his eyebrow pierced like I did – not that you would know now, because my dad made me take it out) and gross-out comedy movies. It's like we were following the same blueprint, without even knowing. Even as adults I would say we're both equally obsessed with (if not dependent on) air fryers – although I suspect he probably has a fancy built-in one, like Tom does. It seems as though it's only in recent years that our paths have deviated, with Caleb going on a reality TV show, but that they're coming back together now that he's becoming an author. It's strange really.

But after reminiscing about old TV shows and swapping embarrassing stories of when we were teens, the tone has just shifted a little.

'Sometimes, I feel like I don't belong in this industry,' Caleb admits, his tone showing a little of his vulnerable side. 'I can't shake this feeling, like when I'm at events, that people are side-eyeing me just because I'm famous for being famous, instead of having a talent like an actor or a musician. I think they question what I've actually achieved, other than being a face on TV.'

Wow, I mean, I know all about imposter syndrome (it's part of the job, being an author) but I never would have thought Caleb felt it.

'Listen, anyone who makes you feel bad is probably just jealous, because you've made such a name for yourself that people will pay you thousands of pounds to, like, hold a mug,' I remind him.

'And you made phenomenal TV. Most actors could never – not without a good script.'

'Did you watch the show?' he asks, in a tone that suggests he assumed I hadn't.

'You know what, I hadn't, until I met you, and then I had a peep because I was curious, and I got hooked,' I confess. 'In fact, the only reason I stopped watching you on TV was because you turned up here. So no spoilers, okay? I'll get back to TV you when real you goes home.'

Caleb laughs.

'Thanks for the pep talk,' he tells me, dipping a French fry into his tomato sauce, before popping it into his mouth.

'Ah, you're welcome,' I reply. 'I totally get it. I often feel like I'm surrounded by more experienced, more successful authors, wondering if I'll ever measure up. Sometimes, I can't help but wonder if they're looking down at me, because I'm younger, less experienced, less settled in life. Everyone seems to have a confidence that I don't think I can unlock with anything but time – the problem is, I could really do with it right now.'

'I guess I have all this to look forward to, huh?' he says with a smile.

'Oh, I'm sure you have nothing to worry about,' I insist. 'With the kind of advance you're probably getting, you don't need to care about what anyone thinks.'

'Yeah, maybe you're right,' he replies. 'It's kind of reassuring, chatting with you about this author stuff. Honestly, I feel like a fish out of water sometimes. I know that it was being on TV that got me a foot in the door, but now that I'm here, the pressure's on.'

I mean, publishing a book that is being ghostwritten for you, and people not liking it, isn't exactly the same as slogging away for weeks, months or even years on a book, only to see it flop – and then having to find the strength to do it all again.

'You've got to have faith in yourself,' I remind him. 'Plus, your publisher wouldn't have offered you a deal, if they didn't think that a book by you would do really well.'

Caleb nods thoughtfully.

I suppose, at the very least, it's something that he recognises his privilege, and why he has a seat at the table.

Neither of us has left so much as a bit of garnish on our plates, in fact, they're so clean you could be forgiven for thinking they hadn't been used. You can't even see a trace of ketchup – although calling it ketchup feels like a bit of a diss, because it's more like a fancy tomato puree.

I notice Caleb gesture over my shoulder at someone.

I just stare at him, silently asking if I need to be worried.

'I've arranged us something special for dessert,' he tells me. 'You're going to love it.'

'I am on the verge of a food coma!' I point out. 'Dessert will send me off nicely, thank you.'

Caleb laughs.

'I'm not specifically doing this to take pictures of the different desserts, but it would be a shame not to,' he says.

'Hey, I'm the kind of girl who takes photos of her food, and I only have like 250 followers, so have at it,' I reply. 'Wait – different desserts?'

'Yeah, it's a tasting menu,' he replies. 'Well, in that we're basically tasting everything on the menu.'

A parade of plates arrives at our table, each one looking more beautiful and enticing than the last. There's crème brûlée, tarte Tatin, macarons, something I don't recognise that looks like layers and layers of chocolate, but yes, please. My mouth is watering just looking at them.

'Wow, Caleb, this is amazing,' I say, grabbing a fork and diving into the tarte Tatin. 'You sure know how to treat a prop girlfriend.'

'It's... never been said before,' he jokes. 'Let me try a bit of that tart.'

'Now that I bet you have said before,' I tease.

We both dig in, savouring each bite, and I have to admit, it's pure heaven. The flavours are rich and decadent, and varied – although that could be because we're having everything on the menu. If you're the kind of person who looks at a dessert menu and struggles to choose (which is what I'm like, and yes, I'm aware that is the opposite of what I'm like with main courses) then it really is a great solution.

But then, mid-bite of the chocolate layered thing that I want to actually marry, something occurs to me. Shiiiit. Bette is cooking dinner for everyone tonight. And I'm supposed to show up and eat it. Oh, God, and I've just eaten so, so much food. Honestly, I've been like a magician, because anything that has been put in front of me I have made disappear.

Panic flickers for a moment, and I know that the best thing to do is to stop eating the desserts, but surely I'm in too deep now, and all of this is far too good to waste.

I'll just have to hope that I can make another dinner disappear – ideally without resorting to sleight of hand.

31

As grateful as I am that Caleb is insisting on walking me back to the château in the dark, I'm a little on edge given that I don't want anyone to spot him. Still, it is dark, cold, and snowy, so it's probably for the best that I'm not doing it alone.

We walk together, along the snow-covered path towards the château, his footsteps crunching softly beside mine. As soon as the château is in sight, I'll tell him that I'll be okay from there, so that he can head back, before the snow starts falling again. I'll just have to hope that he isn't so much of a gentleman that he refuses. No, I never thought I would worry about a man being too much of a gentleman.

'You really don't have to walk me all the way,' I say, glancing sideways at him.

'It's no trouble,' Caleb replies, his breath visible in the chilly air. 'If you slip, fall down the mountain and die, then who will be in my photos?'

I know that he's joking but he actually makes a good point. If I slipped and fell down the mountain, how long would it be before anyone noticed, if it weren't for Caleb being here with me? Even my own parents haven't been taking my calls today.

'Well, I can use my torch, for the last stretch,' I reply. 'And I can always google how to do an SOS.'

I reach into my pocket and pull out my phone, for the first time in ages, and notice a notification from my mum that came through earlier. My heart skips a beat.

'Is everything okay?' Caleb asks, noticing my sudden change in expression.

'I'm not sure,' I say, opening the message. 'I have a message from my mum, it says: "Sorry we didn't answer. Your dad was in the hospital. I'm on my way there now. Will call later."'

Panic sets in. I stop in my tracks.

'Shit, I need to call my mum,' I blurt. 'My dad's in the hospital, and she's just dropping it into a text like that? Fuck, I don't have any signal here.'

Caleb quickly reaches into his pocket and hands me his phone.

'Here, use mine,' he tells me, offering me his phone. 'It has some kind of special SIM. I don't know how it works, I think it uses satellites or something. You should be able to get through.'

I fumble with his phone, my hands shaking as I dial Tom's number first. I can't believe he hasn't let me know.

It rings and rings, but no answer. I try to steady my breathing and punch in my mum's number next. Each ring feels like an eternity, but finally, she picks up.

'Mum! What's going on? Is Dad okay?' I blurt out, my voice a mix of worry and fear.

'Amber, it's you! Okay, calm down,' she says, her voice soothing. 'Your dad's fine.'

She sounds confused that I'm even worried, which only confuses *me* further.

'What?' I blurt. 'You said he was in the hospital...'

Mum laughs.

'Amber, you silly goose, you worry too much,' she says – which is rich coming from the world's most spectacular worrier. 'He was just visiting a friend. You know Elsie, from down the street? Remember her son, Ron, and his wife, Erica? We went to Spain with them, years ago, when you were two – remember?'

'No, Mum, I don't remember going to Spain when I was two,' I reply, my tone totally flat.

'Anyway, he was visiting Ken,' she continues her explanation. 'He's broken his hip.'

I have no idea how Ken connects to Ron, Erica or Elsie, but that's the least of my worries right now.

'Mum, you said he was in the hospital, and that you were on your way there,' I point out.

'Yes, he was in the hospital, visiting Ken,' she says, obviously baffled she's having to explain herself. 'Parking is a nightmare there, so I dropped off and picked up your dad – there's no reason we can't be amicable, Amber.'

I mean, from what Tom has been telling me, it doesn't sound like they're being amicable but, again, that's not the point right now.

'Mum, when someone is admitted to hospital you say they are *in* the hospital,' I remind her. 'When they are vising the hospital you say they are *at* the hospital.'

I notice Caleb smiling, part sympathy, part amusement.

'Honestly, you can tell you're a writer,' she replies with a laugh. 'I'm sorry, sweetheart. I didn't mean to scare you. It's been a long day. I should have worded it better.'

I roll my eyes, but I'm smiling.

'Probably,' I say with a laugh, just happy that everything is okay.

We chat for a few more minutes, and she reassures me that

everything is fine. I feel a wave of relief wash over me as I hang up and hand the phone back to Caleb.

'False alarm,' I say, smiling weakly. 'He was just visiting someone.'

Caleb laughs, shaking his head.

'Your mum has a fun way with words, doesn't she?' he points out.

'Yeah, it seems like it runs in the family,' I reply.

'I think that's one of the things that fascinates me about the English language,' he says. 'How changing one word can make such a difference.'

'Or a comma,' I reply. 'It's that old saying about how a comma changes a sentence, like: helping your brother, Jack, off a horse.'

Caleb laughs.

'Exactly,' he replies. 'The difference between being "shit" and "the shit".'

Another great example. My book is currently shit – if I could just find a 'the' from somewhere.

'Right, here we are, I'll be okay from here,' I tell him, the château in my sights.

'Are you sure?' he replies. 'It's less than a minute out of my day...'

'I'm going to feel guilty that you're walking back alone – what if you slip, fall down the mountain, and die?' I ask, echoing his words back to him.

'That's what this cool phone is for,' he says with a smile. 'Goodnight, Amber. It's been fun.'

'It has,' I reply. 'Thanks for everything. Dinner, use of your phone...'

'You're welcome,' he says with a chuckle. 'See you tomorrow.'

I feel all sorts of things right now. I feel a strange mix of emotions – relief, gratitude, and maybe a hint of something else I can't quite place. Oh, and I feel full. So, so full. Which reminds me...

It's time to face the ladies, and the music, and the second dinner.

I know Bette is preparing dinner for everyone, and the thought of facing more food makes my steps feel heavy, like I'm reluctantly headed for a dentist appointment, but I don't want to be rude – well, I don't want them to perceive me as rude. The warm glow from the dining room spills invitingly into the hallway, casting long, spooky shadows, but instead of feeling welcomed, I feel like I'm walking into a scene from a horror movie.

With each step closer, my resolve weakens. I can practically hear my stomach groaning – screaming, even – in protest. I take a deep breath, hoping it will fortify me, instead it only makes me feel even more full, but I'm here now.

There they are: Bette, Mandy, and Gina, all seated around the table, engaged in lively conversation. In the centre of the table sits a steaming-hot plate piled high with what appears to be stew, and I'm sure it would look appealing – to anyone who isn't already painfully full, that is.

'We were beginning to think you weren't going to show,' Mandy says, her eyes narrowing suspiciously as she watches me sit down.

'Sorry, I got caught up doing some research,' I reply, trying to sound as casual as possible. My voice wavers slightly, because I'm worried my breath will still smell of five different desserts, and they'll realise – even though I'm pretty sure I drank enough alcohol to make my entire body sterile enough for surgery.

Gina raises an eyebrow and grins mischievously.

'Research, huh?' she replies. 'Were you rolling around in the snow with a boy?'

I laugh, though it feels a bit forced, but I'm happy to move the conversation along.

'If only,' I say with an easy-breezy scoff. 'No, just a lot of thinking, looking around and note-taking.'

Bette, playing hostess, takes to her feet and leans over the table.

'Well, if you were, I'm sure you'll be hungry,' she says.

I'm sure she's just being friendly, and that she isn't at all suspicious, but I'm paranoid. Without waiting for a response, she loads my plate high with stew, the thick gravy sloshing around as she does so.

Oh God, I feel sick just looking at it. My stomach, already stretched to capacity, churns in protest, but I force a smile and take my seat.

'Oh, you are hungry,' Bette says, noticing the sound.

Mandy eyes me with suspicion, her fork hovering over her plate.

'So, research, hmm? What kind of research?' she asks.

'Oh, you know, just exploring the area, getting a feel for the place,' I say, trying to keep my tone light. 'It could be a great place to set a book.'

'Come on, dig in, dig in!' Bette encourages me.

I stare at the mountain of food in front of me, and the thought of taking even one bite is just too much. But I can't let them see, I need to keep a lid on it. I pick up my fork and push the stew around my plate, trying to make it look like I'm eating.

The ladies continue chatting about their writing schedules, discussing how relaxed things are, and when their deadlines for their next books are. I try to focus on their words, hoping to distract myself from the smell of dinner.

'I'm actually ahead of schedule for once,' Mandy says. 'It's so much more enjoyable when you're not writing under pressure.'

'Same here,' Gina chimes in. 'I've got most of my first draft done, just need to polish it up – there's months until it's due though.'

Imagine having a first draft and months to spare!

Bette looks at me, her eyes narrowing.

'What's wrong, Amber?' she asks. 'You're not eating.'

'Oh, um, I don't eat meat,' I blurt, because it's the first thing that comes to mind. Of course, now I've left myself open to plot holes, if I don't stick with my story *forever*.

Mandy gives me a quizzical look, her brow furrowing in confusion.

'Didn't we see you eating chicken?' she asks. Suddenly she smiles, excited at the thought of catching me in a lie.

'Uh, it's beef I don't eat,' I tell them.

'This is lamb,' Bette points out.

Oh, for God's sake.

'Right, er, I meant red meat,' I clarify. 'I don't eat red meat. Just chicken and fish. It's okay though, I'll just eat the veg.'

I stab a mushy, gravy-soaked carrot with my fork and pop it into my mouth. It feels like it's dripping with grease, and tastes absolutely minging, but that might just be my overstuffed stomach rebelling against any more food.

'Lovely,' I lie, smiling weakly.

Bette, not missing a beat, smiles back with a touch of understanding.

'Don't worry, dessert doesn't have any meat in it,' she tells me. 'Sticky toffee pudding with custard.'

I never thought I'd say this but no more fucking dessert, God, please.

I continue trying to make it look like I'm eating, in the hope I can say I'm too full for dessert. I feel like I'm a kid again, trying to hide the peas under my mashed potatoes, only I'm trying to hide everything under everything else.

What's more sickening than the food, though, is their attitude. Not that there is anything wrong with it – it's jealousy I'm sick with.

Everyone seems so settled, stable, and happy, with their nice lives and their lengthy deadlines.

Mandy and Gina are back to swapping notes on their upcoming projects, while Bette listens happily. It's a cosy, idyllic scene, and I can't help but feel like an outsider looking in.

Here I am, sitting among accomplished, popular authors, and I'm trying to write a bad book on purpose just to get my contract cancelled.

Still, it's the best idea I've got, and it sounds a lot easier than trying to eat a sticky toffee pudding right now.

32

Absolutely stuffed from trying to eat when I wasn't at all hungry, I drag myself upstairs, each step feeling like a monumental effort. My stomach churns as I walk, gurgling and bubbling, warning me that I'm in for a night of discomfort and acid reflux.

'Amber!' Henri's voice calls out from behind me.

I turn to see him hurrying up the stairs to catch up.

'Hey, Henri,' I say, trying to smile through the discomfort – and hoping he doesn't hear the alien noises coming from my tummy. 'How's it going?'

'I feel like I haven't seen you all day. No one's been walking in on me in the bathroom, and it feels strange,' he says, his grin widening.

As someone who has seen him in and out of clothes, it has to be said, he looks great in them too. He dresses in trousers and shirts that could look like workwear or formalwear, depending on what he was doing. It's that easy French charm that makes him look great in (or out of) anything.

I laugh, shaking my head.

'Some days I leave people to shower in private,' I joke. 'Sorry.'

'No need to apologise,' he says with a chuckle. 'Actually, I have an invitation for you.'

'Oh?' I say curiously.

My tummy gurgles, as if it's echoing my words.

'I was wondering if you'd like to see my private cabin,' he offers. 'It's such a romantic space that I'm working on, and I thought you might find it inspiring.'

'Your *private* cabin?' I reply, more than intrigued.

'Yes, it's my current project – new accommodation for the resort,' he explains. 'It's not creepy, I promise – I've just realised it might sound creepy, in my English.'

'Not at all – that sounds amazing,' I say. 'I'd love to see it.'

'Great,' he says, his eyes lighting up. 'It's a special place. I've been putting a lot of effort into making it perfect. There are stunning views of the mountains, and the surrounding area – it's incredibly peaceful.'

'Wow, it sounds dreamy,' I say, already picturing the scene. 'When were you thinking?'

'I could take you there tomorrow afternoon,' he suggests. 'We can take a walk through the woods, and maybe I'll even tell you some more stories about the area. Perhaps there will be food involved.'

Normally a phrase that would be music to my ears, but I really am so full.

'That sounds great,' I say. 'Can't wait.'

'It's one of my favourite places here,' he tells me. 'I think you're going to love it.'

This could be just what I need. Spending more time with Henri, exploring a private, romantic cabin – it sounds like a great way to get inspired. Between scenes in my own life I keep working on my draft, here and there, adding in scenes that are purposefully awful, or just generally messing up what is already there, but it's never too late to get some good inspiration, right?

'*Bonne nuit*, Amber,' Henri says, flashing me that charming smile. 'Sleep well.'

'Goodnight, Henri,' I reply, feeling a bit lighter despite the heaviness in my stomach. 'I'll see you tomorrow.'

Finally alone, I get to take off my jeans, and plonk myself down on the bed.

Lying face down, I turn my head to the side, to look at my phone, only to see that I have a missed FaceTime call from my dad, from a few minutes ago. Oh boy, I should call him back, shouldn't I? All I want to do is sleep but I've been trying to talk to him all day, and even though it turns out he is absolutely fine, for a few minutes I thought I might lose him. That's as good a reason to talk to him now as any, right?

'Amber!' Dad answers almost immediately, his face filling the screen – why do dads hold the camera so close to their face? 'Finally, you call back.'

'Yep, hello,' I say, giving him a wave. 'So you were in the hospital today, huh?'

'Yeah, I went to see Ken,' he replies, thinking nothing of the wording. Honestly! 'But that's not why I'm calling. You won't believe what your mother has done this time.'

'Oh yeah?' I say, trying to keep my tone neutral. 'What's going on?'

'She's gone completely mad!' he begins his rant. 'She's decided to redecorate the living room without consulting me. Can you believe that? We've had the same wallpaper for twenty years, and she rips it off, like it's nothing, days before Christmas! And don't get me started on the new wallpaper she picked – it's hideous! And she expects me to hang it.'

'Okay, well,' I start, but he doesn't let me finish.

'I'm telling you, Amber, it's like living with a tornado,' he continues. 'One that removes wallpaper, and perfectly good carpet. She's changing everything, and I'm supposed to just go along with it. She hasn't even consulted me and, if she did, she wouldn't listen. She doesn't even listen to my opinions any more. It's like I don't even exist!'

'Dad, I'm sorry you're feeling this way,' I say, trying to comfort him.

If I'm being honest, I'm not used to him being so vocal. Usually he's the strong, silent type.

'Have you talked to her about how you feel?' I ask.

'Talked to her?' he scoffs. 'You know how she is. She'll just say I'm being a miserable old bastard.'

I'm not sure she would drop a B-bomb, but I take his point.

'I could try to talk to her,' I reply. 'Erm, actually, she's calling me right now.'

'Go,' he instructs me. 'Go talk to her. You'll see.'

Ending the call with my dad and picking up a call from my mum feels like a case of 'out of the frying pan and into the fire', but it can't always be on Tom to smooth things over.

I sigh, taking a split second to compose myself before I answer, bracing myself for round two.

'Hello, Mum,' I say brightly.

'Amber, were you just on the phone with your father?' she asks, her tone accusatory as she cuts to the chase.

'Yes, he just called me, to say he was only at the hospital to visit Ken,' I say, already feeling the stress headache forming in anticipation of whatever is coming next. 'Are you okay?'

'Am I okay? Oh, let me tell you,' she starts, frustration building with each word. 'Your bloody dad is being so difficult. I'm trying to make the house look nice, in time for Christmas, and all he does is complain. I'm doing all of this for the house, and he acts like I'm ruining his life. He's so stuck in his ways. It's just a bit of bloody wallpaper, and I've booked someone to do it, they'll get it finished before Christmas. I can't tell if he's mad because he thinks I want him to do it or because he thinks I don't trust him to do it.'

'Mum, I understand,' I reassure her. 'Maybe you two just need to sit down and talk about this. Really talk. It sounds like you're both frustrated and not listening to each other.'

'Oh, I've tried,' she says, exasperated and, ironically, not listening to me. 'But it's impossible to have an adult conversation with him. It's like talking to a brick wall covered in thirty-five-year-old wallpaper.'

I should have known, when they sat me and Tom down and explained to us that they were splitting up, that they were not as chill about it as they made out to be.

'Okay, here's what I think,' I start – for what it's worth. 'The wallpaper is off, right?'

'Yes,' she confirms.

'Right, then it's probably best you go ahead with getting some new stuff up,' I reply. 'You could ask Dad to help you choose one.'

'I've chosen one,' she tells me.

'Okay, but you know what he's like, so he's not going to like the fact you chose without him, even if you gave him the choice initially he would have told you he didn't care,' I remind her. 'So, show him maybe three samples. Whichever one is your third choice, tell him that's the one you want, and then you've got a fifty-fifty chance of him actually picking the one you want. But involve him in the decision.'

'Okay, I can try that,' she replies.

'And, I don't know, tell him you can cancel the decorators, if he wants to do it – it's up to him,' I suggest.

'But he'll do an awful job,' she says.

'But he won't want to do it,' I add. 'Just let him think it's his choice.'

'You're a very clever girl,' she tells me with a smile.

'One who will be back very, very soon,' I remind her. 'Please just hang in there. I can help when I'm home. I just need you all present and alive.'

'Present I can do,' she says, playfully gritting her teeth. 'I appreciate your advice. I really do. Take care, and don't let this ruin your trip.'

She sounds a lot calmer now, thank goodness.

'I won't, Mum,' I say – because I'm perfectly capable of ruining my own trip. 'Love you.'

'Love you too, Amber.'

I hang up and flop back onto the bed, rubbing my temples, taking deep breaths in and out, in and out.

Oh boy, what a mess. The sooner I get home, the sooner I can try to help – not that I have any idea how I'll actually help, which is all the more reason to focus on my book while I'm here. I have my draft, that I hate, I just need to do what I need to do, to get it done so that I can send it.

Then I can worry about how I fix my parents.

33

I don't know who I think I am, sprawled out on a sofa in Caleb's chalet, surrounded by an assortment of jewellery. Some of it I really like, other pieces I'm embarrassed to be wearing even as someone else. Actually, I've just answered my own question. Who do I think I am? I think I'm Annabelle Harvey-Whitaker, clearly.

Each piece has a story, or so Caleb tells me – that's what it says in the info sheet he has that came with the jewellery. Not many of them have a story with a happy ending, clearly, because I don't know anyone who would wear half of these.

Perhaps I have a dirty mind (I definitely do, which makes it ironic I can't write spicy scenes) but the longer I look at certain pieces, the more I'm starting to see things.

'Whatever they are paying you to make your girlfriend wear what looks like anal beads, it isn't enough,' I joke, striking a dramatic pose with the garish necklace dangling around my neck.

Caleb laughs as he snaps away with his camera, taking close-up shots of my neck and chest.

'It could probably pay for that dinner we had last night...

another ten times,' he says with a wink. Then he takes a photo of my dropped jaw.

'Oh my gosh, I love these beads on me,' I say, sarcastic as you like, as I strike another pose.

Caleb laughs, lowering the camera momentarily. He narrows his eyes at them.

'They do kind of look like anal beads,' he admits. 'But you're rocking them.'

'I was starting to think you got them out of the wrong bag until I saw the matching earrings,' I reply. 'Then again, who knows where they're potentially supposed to go.'

Caleb chuckles, clearly having just as much fun as I am with this. He steps back to get a wider shot, and I do my best runway model impression, swaying my hips and pouting ridiculously – even though I'm facing away from the camera, to keep my anonymity.

'Seriously, though, this stuff is a mix of fabulous and fabulously terrible,' I say, adjusting the necklace so it sits less awkwardly on my collarbones. 'But this is kind of fun, isn't it? Playing dress-up. You must have a right laugh, doing this stuff for a living.'

'Yeah, although it's definitely more fun doing it with someone else,' he tells me with a smile. 'Who knows what I would have done with that necklace, if you weren't here.'

I laugh.

'Okay, I am not a necklace kind of guy, but if you can snap some photos of me in this chain, I think we can call it a day,' Caleb says, handing me the camera. He holds up a sleek silver chain with various charms hanging off it then pulls a face as he puts it on.

I take the camera and grin.

'I don't know, I think it kind of suits you,' I tell him, adjusting the lens like I know what I'm doing. 'But maybe that's because it's more subtle than the one I'm wearing.'

'Speaking of subtle,' he starts, shifting his weight and turning his head for a better angle. 'Have you managed to get any writing done?'

I laugh, nodding as I snap a few shots.

'Yes, well, I did a little last night,' I reply. 'Do you know what, it's weirdly fun, trying to do a bad job on purpose.'

'Really?' Caleb raises an eyebrow, clearly intrigued.

'Yeah, it's strange,' I continue, lowering the camera for a moment. 'It's like an extra challenge, trying to take the piss out of myself. It's easy to write all the clichés and use all the plot devices that drive readers mad, but I think the thing that I'm loving the most is just creating absolute chaos.'

'And how do you create chaos in a book?' Caleb asks curiously, resuming his poses with a mix of seriousness and playfulness.

'Almost everyone's name begins with a J,' I tell him proudly, framing another shot. 'Jane, Jade, John, Jack – Gemma, so that it isn't obvious – Jacob, Jenny. Jade and Jane are sisters, and Jack is in love with Jade, no, wait, with Jane, but he's in a relationship with a girl called Jenna. I keep switching tenses, and having characters head downstairs to the loft, and you would be surprised how many different ways there are to type the word "okay". Honestly, it's a mess.'

Caleb shakes his head, laughing.

'I have a headache just thinking about it,' he says. 'Honestly, it sounds infuriating to read. So, good job there.'

'It's kind of liberating too,' I tell him. 'Like, there's no pressure to get it right. It's the opposite, actually. The more chaotic, the better – I'm even finding that I'm doing a good job by accident, from time to time.'

'Sounds like a nightmare and a dream at the same time,' he says with a laugh.

'All right, I think we've got enough shots. You can ditch the ugly chain now,' I tell him, pulling a face.

My phone starts ringing, the screen lighting up with a Face-Time call from Tom.

'It's my brother,' I tell Caleb, holding up the phone as if to explain the interruption. 'Things are a bit weird at home at the moment.'

'Take the call,' Caleb says, waving me off with a smile. 'I'll sit at the table, out of the way.'

'Thanks,' I say, grateful for his understanding.

I swipe to answer the call and Tom's face appears on the screen, looking as exasperated as ever.

'Hello,' I say brightly.

'Amber! Honestly, they're driving me crazy, I can't believe you've left me with them,' he begins, not wasting a second on pleasantries.

'What now?' I ask, already bracing myself for the onslaught of family drama.

'They're like... competing for my affection, like I'm a kid they're fighting over, both trying to get onside, to turn me against the other.'

'Oh boy,' I blurt.

'And the fact that it's Christmas is only making them more nuts,' he continues. 'They're trying to one-up each other with the Christmas decorations too. Mum's got this ridiculously huge wreath for the front door, which Dad hates because he says it makes the door too heavy. So Dad went and bought a Santa that inflates to the size of a small car, and put it right next to Mum's parking space because he knows she struggles to park in tight spots. And now Mum's talking about getting an electric diffuser with cinnamon in it, because she knows it messes with his sinuses. She's basically soft poisoning him, Amber!'

I can't help but laugh.

'But she's the one who finds him the most annoying, when he has a blocked nose, and he acts like he's dying,' I point out.

'Yep, well, they're competing over Christmas dinner too, so you have that to look forward to,' he informs me. 'Mum says she's doing a turkey crown, Dad says it's Christmas and that we should have a "real" turkey, so apparently we're having one of each, and we can all say whose is best.'

'Stunning,' I say sarcastically. 'I'm sorry you're dealing with them on your own.'

'Yeah, I'm sure you're sleeping easy at your five-star resort,' Tom teases, a hint of a smile breaking through his frustration.

'Actually,' I begin, hesitating slightly, 'I'm not sleeping easy.'

Well, technically I'm not falling asleep easily, but he doesn't need to hear that I'm having the best sleep of my life in my super-amazing bed.

'Can't sleep without your beaver cream?' Tom jokes, offering up an in-joke to lighten the mood.

I freeze, my eyes darting to Caleb, who is watching me with mild curiosity, then back to my screen. I can feel my face turning red because obviously I get the joke – he's referring to the lavender balm I used to use to help me sleep, when I was worrying about my GCSEs, that was called Badger Balm, but he used to call it beaver cream as a joke – but Caleb won't know that, and we all know what 'beaver cream' sounds like.

'What? Why are you being weird? Is someone there?' Tom asks, noticing my reaction.

'No,' I say firmly, but he's already peering closer at the screen.

'There is, I can see someone, reflected in the mirror behind you,' Tom says, squinting to get a better look. 'There's a man there, I can see him. That or you've got one seriously chill ghost.'

I glance over at Caleb, who stands up and walks over, clearly deciding it's better to just say hi than to let Tom think some random has his sister held hostage or something.

Caleb stands in front of the camera and waves.

'Hi, I'm Caleb,' he says.

'Oh, hi,' Tom says, taken aback. 'Sorry, I didn't realise Amber had company or I wouldn't have ranted about our parents for so long.'

'No worries,' Caleb replies. 'I sympathise if I'm being honest with you. Not many people know this but my parents broke up when I was a teen.'

'Shit, that's rough,' Tom replies.

'It was a long time ago,' Caleb says. 'But I know what it's like, when your parents split, and to go through it without any siblings, or close family, so I have two things to tell you both. The first thing is that, when my parents broke up, the main thing I remember is that they both stopped trying. When people run out of love for each other, they run out of everything. They don't care, they check out. People who don't want to make things work don't try to push each other's buttons like that. I don't know your parents, so I might be wrong, but they sound to me like two people trying to get a reaction out of each other, and people only do that when they want something.'

'Huh,' I say thoughtfully.

'That's a good point,' Tom chimes in. 'They're not avoiding each other. If anything, they're spending more time together than usual.'

Caleb smiles.

'The two of you have each other,' Caleb continues. 'So long as the two of you stick together, and stay on the same page, you'll be fine, whatever happens with your folks.'

'Yeah, you're right,' Tom says with a half-smile. 'I'm sorry to hear that you don't have any close family, I can't even imagine that. It must be tough.'

'It is sometimes,' Caleb admits. 'But it makes me appreciate the connections I do have, even more.'

I feel a rush of warmth at Caleb's words. He's not just some shallow influencer; he's genuinely thoughtful and caring. He's a real person, not just a series of pretty pictures, and it sounds like he's really been through it. It's like I'm seeing a whole new side of him.

'Thanks for the pep talk,' Tom replies, his voice sincere. 'I've spent the past few days thinking that my family was imploding.'

'No worries,' Caleb says, smiling. 'It's good to remember that family isn't just about who you're related to by blood. It's about who's there for you, who supports you. You don't need a family tree to find people like that.'

By the time the call ends, Tom seems like a new man.

'Thanks for opening up to him like that,' I tell Caleb. 'Honestly, I think it meant a lot to him.'

'I figured,' Caleb replies. 'I'm selective, when it comes to who I open up to.'

'It sounds like you've been through a lot,' I point out. 'Going through that at such a young age – at least Tom and I are adults. Or claiming to be.'

Caleb laughs.

'What actually happened is that my dad left, when things got tough between him and my mum, and he never came back, never bothered on birthdays or Christmases, and we were cut off from his side of the family,' Caleb explains. 'My mum didn't really have any family either, and she died just before my TV debut.'

'Oh my gosh, I'm so sorry,' I tell him.

'She had... she...'

Caleb sounds like he has a bit of a lump in his throat.

'It's okay, you don't have to tell me,' I insist. 'We've got plenty of time to talk.'

'One of the reasons I wanted to do the show was to raise money for her,' he says. 'Anyway, she passed before I had the chance, but I honour her memory by raising money and awareness for charities that will help people who were in the situation we were in.'

'That's so incredible,' I point out. 'She would be so proud of you, if she could see what you were doing.'

He takes a deep breath, as though he's recomposing himself.

'I hope so,' he replies. 'It certainly makes the anal beads a lot easier to wear.'

I laugh.

'I think you're right about my parents, you know,' I tell him, taking his cue to move the conversation along. 'My parents have been referring to whatever they're going through as pre-divorcing.'

'Yeah, they clearly don't want to split up,' he points out. 'Perhaps when you get home you can work out what's the matter, and help them work around it.'

'Gosh, I hope so,' I reply with a sigh. 'Anyway, thanks for cheering Tom up, at least. Even if it just helps him to keep sane until I get home.'

'You're welcome,' Caleb replies.

It's nice, to see Tom and Caleb getting on so well – he didn't have to open up to him like that – and I'm amazed at how Caleb has instantly put Tom's worries to bed. Bloody hell, even I feel a bit better, after hearing his words.

'You know, you're pretty deep, for an influencer,' I point out.

'None taken,' Caleb jokes – implying I should have followed my statement with: no offence.

'Sorry, I didn't mean anything by it,' I reply, laughing awkwardly. 'I meant it as a compliment.'

'I was on this planet for a long time, before this was my job,' he points out. 'I was a teacher, actually, not too far into my career, but it wasn't an easy job to keep up, not when your mum is ill. I've always wanted to help people, I knew that much, so I started training to be a grief counsellor, but ironically, when you're grieving yourself, it's not that easy. I got lucky, with the timing of the show, because it set me on a different path. I do still like to help people, though, so sometimes I can't resist sticking my beak in, offering people advice if I think I can help.'

I smile at him.

'I get that,' I tell him. 'The reason I wanted to write funny books was to make people happy. I always thought that if I could make people smile, even when they were going through a shit time, then I would leave this world a little better than I found it.'

'That's great,' he tells me. 'That's my motto too. And I'm sure you do make people really, really happy.'

'Oh, yeah, I make them happy enough, just not horny enough,' I joke. 'It's always worth it, for the lovely emails and messages I get from people who do enjoy what I do, but you are always going to have people who don't get what you're going for. Lots of people say they enjoy my books, but then follow it up with a comment saying they're not complex, or deep – as though I don't work hard to keep them that way. I don't want to make people think, I don't want to be the reason for anyone's existential crisis, I don't want to make them sad, I don't even really want to make anyone all that horny. I just want to make people smile. To make their dark days lighter. Sometimes it's just not that deep.'

'It was reading that got me through losing my mum,' he tells me. 'Crime books. Nothing too heavy, or deep, just mysteries that needed solving, and detectives picking through the clues to figure it all out. It took me out of my reality and into somewhere I could breathe.'

'People who don't read don't get it, but there's a lot to be said for not getting lost in a book, but hiding away in one,' I reply.

Caleb smiles at me.

'Anyway, I'm just happy to help,' he says. 'It was nothing.'

Maybe there's more to this influencer gig – and to Caleb – than I first thought.

34

Stepping out of Henri's warm 4x4, into the cold outside, is a real shock to the system.

Still, we're here, at the cabin he's working on, and I can't wait to see it.

It's tucked away in a secluded part of the forest, miles away from the main resort. You can tell that it's unfinished, but that it's a work in progress, and I bet it's going to be something really special when it's finished.

The exterior is made of dark, weathered wood, blending almost seamlessly with the trees that surround it. Large windows – even if they are a bit dirty at the moment – promise undisturbed views of the forest that surrounds the place, and the covered porch looks like it's going to be a great spot to watch the sun go down – or rise, if you're into that sort of thing.

'Here we are,' Henri says as he holds the door open for me, and I step inside.

'Oh, wow,' I say – meaning it mostly in a good way.

The interior is sparse but inviting. The walls and floors have been redone (oh, come on, like I know the technical term for it) with raw timber, giving the place more of an inside feel and the most amazing smell. The only furniture in the room is a bed in the corner and two armchairs positioned near a fireplace. It's all clearly seen better days which makes me think that it's only here for Henri, or whoever, while they're working on the place.

'I want this place to be a romantic escape,' Henri says, his voice filled with passion. 'Somewhere lovers can come to get away from it all. It's kilometres from the main resort – too far to walk – and there's no phone service. Eventually, there will be Wi-Fi, but I think there's something romantic about being cut off from the rest of the world, don't you?'

I nod, imagining how cosy the cabin will be when it's finished, and how nice it would be to be trapped here with a dreamy man – definitely something that could go in one of my books.

'It does sound wonderful,' I reply. 'Is there a kitchen?'

I don't mean to make it sound like food is all I care about but I'm also in no position to deny that's true.

'Not yet,' Henri replies. 'Which is why I brought a picnic.'

He lays a blanket on the wooden floor and starts unpacking the basket he brought with him. He pulls out a variety of foods: breads, a selection of cheeses, charcuterie, grapes, and a small jar of honey. There's also a bottle of red wine and two glasses.

No, I don't know how much cheese is too much cheese, I just know that I'm nowhere near my limit yet.

'It's a bit chilly in here,' I remark, rubbing my arms.

Henri nods and moves to the fireplace, expertly arranging the logs and kindling. Within minutes, a warm, crackling fire springs to life, lighting the room with a romantic glow.

I sit on the blanket, appreciating the warmth as it slowly spreads through the lodge. Yep, this is definitely romantic.

'It will be warmer when it is finished,' he explains. 'But for now it's okay, to spend a few hours here, away from everyone else.'

I smile. I can definitely brave the cold for this. I've never done anything like it before.

Henri joins me on the blanket, handing me a plate before loading up his own.

It looks so, so good. The food doesn't look bad either.

'So, tell me more about your role here,' I say, genuinely curious. 'I know you look after the château, but this seems like a real pet project of yours.'

Henri leans back on one elbow, his face illuminated by the firelight.

'This place is owned by my family,' he tells me. 'My dad is technically in charge, but I run the day-to-day operations. And one day it will be mine, so I like to do a good job.'

I laugh.

'Wow, that's amazing,' I reply. 'I had no idea.'

'No, I don't usually tell people who stay at the château,' he replies. 'And no one would guess, because I actually work hard. My siblings are just happy to live off my family's money but I could never do that. I love to work.'

Jeez, imagine loving your job. I'm more envious of the fact he loves what he does than I am of the fact that his dad is clearly a millionaire – probably a billionaire. No, wait, what am I saying? I'm sure if I had family billions I could have a job that I loved – I could start my own publishing house, and publish my own books, whatever genre I wanted.

'Do you like the wine?' he asks me, changing the subject.

'Yes,' I reply. 'I usually only drink white but this is nice.'

He narrows his eyes at me, unconvinced.

'I have white in the car,' he says with a smile. 'Let me get you some.'

'Oh, you don't have to do that,' I reply.

'It's no problem,' he insists.

I pop a piece of cheese in my mouth. Wow, so Henri is the heir to all of this? Can you imagine if Mandy, Bette and Gina knew that? The banging-a-billionaire trope would be straight to the top of their list – and yes, I know the wager is off, but I still think they would be all over it.

A few minutes later, Henri returns with a concerned look on his face.

'What's wrong?' I ask, sensing his unease.

'It seems like my car battery is flat,' he says. 'I can't unlock it.'

My heart sinks.

'Can we walk back?' I ask him. 'To the château, I mean?'

Henri shakes his head.

'It's too far, and it's getting dark,' he tells me. 'But don't worry, I have a meeting later, and I told the person I'm meeting that I would be here first. When I don't show up, he'll know to come here and get me. Everything will be okay.'

I nod, trying to shake off the anxiety that is building inside me. I don't want to sound like I'm addicted to my phone but I do feel kind of edgy when I know I'm somewhere without signal.

'Okay,' I say, forcing a smile.

Henri sits back down, and we continue our meal in silence for a few moments. Then, sensing my discomfort, he reaches over and takes me by the hand.

'I promise, it will be okay,' he reassures me. 'In the meantime, let's enjoy our picnic, and the fire, and each other's company.'

'Yeah, you're right,' I tell him, trying to sound like I mean it, and like this hasn't totally distracted me.

I pick up another piece of cheese. Then another, as my mind races with worry. After all, nothing good ever happens in a cabin in the woods, does it?

35

Pacing the floor – treading the creaking floorboards, which only makes all of this even more creepy – I try to steady my racing heart and my sharp breaths which are, probably technically speaking, in panic-attack territory, but I'm trying to run it in the background, so that Henri doesn't think I'm a dork. Hopefully I'm coming across as fidgety, rather than like I'm freaking out.

The cabin would be completely dark were it not for the flickering glow of the fire – although somehow this only makes things seem creepier. It's marginally better than total darkness, of course, and I'm grateful for the warmth.

It's late now, and no one has turned up to rescue us. Every creak of the wood, every gust of wind outside, every*thing* sends shivers down my spine. Even without everything I've ever seen in every horror movie *ever* running through my mind, it's cold here, and we only have so much food. It's glorified camping.

Henri is much more chill about it. He's sitting by the fire, the reflection of the flames dancing in his eyes as he warms his hands.

'Don't worry, Amber,' he reassures me, his voice calming.

'People knew I was coming here. I'll be missed – the resort relies on me for too much. Someone will come.'

I nod, but I'm not convinced.

'Even if they don't come until morning, it will be okay,' he continues. 'If you want to take the bed, wrap yourself up under the covers, and I'll add more wood to the fire. I'll wake you, if anyone comes, but otherwise try to get a good rest. I will take care of you.'

Oh boy, now we're going to have to sleep here? Really? I mean, at least it's warmer in here than it is outside, and slightly less scary, but... come on.

As I glance around the cabin, I can't help but smile to myself. I can't believe I've walked right into a classic trope – perhaps the most iconic one there is – there's only one bed. Oh my God, there's only one bed. What am I going to do?

I shake with cold as I watch Henri push the two small armchairs together. He tries to get on them, to make a sort of bed out of them, but he looks like he's struggling to keep his balance.

Shivering, I get into the bed, pulling the blankets around me tightly. My teeth are chattering, and I can't seem to get warm.

I can see Henri, still struggling to keep his balance on the chairs – and without a blanket – and I feel a pang of guilt.

'Henri, you can't sleep like that,' I tell him. 'Just share the bed with me. I don't mind.'

He looks at me with a playful glint in his eye.

'You just want my body heat,' he says.

I laugh, despite the cold.

'I mean that won't hurt, come on, I'm sure we can both fit,' I tell him.

It's one of those beds that is a little bit bigger than a single, but a little bit smaller than a double.

Henri hesitates for a moment before climbing into the small

bed beside me. The lack of space forces him to spoon me but I can't complain because his body heat almost instantly calms my shivers. As his arms wrap around me, suddenly I don't feel so scared any more.

'I am actually much warmer,' I murmur, snuggling closer. 'God, I can't believe we're stuck here.'

Henri chuckles softly.

'You know, there are rumours of a yeti in these mountains,' he says, his voice like he's telling a ghost story around a campfire.

I roll around to face him, playfully swatting his chest.

'Stop trying to scare me!' I tick him off – although it does lighten the mood. Obviously I'm not worried about a yeti.

His laughter rumbles in his chest, and our faces are so close that I can feel his warm breath. Things are playful for a second or two until there's a shift. It's like the air changes as his eyes lock on to mine, and slowly but surely I notice his lips heading for mine.

I don't know what to do, other than hold my breath, and freeze (it's oh-so easy to freeze right now). Our lips brush together, very lightly, for a split second, before a loud knock on the door makes us both jump.

Henri bolts from the bed, rushing to the door. He speaks in rapid French with the person outside. After a moment, he turns back to me.

'It's okay, it's my colleague,' he says, relief evident in his voice. 'He's come looking for me. He says he'll take us back to the château.'

It's only now that I can exhale. Henri helps me up, and we gather our things quickly, and in awkward silence. As we step outside into the cold night, loading our things into Henri's colleague's car, I can't help but glance back at the cabin. I'm so, so glad that I didn't have to spend the night there, not just because it was cold, or because of the potential yeti outside, but because things with Henri were heating up, and I'm not exactly sure it's what I wanted.

36

Waking up in my bed, at the château, I think about how different things could have been, if I were waking up with Henri, in his cabin.

He was going to kiss me – he practically did – but why? Was it just to keep warm? To pass the time? Or... because he likes me? I don't want to sound like a teenage girl but... does he like me? I mean obviously he likes me, or he wouldn't be hanging out with me, but I mean *likes*-me-likes-me and, yep, I definitely sound like a teenage girl.

I certainly wouldn't be waking up as comfortably, that's for sure, because this bed is everything.

I think my best move today might be to give Henri a bit of space, and to absolutely avoid the ladies, just in case they noticed I was missing, because I'm not quite sure how I would explain that one.

I roll over and grab my phone from the bedside table, noticing several missed calls from Caleb. I feel a pang of guilt and quickly call him back.

'Amber? Are you okay?' Caleb's voice is filled with concern as he answers the phone. 'I was so worried when I didn't hear from you last night.'

'I'm fine, I'm fine,' I assure him, though my voice sounds unconvincing, even to my own ears. 'I'm at the château – I slept in.'

'I'm outside, in the front garden,' he tells me. 'I didn't know what else do to, so I came looking for you. Is everything okay?'

He's outside? Shit. What if someone sees him?

I jump out of bed and run to the window and, yep, sure enough, there he is, for everyone to see.

I take a deep breath, trying to steady myself.

'I'll tell you what, start walking back to the resort, and I'll catch you up,' I tell him.

'I don't mind waiting for you,' he replies.

'It's okay because I need to throw some clothes on,' I insist. 'And obviously we don't want anyone to see you.'

'Oh, okay, good point. I'll stroll around a bit and come back for you, it's no trouble,' he says. 'It's not like I have anything else to do.'

I laugh awkwardly.

'Okay, see you soon,' I tell him.

After we hang up, I watch him for a second. Go on, Caleb – and I say this in the nicest possible way – go away. Eventually he walks off and I spring into action.

I quickly get dressed, throwing on a pair of jeans and a warm sweater. I brush my hair, and do the quick version of my make-up – although, thankfully, I know there is plenty of make-up at Caleb's chalet.

I grab my laptop, shoving it into my bag, and head out the door. The château is still quiet, so I'm relieved that I don't see any sign of anyone as I dash out. I walk briskly, my breath forming clouds in front of my face, clouds that grow bigger as I get out of breath.

I glance back at the château, feeling a mix of relief and apprehension, as I realise that the coast is clear, and that I'm out of the woods – although, ironically, walking through them too.

Eventually I catch up with Caleb a short distance down the road. He's waiting by a large pine tree, his hands stuffed into his pockets, looking a bit bewildered.

'Hey,' I say, all easy-breezy, as I approach him.

'Hey,' he replies, studying my face. 'What's going on? You seem... I don't know. You seem off.'

'Oh, no, I'm fine, honestly,' I reassure him. 'I just didn't want anyone to see you.'

'It's okay, I'm safe here,' he reassures me. 'Everyone here wants privacy.'

I'm not sure Mandy, Bette or Gina would be so obliging.

'Better safe than sorry, right?' I reply.

'You worry too much,' he tells me. 'Anyway, breakfast? I'm starving.'

'That sounds great to me,' I say with a smile.

Obviously I don't want anyone in the château to see Caleb but, for some reason, I don't want Caleb to see any of them either. I mean, I can't imagine the ladies being kind about any of this, but the last thing I want is for Caleb to think that I set out to spend the night (or even part of it) in bed with Henri. Why? I'm not sure. This is all just business, after all.

37

I'm sitting at the large wooden table in Caleb's chalet, the morning light streaming in through the windows, casting a beautiful glow on everything – Caleb says this kind of light is one of the best for taking photos.

Caleb is across from me, meticulously arranging his breakfast plates, angling his coffee cup just right.

'I've never seen someone take so many pictures of scrambled eggs,' I point out.

That said, breakfast was delivered from the resort kitchen, and they've somehow managed to make them in the shape of a rose, which really is quite impressive.

'Of course! Look at them – they're practically art,' he points out.

'They do look good,' I admit, taking a sip of my coffee. 'But I'm just so hungry.'

Holiday Amber, it turns out, is absolutely starving all of the time, although I suspect it's just because the food here is so good.

'Almost too beautiful to eat,' he replies, snapping one last photo before digging in. 'But not quite.'

As I glance around the table, I notice notes scattered everywhere – pages of scribbled handwriting and printouts. Curiosity gets the better of me.

'What's all this?' I ask, picking up a sheet, careful not to get ketchup on it.

'Oh, that's my book,' he says nonchalantly between bites. 'Well, parts of it.'

'You're actually writing it?' I say, genuinely impressed. 'I assumed you would have a ghostwriter doing it.'

'No, I'm writing it,' he says – again, so casually. 'I studied English lit at uni, which admittedly feels like a lifetime ago. I thought I was doing a great job but my editor is on my case about it.'

Oh, boy, does that sound familiar.

'Can I read it?' I ask, genuinely desperate to get a peek at what he's working on.

He hesitates for a moment but then nods.

'Sure, if you want. But only if I can read yours,' he says.

'Deal,' I say, grabbing my laptop from my bag. 'And feel free to add things in, make it worse. Have fun with it.'

Caleb laughs.

'Make it bad on purpose – I'm excited to try that, rather than just doing it naturally,' he jokes.

Having already finished my breakfast – because I was too hungry to photograph it – I head for one of the armchairs, sitting on my legs, ready to dive in.

Oh, it's a fun murder mystery set on a cruise – exactly the sort of thing I wish I could write – and I find myself getting completely absorbed. The plot is genuinely gripping, the characters are interesting, and he's great at creating tension.

'This is really good,' I say, eventually looking up from the pages with no idea how much time has passed. 'I'm genuinely impressed and sort of jealous.'

'Thanks,' he says, though he doesn't look entirely convinced. 'My editor thinks it lacks universal appeal. He says men will love it, but women will hate it.'

'What?' I say, frowning. 'That's ridiculous.'

I think about it for a second, trying to work out what Caleb's editor could have meant, based on the chunk that I read.

'I suppose it is a little geared towards male readers,' I point out, chewing my lip thoughtfully. 'It just needs a little something extra, something like...'

I think for a moment. This is exactly the sort of thing I wish I could write, it's just that I wanted to... oh my God, I've got it.

'You know what you're missing?' I say, smiling smugly. 'A romance arc.'

Caleb looks dubious.

'I'm hopeless at writing romance,' he says. 'I write romance about as well as you write spice.'

'Oi,' I reply with a laugh. 'But, honestly, I'm serious. I'm guessing your editor wants this book to appeal to women too, so a romance arc will win over a few die-hard romance readers, and, to be honest, just having a woman edit it will help. I'm starting to realise why you suggested I write "suck a tit" – it just needs that blokey edge taking out of it.'

'Okay,' he says, a little hesitant but clearly willing to give it a try. 'What do you suggest?'

'How do you fancy working on it together for a bit?' I suggest. 'My reluctant speciality could be just what you need.'

'Yeah, all right, so long as you don't mind?' he replies.

'No, of course not,' I reply. 'This sort of thing is fun to me.'

We spend the next hour tossing ideas back and forth, and I can't help but get more and more excited – about Caleb's idea, not my own. Caleb listens intently, taking notes, and I can see him starting to warm up to the idea of having a love triangle running through his murder mystery.

'You really seem into this,' he says, looking at me with a smile.

'I am!' I say, laughing. 'This is why I wanted to write a book like this. With a murder mystery, you know what you're going to get – the murder is guaranteed. So, how do you raise the stakes, and give someone something to care about? You give them a romance to get invested in. Can I try to write you a chapter? It might help, to show you what I mean.'

He nods.

'Go for it,' he says. 'You seem really passionate about it, who am I to stop you?'

I laugh, but only for a second, before I'm grabbing my laptop and typing away. Honestly, I don't remember the last time I typed this much, this quickly, there's practically smoke coming from my fingers as I pound the keys. Even my document is struggling, seemingly like there's a delay between me typing a letter and it appearing.

Doing this, crafting a romantic subplot that weaves seamlessly into his murder mystery, is so my shit. I'm having so much fun, and I can see Caleb getting excited too, as he reads over my shoulder, occasionally laughing in approval.

'This is perfect,' he says. 'I can't believe how well it fits.'

'I told you!' I say, beaming. 'A little romance never hurt anyone.'

We spend the rest of the morning working together, bouncing ideas off each other, and I can't remember the last time I had this much fun working on a book.

It's just a shame it's not my own.

38

'Do you think we have everything we need?' Caleb asks, flashing me that irresistible grin of his.

'Absolutely,' I reply. 'I suppose pancakes are the kind of meal where you can just buy endless ingredients to put on top of them. But we have the basics, and if I buy any more fruit, spreads or sauces I will officially be eating more topping than I am pancakes.'

Caleb laughs.

I feel like I'm in a bit of a dream today. I mean, Caleb Carney is cooking me brunch, which is something I never thought I would say, but everything feels strangely perfect. It's like the scene has been set, just for me. The air is crisp, the sky is a perfect shade of blue, and I'm pretty sure I hear upbeat music playing somewhere in the distance as we walk back to the chalet, from the food shop in the resort.

We've been talking about his books all day – and ideas for future books too. I feel like my suggestions for how to give his books more universal appeal have lit this creative fire under him, and now he can't stop. He's got so many ideas, and I'm genuinely surprised by how well we riff off each other. It's like we're on the same wavelength, each idea rolling back and forth between us, like a snowball, getting bigger each time.

'Okay, how about this,' Caleb starts, his eyes darting around with excitement. 'A famous chef is found dead in his own kitchen. The detective assigned to the case is this brilliant but reclusive guy with a twisty backstory. He starts falling for the chef's sous-chef, who is also the prime suspect.'

'Oh, that's tasty,' I say, naturally moving closer to him as ideas pop into my head. 'And maybe the sous-chef has her own twisty past. She's been running from something, and she's got secrets that make her look guilty, but she's not.'

'Exactly! And as the detective digs deeper, he realises that the chef's death is connected to a string of unsolved murders from years ago,' he continues. 'The sous-chef's past might hold the key to solving them all. Oh, I know, I'm a big fan of *Vertigo*, so what if the sous-chef looks exactly like the detective's dead ex-wife, to the point where he is suspicious that it might actually be her.'

'Oh, I love that!' I exclaim. 'And the romantic tension builds as they work together. Maybe they start out distrusting each other, but there are all these moments where they have to rely on one another. They realise they misjudged one another, and it's only through working together that they get the chance to realise they should be together.'

'Yes!' Caleb says, practically dancing on the spot. 'And there could be this big twist where they discover that the real killer has been watching them the whole time, trying to manipulate them into turning against each other.'

'I have about ten different ideas, for who the real killer could be,' I tell him.

But then my logical brain catches up with my creative one, when I remember that this is Caleb's work, not mine.

'Right, I'm making brunch, you just relax,' Caleb insists as we step into the warmth of the chalet.

'I feel bad, you doing all the work,' I say. 'Is there anything I can take photos of?'

'Have a look through the bag of stuff,' he tells me. 'There are some skincare products – face masks and stuff like that – if you wanted to have a play around with those. We'll have to get creative, with the angles, maybe photograph the product on your hands, the back of your head as you reach to apply it – I don't know. See what you can find, and what you think we can make work.'

'Okay, sure,' I say.

I rummage through the case full of things to promote and notice some lingerie mixed in with the skincare products. Caleb had mentioned that these items come with the biggest price tag, and while I always thought he was all about the money, knowing how much he donates to charity makes me more eager to help out. Plus, you know, with my own latest project being destroying my own career, my share of the proceeds will definitely go to good use.

I figure I can wear the lace cami and use some of the skincare products at the same time, killing two birds with one stone. The focus on my face (while still trying not to show too much of my face, bizarrely) will make the underwear shots more subtle? Maybe? The voice in my head doesn't even sound convinced, but it's worth a go.

Holding my glasses in one hand (they don't fit the character I'm playing, and I have a sticky green face mask on), I wander into the living room to get Caleb to carefully snap the photos for me.

'Hey, I have an idea,' I say, explaining my plan. Caleb seems to be staring at me, but without my glasses, I can't see his expression.

'If you've got a spare minute, I thought we could combine the lingerie shots with the skincare ones? It feels like a sneaky way to plug the undies, without me having to go full glamour model, because I am neither glamorous, nor a model, so...'

I can just about tell that he's looking at me but I still can't make out his expression, and he seems awfully quiet.

'Yeah, that sounds great,' he eventually says. 'I'll grab my camera. You look amazing, by the way.'

Hmm, I'm not sure about that one. I feel like my general awkwardness is making me look stiff and strange, like I'm not at home on this planet, never mind in fancy underwear. But I'm being motivated by the money. More money for me, more money for Caleb, more money for charity. Can you think of a more noble reason to slip on a nightie?

I blush, glad he can't see my face clearly under the mask.

'Thanks,' I mumble, feeling a mix of nerves and unexpected excitement.

'Honestly, you look great,' he says again, clearly picking up on my body language. 'And you know you don't have to promote this stuff if you don't want to, we've got plenty of other bits.'

'No, no, it's fine,' I insist, literally trying to shake it off – but carefully, so I don't flash him. 'I was thinking you could just get arty shots – just glimmers of what I'm wearing, rather than body shots. Either way... I just feel a bit silly.'

'Hey, if you feel silly, I'll just do my best to focus on your face this time.'

'Fab,' I say, feeling more at ease already.

He starts lining up shots, and although I don't feel uncomfortable with him, I do feel a bit like an underwear model. Oh, if my parents could see me now.

'Amber?' I hear my dad's voice call out.

I freeze on the spot. I imagined that, right? My dad isn't here, he can't be, and even if he were, how would he get in the chalet?

'Amber,' he calls out again.

Right, that's definitely my dad's voice.

I grab my glasses from where I set them down on the table, next to my laptop, and pop them on my face – face mask be damned – and that's when I notice my dad's face on my laptop screen. Oh, shit. He's right there, in real time, looking bewildered, and I am just gawping back at him.

Panic mode: activated. I bolt from the living room, sprinting to the bedroom, and then into the bathroom, slamming the door behind me. What just happened? I try to piece it together, my heart racing. My laptop must have heard something that sounded like a request to FaceTime my dad, I'm guessing, because there he was. Oh God, there he was. And there I was, in full view of the camera, posing for photos in my underwear.

I wipe off the green face mask, hoping the redness on my face is from some kind of reaction to it, but no, it's sheer embarrassment.

I can hear voices in the other room – my dad and Caleb chatting. Oh, why are they still chatting? Great, just great.

I lean against the bathroom door, debating my next move. I can't stay in here forever, can I? *Can I?* No, I can't.

Eventually, with a deep breath, I put my top back on – a real top – and reluctantly head back out into the living room.

As I approach the dining area, I see Caleb and my dad deep in conversation. Caleb spots me and grins, then turns to the screen. 'Ah, Johnny, here she is.'

I approach the laptop cautiously, like I'm a teenager again, and like my dad has the power to reach through the screen, grab me, drag me home, and ground me for catching me with a boy.

'Hi, Dad,' I say, trying to sound casual, like this isn't the most embarrassing moment of my life – and, believe me, there are some other strong contenders this week alone.

Dad looks... happy? That's odd. I'm not sure I've seen my dad look happy since, I don't know, the nineties.

'Amber, Caleb explained everything. I get it – good work if you can get it,' Dad tells me.

I laugh awkwardly.

'Erm, thanks, Dad. Are you okay?' I ask.

'Yes, I'm fine. Just checking in,' he says. 'Nice to meet you, Caleb. Thanks for the chat.'

'Nice to meet you too, Johnny,' he tells him. 'Anytime.'

After a bit more small talk between the three of us, we end the call.

Caleb turns to me, still smiling.

'Your dad is great,' he tells me.

'Is he?' I reply, almost suspiciously. 'I feel like the two of you were talking for ages, while I was dying of shame in the bathroom. Historically, the longer people chat with my dad, the less likely they are to refer to him as great...'

Caleb just laughs this off.

'We were just chatting,' he tells me again. 'And he really does seem great. You're lucky to have him.'

I don't think he was trying to make me feel bad with that comment, I think he genuinely meant it, but it does give me a reality check. I'll bet Caleb would love to have a dad like mine and, jokes aside, I know that I'm lucky to have him really. Even if he is stressing me out lately.

'Thanks for smoothing the awkward situation over with him,' I tell him. 'I don't know what I would have said.'

'Oh, it's fine,' he replies. 'He really was chill about it and, look, we don't need to take any underwear photos. To be honest, we've taken plenty of photos, we don't need to do any more. I know you've only got a couple of days left so I thought I would take you out for the day tomorrow, what do you say?'

'Oh, you don't have to do that,' I reply.

'I've got it all planned out,' he insists. 'Plus, it might be good for book inspiration – bad or good. What do you reckon?'

He smiles at his little joke and I can't help but smile back.

'Okay, yeah, sure,' I say, my excitement building. 'Sounds great. Just when I think I've seen everything the resort has to offer...'

'Well, I don't want to ruin the surprise, but I'm taking you out of the resort,' he tells me. 'But that's all I'm saying.'

Oh wow, outside the resort. This place has so much going on, I hadn't even considered the idea of leaving. Then again, I am supposed to be on a writers' retreat, but also, it turns out it's a writers' retreat where no one actually writes, they just drink wine and try to bang the staff.

I wonder where Caleb could be taking me, and I can't wait to find out, but first it's time for pancakes. This day just keeps getting better and better.

39

I arrive back at the château to – surprise, surprise – find Mandy, Bette, and Gina lounging on the sofas, glasses of wine in hand.

'Here she is,' Mandy says, and I can't quite place her tone but have you ever had that feeling that everyone was in on a joke apart from you? 'Henri's been looking for you,' she tells me. 'He said he'd be in the study before bed, and that we should tell you to see him there.'

I raise an eyebrow, my curiosity piqued.

'Did he say why?' I ask.

Mandy shrugs, swirling her wine.

'He didn't. Just that he was looking for you,' she tells me. 'You know, we were only having a bit of fun with the wager, but you've clearly taken it too far.'

'What do you mean?' I dare to ask.

'We know you spent the night with him,' she replies. 'We saw the two of you head out together.'

'He was just showing me his private cabin in the woods,' I say innocently – as though that's a normal-sounding thing to say.

Gina remains silent, her eyes darting between me and Mandy.

'Come on, Amber,' Bette says, in a knowing tone. 'We're all adults here.'

Mandy leans back, a smirk playing on her lips.

'We know you were both missing last night,' she says. 'Come on, Amber, just admit it.'

'His car broke down,' I explain. 'Honestly, it's not what it looks like.'

'Oh, don't be so dramatic,' Mandy says as she waves her hand dismissively. 'Bette is right, we're all adults.'

'And Henri is seriously delicious – who would blame you?' Gina says.

'It's just that we don't usually, you know, sleep with the help on these things,' Mandy points out in a tone that makes me want to throw a glass of wine over her. 'We usually just spend time together – that's the whole point.'

Is she serious? She was the one saying we should all try to woo him and now she's saying this, which is all kinds of offensive, on so many levels.

Now the other two are saying nothing, their silence more telling than words. I wonder if anything could make them disagree with her.

'I'm sorry I haven't spent more time with you,' I reply, focusing on that part. 'I've just been trying to finish my book, and trying to find inspiration here at the resort.'

I mean, I've been trying to finish it in that I've been pasting in chunks of absolute garbage, whenever I've found myself with a spare minute, but I can't tell them that.

'And you found it in Henri,' Mandy points out. 'Anyway, it doesn't matter, with only a few days left there is no point trying to join in now. You might as well make the most of your holiday romance – for as long as it lasts, before the next guests check in.'

I sigh. I never really felt like I fit in with them before but now, after spending time with them, things feel even more impossible. Honestly, it's exhausting, trying to break into their tight-knit circle and to get them to like me. I can't be bothered to try any more.

'Okay, well, goodnight then,' I say, forcing a smile before turning and heading to the study.

This is the first time I've seen him, since we were rescued.

Thankfully the door is open. Henri is sitting in a leather armchair, reading through some documents. He looks up as I enter, a warm smile spreading across his face, which quickly puts me at ease. See, it's so easy, to just be welcoming and nice.

'Amber,' he says, standing up. 'I was beginning to think you were avoiding me.'

I laugh lightly, shaking my head.

'No, I'm not avoiding you,' I reassure him. 'Are you avoiding me?'

Well, he was the one who mentioned the A word.

He chuckles, probably picking up on my nervous energy as he moves closer, closing the gap between us.

'No, I've just been busy with some publicity work today,' he reassures me. 'But I would like to take you to dinner tomorrow evening, if you're free.'

I'm taken aback – and smiling like a maniac.

'I'd really like that,' I tell him.

It sounds like it's just dinner. Not book-inspiration dinner – dinner-dinner. The two of us, eating, spending time together. That's exciting, right?

Henri hands me a slip of paper with his number on it.

'So that I don't need to search for you when I want to find you,' he tells me. 'Send me yours.'

I take the paper, our fingers brushing for a moment.

'I'll do that,' I tell him.

He gives me a lingering look before nodding.

'Okay, that's good,' he replies. 'Then I will see you tomorrow. *Bonne nuit*, Amber.'

'*Bonne nuit*,' I reply, probably not nailing the accent, but giving it my best.

As I head up the stairs, I take my phone from my pocket and add Henri's number to my contacts. Then, so that he has my number, I send him a message.

> See you tomorrow. X

A reply comes through almost instantly.

> Looking forward to it xxx

I know what they say, sisters before misters and all that, but I don't think I have any sisters here and, anyway, Henri isn't a mister, he's a monsieur.

40

The day I am having with Caleb might honestly be the best day of my life and I am in no way exaggerating when I say that. He's just so much fun, and so thoughtful, and he really knows how to show a girl a good time. The effort he has put into today so far is just... wow. And it's only lunchtime.

It all started when I arrived at his chalet earlier and found out he had hired a car, complete with a driver, who took us to Switzerland for breakfast. Actual Switzerland. Okay, sure, it's not that far from the resort, but no one has ever taken me to another country for breakfast before. We had pastries and coffee, and then strolled through the quaint streets, breathing in the crisp morning air, chatting – and honestly, I thought that was it. How wrong I was.

As if breakfast in Switzerland wasn't enough, we got back in the car and headed to Italy for lunch. Yes, Italy. Another country. How amazing is that?

Right now, we're sitting outside a charming little café, eating fresh focaccia, drinking cocktails, taking in everything this piazza has to offer, and although it's not exactly summer here, it's a lot less wintry than the resort. It's nice to be outside and to not be freezing.

Caleb leans back in his chair, looking at me with a satisfied grin.

'So, are you having a nice time?' he asks.

I smile back at him, feeling genuinely happy.

'I'm having an amazing time,' I tell him, making sure he can tell by my tone that I mean it. 'The furthest a man has ever taken me before is Thorpe Park.'

Caleb snorts with laughter, then tries to contain it.

'I shouldn't laugh, but as great as Thorpe Park is, that's just not good enough,' he replies.

I laugh along with him – well, if you can't laugh at yourself...

'Well, thank you for ruining men for me,' I tell him. 'I'll never be impressed again. You'll always be the guy who took me to three countries in one day.'

He smiles.

'Oh, this is nothing,' he says. 'Imagine how great a date this would be if I was actually trying.'

I tilt my head, curiously.

'Is this a date?' I dare to ask.

'Of course it is,' he replies, leaning forward. 'If you're pretending to be my girlfriend, you deserve a real date. Some might say you deserve a medal.'

'In all honesty, you're a great fake boyfriend,' I reply. 'I can't imagine ever fake dumping you.'

Caleb's expression shifts slightly.

'Well, Annabelle didn't have a problem real dumping me,' he says.

I hesitate, but then curiosity gets the better of me.

'If you don't mind answering, why did you two break up?' I ask.

He sighs.

'It's a tale as old as time, really,' he replies, trying to keep it light, but I can tell that it bothers him. 'She realised that being really beautiful and really famous meant she could have anyone she wanted. And, hey, there will always be someone hotter than all of us, right? And if people think they can do better, there's not a lot you can do about it.'

Wow. That's brutal. Did she really think she could do better than Caleb? Mr three countries in a day, who has done nothing but try to help me over the past few days.

'That's why you should go for an average chick,' I joke, trying to make him smile. 'We'll never let you down.'

Caleb takes my face in his hand, stroking my cheek gently. His eyes are intense as he looks at me.

'You are not average, Amber,' he says, the most serious I have seen him. 'You're beautiful. Really beautiful.'

For a moment, it feels like he might lean in and kiss me. My heart skips a beat, and I can't help but wonder what it would feel like. But before anything can happen, a musician with an accordion appears, shouting something excitedly at us in Italian before launching into an intense rendition of 'That's Amore'.

All we can do is laugh – and listen, because this guy is not going anywhere. Caleb wraps his arm around me, pulling me close as we listen to the song, moving us both gently to the music.

As fake boyfriends go, Caleb might just be the best I've ever had.

41

I'm feeling on top of the world. I mean, technically, I'm nearing the top of the mountain, where the resort is, but genuinely I feel sky-high right now.

Today has been, hands down, the best day of my life. I've experienced so much in such a short space of time that it almost feels like a movie I watched, rather than something I lived through. But I did live it, and I savoured every moment. I don't think I'll ever forget this day – even if it's just because of the sheer volume of photos we took, although somehow they didn't feel like they were for content, they were for us. The fact we took so many selfies, when we're not supposed to be showing my face, is proof of that.

For one reason and another, we're back later than we intended. This means my dinner plans with Henri are ruined, but I messaged him ahead of time to let him know that I was held up on my research trip (yep, that's what I'm calling it). He messaged back to say it was okay, and that whatever time I get back, I should join him for a drink, and that we can do dinner tomorrow, so that's good.

I do feel a bit bad, ditching Henri to hang out with Caleb, but hey, this is technically work, right? Taking photos is what he does, and research is a big part of writing, and it worked because I've never felt more inspired to write something romantic.

As we drive back, the dark, winding mountain roads are as thrilling as they are terrifying. I have no idea if we're next to a wall of trees or a sheer drop, and honestly, I think I'm better off not knowing. I just hope our driver knows the way.

'Thanks for such an amazing day,' I say to Caleb, breaking the comfortable silence.

'You're welcome,' he replies with a smile, lightly knocking my shoulder with his. 'I've had a really great time. Thanks for making it so special.'

'Hey, this was all you,' I remind him. 'And you can do this sort of thing all the time.'

He looks at me, his smile widening.

'No, I can't. It wouldn't be the same without...'

He trails off as our driver interrupts our conversation.

'There's something blocking the road up ahead,' he tells us.

We both peer through the windshield and see that a crowd of people has gathered at the resort entrance.

'Oh, shit, they're photographers,' Caleb says. 'They look like paparazzi.'

'Do they know you're here?' I ask, my heart racing.

'No, I've been so careful about what I post,' he replies. 'Maybe they're here for someone else, or just trying their luck, but there's no way they're not going to see us if we drive past them.'

'I can't turn around, unfortunately,' the driver tells us. 'The road is too narrow; I need to go into the resort to turn around.'

It feels like we're approaching the photographers in super-slow motion, but everything happens in an instant. I try to think fast, to come up with a way to hide my face. With no better options – although now that I'm down here, I can think of several – I bury my face in Caleb's lap, hoping the paparazzi won't be able to snap anything but the back of my head. Of course, thinking about it, I realise that my blonde hair is going to really pop against his dark outfit, and it's going to look like I'm... like I'm... oh boy.

'Okay, you can come up for air,' Caleb says after a moment, laughing, once the coast is clear. 'But they definitely got that Kodak moment.'

'At least they didn't see my face,' I offer up hopefully.

'No, but they saw mine,' he replies, pulling a funny face.

Thankfully he seems highly amused, and not mad, and hey, it did work, but it might have been less strange if I just, I don't know, put my hands over my face or something. I'll know for next time, not that there will be a next time, I'm astonished there was a first time. I very much feel like I'm living someone else's life right now, and I suppose I am, I'm living Annabelle Harvey-Whitaker's life, but you know what I mean.

The driver drops us right at the chalet door. Now that we're inside the resort we're safe from photographers but, even so, we make a dash for it.

We practically fall through the door, laughing as we go, and then we open more wine – even though I'm still buzzing from all the drinks I've had today.

'Those photos are definitely going to take some explaining,' Caleb says, pouring us each a glass.

I laugh – well, what else can I do now?

'Your career could take a sexy turn – you already have under-wear to promote,' I point out.

'Yeah, true, there's always the adult entertainment industry, if you get me cancelled,' he jokes.

The wine is kicking in, topping up my already healthy (or unhealthy, I guess) blood-alcohol level, and the intrusive thoughts (the ones we all get, you know, when you're standing on a bridge, and a little voice tells you to jump off) are clearly drunk too, because they're telling me to do something wild.

'You know what? Let's do those big money photos,' I suggest. 'Grab the stuff the adult store wants you to promote.'

'Really?' Caleb replies, his wine glass hovering in front of his lips. 'Because we've got plenty of photos of other things, enough for a decent payout for us both. We don't need to bother with the really sexy stuff. I probably would have skipped it anyway.'

'Yeah, go on,' I push him. 'We don't have to share the photos, live a little, let's see what they've sent.'

The irony of me telling a TV star with a fabulous life to live a little isn't wasted on me but, well, wasted is the word, I'm kinda drunk and I'm having a blast.

'Are you sure?' he asks, looking at me intently.

'Yes,' I say, grinning, probably not looking as sultry as I'm trying to. 'My career is going down the drain, so the money would be good.'

I pout at him but he doesn't need telling again. He hands me a bag of lingerie, and I choose something to put on – a really complicated hot pink set, with peepholes and trapdoors, which basically covers the things you don't actually need to cover, and keeps the important bits ready for action. However, I'm not about to walk out there with my nipples out, because I'm still me, and that feels like low-key sexual harassment, so for a little modesty (ha!) and good measure, I throw on a saucy French maid's outfit over the top (which even comes with a brunette wig, because apparently to fit the part you can't be blonde). Well, when in France, right?

Caleb looks stunned when he sees me, standing there in my French maid's outfit, complete with a feather duster in hand. Well, the entire time I've been here I've been nothing but a little doom cloud.

For a moment, I think he might be speechless, but then he breaks into a grin.

'Well, if you're going to clean, you might as well start with my room,' he says, waggling his eyebrows.

I burst out laughing, instantly feeling more at ease. He's standing there in a pair of silk boxer shorts, looking like he just stepped out of a luxury sleepwear catalogue. Honestly, why is men's lingerie always so simple and relatively normal-looking? Meanwhile, I'm in what is basically a Rubik's cube in underwear form.

'Yeah, yeah, keep dreaming,' I say, giving him a playful swat on his bare chest with my feather duster. 'But I will pretend to clean, for the sake of the photos.'

I playfully bend over the sofa, to dust the coffee table, ready for my close-up.

Caleb walks over to me, makes a camera gesture with his empty hands – the millennial kind with a shutter button, not the Gen Z mime that is basically holding up a smart phone – pretending to take a photo of me.

We laugh as we start posing for more fake photos. The absurdity of the situation makes it all the more fun. Caleb strikes a few ridiculous poses, and I follow suit, each shot getting sillier than the last, and yet still so undeniably sexy. There is something kind of horny about having a laugh in the bedroom, right? Or the kitchen area, in our case, but you know what I mean.

Every time our eyes meet, there's a spark. It's like the air between us is charged with electricity. We move closer, posing together for absolutely no reason, his arm around my waist, and I can feel the warmth of his skin against mine. The laughter dies down, replaced by a comfortable, almost intimate silence. I can't help but feel a flutter in my chest. I'm almost worried he'll be able to hear my heart beating, or feel it, now that my body is pressed against his.

'You look incredible,' he says, and there's no trace of a joke in his voice this time.

'Thanks,' I reply, feeling a blush creep up my cheeks.

I notice him notice the pink strap of the bodysuit I'm wearing.

'Was that in the bag?' he asks. 'Or is that yours?'

'It was in the bag,' I reply. 'I couldn't have walked so many steps today in this thing. It's so, intimately tight, I think I'm having sex with it right now.'

Caleb laughs lightly for a split second but then his expression goes serious again.

'Is it weird that I'm jealous?' he asks.

'Is it weird that I'm glad?' I reply, my heart absolutely pounding in my chest now.

For a moment, we just stand there, the room around us fading away. I can feel the pull between us, stronger than ever. It's as if the world has stopped, and it's just the two of us, caught in this perfect, surreal moment.

He reaches out, tucking a loose strand of hair behind my ear. His touch is gentle, and I can feel my breath catch in my throat. We're so close now, I can see every detail in his eyes, feel the heat radiating from his body, the excitement building in him too, as every part of him tenses up.

'Amber,' he says softly, and there's a question in his voice.

'Caleb,' I whisper back, not sure what I'm saying, only that I don't want this moment to end.

Whenever I've seen people get together in movies, and they've had that synchronised, unspoken moment where their bodies just snap together, because they know the time is right, I've always wondered if that actually happens. It turns out it does. It's like our bodies are speaking to each other, going over our heads, making plans of their own, and all we can do is go along with them.

As we kiss, Caleb scoops me up in his arms, grabbing me by the bum as I wrap my legs around his waist and my arms around his neck.

'Bedroom,' I mumble to him between kisses. 'I don't see why this underwear should have all the fun, it's you that I want.'

'And you told me you didn't know how to be spicy,' he replies, in a breathy voice, as he does as he's asked.

Caleb lies me down on his bed and slowly removes my stockings, one after the other, unwrapping me, like I'm a present that he wants to savour.

I bite my lip as I watch him at work. He kisses his way up my leg, until he's at eye level again, and as his body presses down on me, and his lips meet mine, everything falls into place. It's not that I'm not a spicy kind of girl, I just needed the right person to bring it out of me.

42

Waking up in Caleb's arms, everything just feels right.

Last night was beyond incredible. I didn't think nights like that existed outside the movies, but it turns out they do.

Caleb is nothing short of phenomenal in the bedroom. I remember once having a taster session with a personal trainer, during a brief stint where I had a gym membership (which, hilariously, was only for research for a book, not to be healthy), and the whole time I was there it felt like he was carrying me. He was great, strong, agile, and just generally knew what he was doing, and I was just doing my best to keep up. It was a bit like that. Actually, it was a lot like that.

He has retrospectively obliterated every other man I've slept with by being so, so much better than them in every way. I can still feel it all, if I let my mind wander back a few hours.

The soft rise and fall of his chest beneath my head feels like the most comforting rhythm in the world. Caleb is still sleeping, and even though I'm awake I'm tempted to stay here forever, basking in the warmth of his arms. I could get up, and I could write, because I have never felt so inspired, but, really, I just want to be here, with him, like this. I just want to lie here, tracing the contours of his abs with my fingertips, and smile smugly to myself.

Life has other ideas, though. There's a loud banging on the door and the sound of a woman shouting, which makes me jump and wakes Caleb up. He listens for a moment and then groans.

I look at him, as if to ask what's going on, only to see his expression shift from confusion to recognition as the familiar voice of his ex, Annabelle, echoes through the chalet.

'It's Annabelle, and I'm not going anywhere until you let me in, we need to talk,' she calls out.

Her tone is like a siren, demanding attention (or warning of danger), and I can't help but wonder why she's here, why she's so mad, and what she will do when she finds out I'm in here.

Caleb grabs his phone from the bedside table and his face drops as he scans his notifications. Whatever he sees doesn't seem to sit well with him.

'Shit,' he says to himself softly. His tone seems to change all of a sudden. If I didn't know better, I would think he was mad at me.

'Stay here and stay hidden,' he tells me, with all the warmth of a drill sergeant. 'I'll go get rid of her.'

'Okay,' I reply softly.

I do as I'm told and stay in the bedroom while Caleb goes into the living room, to let Storm Annabelle inside.

As I strain to listen from my hiding place – aka Caleb's bed – while he chats to his ex in the other room (standard stuff), I'm almost impressed at how Annabelle's voice pierces the air with a mix of anger and hurt.

'I can't believe you, Caleb! How could you let people think those pictures are me?' she snaps at him. 'The one that hit the net last night, oh my God, everyone thinks it's me, going down on you in a car, and then I look on your Insta, to see where you are, and I find out that it is you, you are here, and you're parading around with some weird body double of me, posting pictures of the two of you, do you know how messed up that is?'

I don't know if Annabelle gives Caleb a chance to reply, or if he has nothing to say for himself, because the next voice I hear is Annabelle's.

'What the hell is wrong with you?' she presses him. 'Do you really think this is okay?'

'You broke up with me,' he reminds her. 'I thought you would be happy, to see me moving on.'

'But have you moved on, Caleb? Have you really?' Annabelle's voice wavers with emotion. 'Because you're running around France with some kind of cheap knock-off, and I'm seeing pictures of you, and her, and you're up to all sorts and... and you just look so happy... and, truthfully, it was like a knife to the heart.'

Eh?

'It's obvious that you still want me and, seeing you with someone else, well, it's reminded me that I still want you,' she tells him. 'I'm sure we can smooth all of this out, we'll say that photo was a joke, and we'll post some real photos together – what do you say? Can we give it another go?'

Oh boy, she's gone from bollocking him to pretty much begging for him to take her back and, worst of all, Caleb isn't saying a word. He isn't telling her he's moved on, he isn't trying to get rid of her, he's obviously just standing there, like a lemon – oh, God, do you think it's because he wants to say yes, but he knows I'm in here, so he doesn't know how to say it? I need to get out of here, right now, because I don't want to hear what comes next.

Oh, the sicky, sinking feeling in my stomach, when I realise that my actual clothes are in the other bathroom, on the other side of the living room, and that the only thing I have in here is the French maid's outfit. I suppose I'm lucky that I have anything but, come on, it's a fucking French maid's outfit from a fucking sex shop.

With no other choice, I put it on, along with a pair of Caleb's trainers that are too big, but beggars can't be choosers – I'm not sure how long I would last barefoot in the snow, although at this stage I'll be lucky to find a way out.

How on earth am I going to get out of this chalet, when the only external door is the front door? As I try to open the window – not that I know how I'll get myself out through it – I knock over an ornament, which hits the floor, and while it thankfully doesn't break, it does land with a thud. I freeze, hoping they didn't hear that.

'What was that?' Annabelle asks.

Oh, I can't catch a break.

'Do you have someone in there?' she asks angrily. 'Is it her? Is it my crappy clone? I'll rip her cheap blonde extensions out.'

I mean, I'm mildly offended that she's referring to my actual hair that I have actually grown on my actual head as cheap extensions, but that's hardly the pressing issue right now, is it?

'Annabelle, wait,' Caleb pleads with her. 'Don't go in there, it's...'

Panicking, I try to hide under the bed, but it's no good, it's too close to the floor, I can't get under it.

Spotting the brown wig and feather duster from last night, I quickly grab them, wrestling on the wig as fast as I can, before popping up just as Annabelle and Caleb walk through the door.

I dust the bedside table, trying to blend in, to make it look natural.

'Ah, *bonjour*,' I say with a big smile, in my best attempt at a French accent.

The two of them just stare at me for a moment.

'*La lit, c'est bon. La chambre, c'est bon*,' I babble, mustering up as much GSCE French as I can, but there's only so much that sticks in here, when you only scraped a D grade. I'm sure none of this is right, but I'm hoping Annabelle won't know any better.

The two of them continue to stare at me.

'All clean,' I say, in a French accent that is supposed to sound like English isn't my first language. '*Merci.*'

'I was just going to say, don't go in there, the cleaner is in there,' Caleb tells Annabelle, his face etched with relief.

'Christ, do they really make the poor cow clean dressed like that?' I overhear Annabelle say, as I head for the door.

'Yeah, she must be freezing,' Caleb adds ever so considerately.

I quickly grab my bag, coat, and Uggs from next to the door, throwing them on as I make my escape onto the porch.

Breathing a sigh of relief (although not a very big one, all things considered), I glance back at the chalet one last time before heading back to the château. So that's that then, right? He didn't defend me, he played along with the cleaner story, and she wants him back so, yeah, that's that. I mean, a holiday romance, even a brief one, was more than I was expecting but, I don't know, I really thought we had something.

I guess it turns out I was just under the influence, in more ways than one.

Fab.

43

I almost take a tumble, slipping on a bit of icy sludge that has clung to my boot, as I walk into the château. I'm out of breath, shivering, and fucking starving now. I kind of wish I had kept the wig on, to keep my head warm, but I dropped it in a bin back at the resort.

The first thing I do is head toward my room, because right now all I can think about is getting out of this French maid outfit, because I feel like an absolute clown in it. Last night I felt great, and sexy, and fun, and today I just feel stupid.

I head up the stairs, turn the corner and bump straight into Henri (not literally, for a change), who's hovering outside my bedroom door in a way that makes it seem like perhaps he was waiting for me. His eyes widen, and his jaw drops as he takes in my outfit, peeking out from behind the coat I just unzipped.

'It's a long story,' I say quickly, hoping to brush past him.

'Oh, I'd love to hear it,' he replies, a smirk tugging at the corners of his mouth.

'I just need to get changed first because... yeah.' I gesture down at my body.

Henri follows me into my room, ignoring any semblance of personal boundaries.

'You don't need to do that on my account,' he says with a wink. 'And you don't even need to explain. Sometimes, the imagination is better than the reality.'

I can't help but think to myself that sometimes it's the other way around.

'Sorry for bailing on you last night,' I say, trying to steer the conversation away from my attire, as I pull on an oversized jumper that more than covers my maid clobber. 'It was for work, and I definitely feel like I've learned a lot, so...'

'It's okay, I understand,' he replies, nodding. 'I work hard too. In fact, I've been busy with a secret project, but I can tell you all about it, I'm sure. We had a big influencer here, from London, who didn't want to stay for free in exchange for promotion. It would have been great publicity for us, too great to miss out on, so I had to leak that he was here, to have photographers show up, so that the world would know he was staying here. It's incredible, how good it is for business.'

My heart sinks. So, Henri is the kind of guy who would use his guests for money and publicity, not only without their consent, but even after they make clear that they want privacy – and I thought this place advertised privacy? And he looks so, so proud of himself. He clearly has no idea what kind of mess he's made, and how it's going to affect me. Suddenly, Henri is the last person I want to be around – and to think, I was feeling so guilty, when I thought I had stood him up to be with Caleb.

Boy, am I glad I'm going home tomorrow.

'How about we grab some breakfast?' he suggests, looking hopeful. 'I don't mind what you wear.'

'I'm really tired,' I tell him, yawning for effect. 'Maybe I'll catch you later.'

'It's your last night here,' he reminds me, 'and I've got some work to do later today…'

'I have work to do too,' I say, forcing a smile. 'Maybe next year.'

Though I know full well I won't be back next year.

Henri looks disappointed but nods.

'Okay. See you around, Amber,' he tells me.

I mean, he seems disappointed, but he doesn't seem bothered. I'm getting the feeling that he does this sort of thing often. No wonder he's a live-in caretaker, he's having the time of his life.

I close the door behind him and finally exhale. My amazing day and night with Caleb seem like a distant dream now, replaced by the harsh light of day and the realisation that I need to leave all this behind, only now things feel like even more of a nightmare than they did before.

I strip off the French maid outfit (which only reminds me of last night) and throw on some comfortable clothes. Flopping onto the bed, I let out a deep sigh. I've gone from sky-high to rock bottom in record time.

Oh, and to top it all off, inspiration has once again been totally drained from my body.

The holiday really is over.

44

I'm all washed up – I was going to say 'so to speak' but, now that I think about it, maybe I'm as washed up as a girl can be – and dressed in my own, regular clothes, finally feeling like myself again. Well, that girl last night was not me, and neither was the French maid's outfit, and neither was my brief stint pretending to be a cleaner. I'm Amber Page, writer, and all-round dull person, and that's just the way I like it. All of this chaos is not for me. I'm not enjoying it, I'm not good at it, and I'm not playing these games any more.

Sitting at my laptop, I skim over the draft of my book. It's a mess, full of deliberately awful writing, cringey clichés, and plot holes the size of craters. This is what I wanted, right? The whole point is for my editor to hate it so much that she'll terminate my contract. I still can't believe this is the plan – trying to lose a book deal after it took me so long to get one in the first place, but sometimes you've got to do what you've got to do.

I lean back and sigh. I'm really not sure if I'm failing or succeeding right now.

My thoughts are interrupted by the familiar ringtone of my phone, and my mum's name popping up.

'Hello, Mum,' I say, trying to hide my sigh, but I'm expecting another round of complaints about what my dad is up to now.

'Amber, darling, how are you?' she asks, her voice sounding unusually bright. Suspiciously, even.

'Yeah, I'm okay, thanks,' I reply. 'How's it going?'

'Yes, all good, thanks,' she tells me. 'I was hoping to speak to Caleb.'

'Caleb?' I repeat, bewildered. That's the last thing I was expecting her to say. I haven't even told her that he's here. 'He's not here right now. Why do you need to talk to him?'

'Oh, Amber, it's amazing,' she gushes. 'Caleb spoke to your dad. He told him a few home truths, and, honestly, he's like a changed man now.'

I blink, rapidly, my eyes like a camera shutter that's taking a burst of photos to capture a moment in time. Well, it is an unexpected one. He did say that he liked to stick his nose in, if he thought he could help, and it sounds like he really has.

'Wait, what?' I reply.

'Oh, he's wonderful,' she continues. 'Caleb, that is. He's... well, I don't know what he's done, but he's knocked some sense into him. Your dad is doing everything he wasn't doing before – paying attention to me, being helpful around the house, generally being a joy to be around. That's why I asked him for the divorce, because I just wanted him to realise, to see what I was missing, and what he would be missing without me, and it all went a bit far, but it's all perfect now, we're going to give it another go.'

I feel kind of stupid, in hindsight, for not questioning why Mum would be choosing wallpaper she loved for a lounge in a house she reckoned they were going to have to sell.

'Mum, that's great news,' I tell her, genuinely. 'I had no idea

Caleb talked to Dad. Oh, actually, they spoke on FaceTime a few days ago, while I was... in the bathroom, but I didn't know what they talked about. I thought they were just making small talk.'

'I only just found out myself, and at first I was jealous that he got to speak to him and I didn't,' she admits. 'But whatever Caleb said to him, it worked.'

Wow. It sounds like Dad just needed someone like Caleb, who's been through so much, to point out what he has, and what he was taking for granted.

'That's the best Christmas present ever, Mum. I'm so happy for you,' I say with a smile.

It's not just a Christmas present, it's a Christmas miracle.

'Thank you, darling,' she says. 'We both needed this. I just wanted you to know, and to thank Caleb if you see him. But I would love to thank him myself.'

'I'll let him know,' I say, not wanting to get into anything else right now. 'And I'll see you very soon.'

'Yes, not long to go,' she says excitedly. 'And even more Christmas plans to make. It's going to be an even bigger and better one now.'

Christmas is one of those things where, sure, it can be bigger, but that rarely makes it better. The fewer extended family and friends around on Christmas Day, the more relaxing it tends to be.

But, hey, at least we're ending the call on a happy note, and I won't have to take any more calls, and Tom's life will be much easier. I guess everything is working out for the best. Well, almost everything.

I'm feeling a real mix of emotions right now – I can hardly pick them apart. I'm thrilled that my parents are working things out. It's a huge relief, and I'm grateful to Caleb, for the part he played. But the way things have played out between us, ugh, that I'm not happy about. I always assumed he was just another *him*bo influencer, all sponsorship deals and no substance, but he's actually a really sweet, thoughtful guy, with a difficult past behind him, but one that hasn't ruined the way he feels about the future. And, annoyingly, I like him. I really like him – so obviously his ex has shown up, and it seems like he's going to choose her.

Will he choose her? Am I definitely going to lose him to his ex, or can I still do something about it? I've never been the type to make grand romantic gestures – off the page, anyway – but maybe it's time that changed. Maybe I should go to Caleb, thank him for whatever he said to my dad, tell him how happy he has made my parents – and me. I should tell him how happy he makes me, and I should tell him exactly how I feel. No misunderstandings, no room for interpretation. Then it's up to him, what he decides to do, who he decides he wants to be with. Gosh, I really hope it's me but, if it's not, I will always be able to tell myself that I was bold and brave and I gave it a fucking go.

While the newfound determination is raging, I grab my coat and head for the door.

Maybe this is a mistake, maybe it isn't. Either way, it's worth a shot.

45

Standing outside Caleb's chalet door, I take in a deep breath of cool air and remind myself why I'm here. I can't leave without knowing for sure where we stand and, even though this is way out of my comfort zone, and that I really, really, truly, honestly never, ever do anything like this, I would kick myself forever if I didn't try.

My heart pounds like a drum inside my chest, each beat reminding me of just how much is riding on this moment. I lift my hand and knock, trying to steady my nerves.

It doesn't take long before the door swings open, and there he is, Caleb, which is a huge relief already.

My relief is short-lived, though, because the moment he sees me, his face falls, and a heavy, sinking feeling punches me in the stomach.

'Who is it?' Annabelle's voice calls from inside, her tone sharp and impatient.

Oh, great, she's still here. Wonderful. I'm sure that's a *great* sign.

'It's someone from the hotel. I'll be back in a minute,' Caleb shouts back.

He steps outside, closing the door firmly behind him. Shit, this is not a good sign, is it? I try to read his expression, but his eyes are guarded, his lips are saying nothing.

I force a smile, trying to act like things are normal.

'Is everything okay?' I ask, trying to keep my voice casual, even though my heart is playing battering rams against my ribcage.

Caleb sighs heavily, running a hand through his hair. He seems frustrated and kind of disappointed.

'I'm sort of in the middle of something, Amber,' he tells me plainly. 'I have a big mess to clean up, given that I've been photographed here at the resort.'

He surely can't think this is my fault, can he? He approached me, he stalked me across Europe, and he took me on the kind of dream date that would make a woman pounce.

Desperation claws at me, and I grasp at humour like a lifeline, like I always do.

'Need a maid to help clean up?' I joke, flashing what I hope is a disarming smile.

But he doesn't laugh. Not even a glimmer of amusement is anywhere to be found on his face. Instead, he just looks at me, his expression unreadable, almost distant.

'I really need to go back inside,' he says, his voice flat.

'Okay, see you later then?' I say, trying to mask my disappointment with a breezy tone – everything is normal, everything is fine – but it comes out sounding forced.

'Yeah, see you later,' Caleb replies, already turning back to the door.

And then he leaves me standing there, out in the cold, the door clicking shut behind him with a finality that really stings.

I stand there for a moment, staring at the closed door, as though I'm expecting him to come back out, to tell me it's all okay, but he doesn't. I still can't get over that he really does seem mad at me. What did I do wrong? Maybe he feels guilty about last night and doesn't want Annabelle, his true love, to find out what happened. Which is just, wow, chef's kiss, great. Perfect ending to this twisted fairy tale.

Oh, well, at least now I know where I stand, and I can go home, back to my life, and focus on me and my family. I need to be a big girl, to pick myself up, and remind myself that no one died. I guess, if they had, he could use it as inspiration for one of his books, like the one I helped him to write, the arsehole. I can't believe he's dropping me like this.

No. No, no, no. I'm not doing this. I'm going home, with my head held high, I'm not beating myself up over someone else's love story.

Timing is just as important in romance as it is in comedy and, as perfect as Caleb and I seemed for each other, we just had bad timing.

Sometimes it's as simple as that but, wow, what a waste.

46

After dragging my feet back to the château, with my tail between my legs and my heart pretty much in my arse, I get to step into the warmth of the hallway – probably for the last time.

I'll miss that feeling, of leaving the cold air outside, to step into the warmth of the château, the smell of burning wood greeting me, making me feel like I'm home.

However cold it is outside today though, honestly, Caleb was colder. Now that I'm back here, and the icy winds have blasted some sense into me, it's a little easier to remind myself that I don't need him, and that I don't need anyone treating me this way. I don't deserve it, and I can do better.

I mean, I didn't need him, I wanted him, but... yeah, I can do better, I can do better. And if I chant it enough, I might believe it.

I need to pack my bags but, before I do, I've got some goodbyes to say – and maybe some apologies to make.

I step into the inviting glow of the lounge. Mandy, Bette, and Gina are sitting around the fire, drinking wine and nibbling on olives. They're laughing and chatting, clearly enjoying their evening, but the moment they see me their mood shifts and their laughs fade out into awkward silence.

'Hey, ladies,' I say, attempting to muster up a smile that doesn't quite reach my eyes – hopefully they can't sense my fear, or tell that I have a nervous lump in my throat. 'Listen, I'm really sorry I've been MIA for the last few days. I've had some things going on, and... long story short, I think it might be time for me to step back from writing for a bit.'

Mandy raises an eyebrow, her lips flickering a hint of smile for a split second, before she settles on something that looks more understanding.

'That's all right, Amber,' she tells me. 'This job isn't for everyone. Not everyone is cut out for this life.'

So nice of her to make this a personal failing on my part.

Bette nods in agreement, reaching for another bottle of wine and expertly popping it open with ease.

'She's right,' Bette chimes in, her eyes firmly on her glass. 'This job is so hard. Sometimes I wonder how we do it.'

She isn't making it look hard, pouring herself a glass of wine, on her French retreat. Perhaps it's just what I've seen here, and what they show people on social media, but their lives seem filled with leisurely wine evenings, laughter, and each other. I don't think I've ever seen or heard a hint of struggle from any of them. Then again, I assumed Caleb had always had a perfect life too. Who knows what things are really like for them? One thing I can say for sure is that, whatever I'm going through, they're not all that bothered.

'Well, I need to pack my bag, to head home, but I just wanted to say thank you so much for the opportunity, and maybe I'll see you later.'

'Oh, I'm sure you'll see us again,' Mandy replies.

We exchange brief, half-hearted goodbyes and – honestly – I

can't leave the room fast enough. I head for the stairs, picking up the pace, keen to get back to my normal life.

As I reach the end of the hallway, I hear footsteps rapidly approaching behind me.

'Amber, wait!' Gina calls out as she catches up with me. 'Can I talk to you for a second?'

I turn to face her, surprised to see genuine concern in her eyes.

'Yeah, of course,' I reply, keeping my guard up just a little. 'What's up?'

'You need to take care of yourself, Amber,' she tells me firmly, but sincerely. 'Sometimes we all need a break so take some time and figure out what you want to do. There will always be other books, but there's only one you – take care of yourself.'

Her words are filled with a warmth and understanding that I didn't get from the other two, and I'm touched that she has come out of her way to offer me some advice.

'Thanks, Gina. I really appreciate that,' I say, my voice wobbling slightly. 'That means a lot to me.'

She gives me a quick, reassuring hug.

'Just remember that it's okay to take a step back and breathe,' she adds. 'And don't be too hard on yourself. Save the spanking for the book.'

I laugh, feeling a bit lighter for the first time in days. She's right, a break is exactly what I need.

'I'll try. Thank you,' I reply, genuinely grateful for her support.

Gina heads back to the lounge, and I continue on to my room.

I grab my things, stuffing them into my bag, pausing for a second to smile to myself as I pack the lingerie I flashed Henri in. I'm not sure I'll ever wear it again but, weirdly, I feel like it has sentimental value now. How often do you think people say that about raunchy lingerie?

I'm grateful to Gina, for her kind words, and for the time I got to spend with Henri, and all of the inspiring places I saw, and the stories I heard, and yes, I'm grateful for Caleb. Not just for the money he's paying me for the photos I helped him with, or for seemingly repairing my parents' marriage, but for the time I got to spend with him too.

Life is just a mess of ups and downs and all we can do is ride the waves as they come at us. At least I can go home to my family – my happy family – and Christmas.

I just need to focus on the positives and get home safely. Although I think perhaps I need something different to watch on the flight on the way home.

I'm not sure I'm in the mood for any more *Welcome to Singledom*.

47

I spot Tom in his shiny new BMW, waiting for me outside the airport. I reckon he would have picked me up from France, if it meant he got to drive it, because living in London means that, unsurprisingly, a car might just be the slowest form of transport.

The cold nips at my face, but it's a different kind of cold from where I've just been. Even though I think it's technically not as cold here, the UK cold is damp and dreary in comparison, but that might be because we've got icy rain instead of snow. Maybe the grey of the city and the exhaust fumes I'm breathing in aren't helping, or maybe it's just my mood. No prizes for guessing which one.

Tom waves energetically from inside his car, his grin wide and welcoming.

'Hey, sis! How was France?' he asks, the second I get in the car.

He is almost unnervingly chipper.

I make myself comfortable, immediately appreciating the warmth of the heated seats.

'Hey, yeah, it was good,' I say, not giving anything away, but also not sounding like I've had the best time.

'How's Caleb?' he asks. 'Is he still in France or has he come home? He seems like a top bloke. Honestly, that talk he gave me was so encouraging. And, bloody hell, he really worked his magic on Mum and Dad, they're over the moon. Actually, they're annoyingly happy. All over each other – it's a bit much. You'll see when you get there.'

I laugh, trying to picture our parents all loved-up, but I'm guessing it has to be seen to be believed.

'I can't wait,' I say with a chuckle.

'Their happiness is having a knock-on effect on Christmas,' Tom continues. 'We've got a big party planned for Christmas Eve, so you've got that to look forward to in a couple of days. They've invited absolutely everyone. They even told me to bring a plus-one – not bloody likely though. Watching our parents French kiss under the mistletoe would scare anyone away.'

I burst out laughing. Now there's an image.

'Yeah, I think that would test any potential relationship,' I tell him. 'Do you think we ought to try to break them up again?'

Tom almost cackles with laughter because that one caught him off guard.

'You've got a plus-one too, you know,' Tom adds, glancing at me as he pulls out of the car park. 'You could invite Caleb.'

I shake my head.

'I don't think so, we only really had a working relationship,' I tell him. 'Plus, he has a lot going on. His girlfriend wants him back, and he is busy dealing with a PR problem. It turns out the guy who runs the place where we were staying set him up and tipped off the paparazzi about him being there.'

Tom's eyes widen.

'Wow. How do you know?' he asks curiously.

'The guy told me himself,' I say, shaking my head. 'He lived in the château where I was staying. He just proudly blurted it out to me.'

'He sounds like a dick,' Tom replies.

'Yeah, I guess he was,' I agree, feeling absolutely zero regrets that I didn't spend more time with Henri.

'Ah well, at least it's Christmas,' Tom says, giving me a nudge with his elbow. 'Let's go to our no longer broken family home, start drinking, and not stop until the new year.'

'Sounds like a good plan to me,' I say, trying to snap myself out of my funk. 'Did my shopping all arrive?'

'Yeah, there are loads of packages for you,' Tom replies. 'I hope you got me something decent. I think I've got something great for you.'

'I can't wait to open it,' I say, finding a bit of genuine enthusiasm.

Despite feeling down in the dumps and a bit sorry for myself, maybe Christmas is exactly what I need. I've sent my latest (car crash of a) book to my editor, so I can stop thinking about that disaster. Spending time with my family is the perfect escape. I can take a break from reality, reset, and hopefully, in the new year, I can be a whole new me.

Yep, that old one. I don't believe it either.

48

Tom wasn't kidding when he said our parents were having a big Christmas Eve party – the house is practically bursting at the seams. Mum has gone all out with the decorations this year. The hallway is decked with garlands, each one twinkling with so many fairy lights they're actually brighter than the big light in there. There's a gigantic tree in the living room, adorned with a mish-mash of old family ornaments, and new, shiny baubles ping light around the room like a disco ball. Honestly, the whole place looks like something she should have charged admission for, like a Christmas wonderland, if wonderlands were full of random friends and family who are all drinking way too much.

Hilariously, you can't really see the decorations any more. The place is overflowing with people, all talking and laughing over each other. I cradle the super-strong cranberry cocktail that Tom made for me – he called it a 'Cranberry Death', which sounds like, well, something that will kill me with Christmas. I nibble on a mince pie as I scan the room for a familiar face. Well, someone familiar who I actually want to talk to, at least.

It weirdly feels like everyone and no one is here. I know my auntie and cousin are somewhere in this sea of festive cheer, but I haven't seen them for ages. The local vicar is chatting animatedly with Val from down the street. Oh, and there's her husband, Pete – the one who always asks if I'm still a writer and, when I say yes, gives me a patronising pat on the back and tells me to hang in there. He once suggested I apply for a job at his son's garden centre. Hey, I wonder if it's still going...

With no one I really want to engage with, there's only one thing for it: hit up the buffet table *again*. It's Christmas, so all conventional food rules are out the window. Despite just finishing a mince pie, I pick up a giant Scotch egg and start munching on it like it's an apple. If you were supposed to eat beige snacks five times a day then let's just say I'm smashing all expectations.

I spot Mum and Dad across the room. Dad's hands are on Mum's hips, and they're swaying to the music. It's like they're loved-up teenagers again. Who knew Dad even knew Mum had hips? They're acting like newlyweds, in a way I suspect they didn't do when they were actual newlyweds. Say what you want about Caleb – and believe me, I've been saying a lot, none of it flattering – but he's done something right. If nothing else comes from this whole mess other than my parents giving things another go, then maybe it was worth it. It might not feel that way now, but maybe in the future I'll see that everything happens for a reason.

I pull out my phone. The one thing I told myself I wouldn't do is check my work emails. It's unlikely Jen will read my book until the new year anyway. But here I am, bored enough to break my own rule.

There is an email from Jen, it turns out, with the subject line 'New Book'. I open it, and my face contorts with confusion. Eh? None of this makes sense. Jen says she's read my book – my awful, purposefully bad book – and she loved it. She's signing off for

Christmas but is excited to discuss new contracts and advances in the new year.

What? Advances? I don't get advances, I'm not important enough, I'm an author, not a celebrity. Plus, I only sent her it yesterday, so she can't have sat and read the whole thing? Even if she just read the new bits, it still doesn't seem likely, because I've changed little bits here and there all the way through. Has Jen started on the sherry early or something, or has she just had enough of me to the point where she'll publish any old shite I write? But, then again, why would she give me an advance, if that were true?

'How would you like your present early?' Tom asks, snapping me out of my thoughts.

I decide to keep the email to myself. There must be some kind of mix-up.

'I should wait until tomorrow,' I tell him. 'Them's the rules, right?'

Tom grins.

'I've got two presents, so you can have one today if you follow me,' he replies.

'Okay,' I say with a heavy sigh, grabbing my cocktail and half-eaten Scotch egg, and following him through the house. 'Where are we going?'

'To the garage,' he tells me.

'Ooh, have you got me a BMW too?' I joke.

'Could you drive one even if I did?' he laughs. 'But no. I just put it in there because it's the only part of the house without people in it.'

'Fair enough,' I reply with a laugh.

'In there,' Tom says, pointing to the garage.

'I know where the garage is,' I laugh.

'Yeah, I know, I'm saying go in there. I'll wait here,' he continues.

'Is this something awful? Is something going to go off or go "boo" or... I don't know?' I ask suspiciously.

'It's nothing bad,' he insists. 'Merry Christmas.'

I give him a sceptical look but my curiosity gets the better of me.

'I will throw your present in the pond if this is a prank,' I warn him.

I step into the dark garage but pause for a moment.

'Can I have the light on?' I call back.

'I'll turn the light on when you close the door,' he insists. 'Humour me, it's just because I haven't wrapped it.'

'It better be a car,' I mutter under my breath.

The door clicks shut, the light flicks on, and there he is – Caleb, standing next to the deflated inflatable Santa Claus that Dad retired once he stopped warring with Mum.

'What are you doing here?' I ask, almost accusingly.

'Tom invited me,' he says simply.

'How?' I blurt.

'He had my number, from when you used my phone to call him, so he gave me a ring,' he explains, like it's a perfectly normal thing. 'We had a chat, about a few things, and then he invited me, so here I am.'

'But why did you come?' I reply. 'Why didn't you say no?'

'Because I wanted to see you,' he tells me.

I pull a face, somewhere between confused and irritated.

Caleb laughs, probably at my teenage-girl level of moodiness, and steps forward. He takes my cocktail and my Scotch egg, placing them on the side before taking my hands. 'I owe you a few apologies,' he begins, taking a deep breath. 'That morning when Annabelle turned up, I saw a photo of myself online, taken from the château window. I assumed it was you who had taken it because, well, who else could it be? You told me you had seen me out of the window, and then a photo of me out of the window was leaked to the press, so I put two and two together, but I was always better at English than maths.'

'Oh,' is all I can say. 'No, that wasn't me. That was Henri, the guy who runs the place. He told me it was him, that he did it because you wouldn't post promo stuff about the resort. I tried to come see you after, to tell you, but Annabelle was still there and you were kind of rude, so...'

My voice trails off.

'I should have known you wouldn't have done that,' Caleb tells me. 'Instead, I acted like a baby, and I'm sorry. I think it just freaked me out, how much I was enjoying spending time with you, and then thinking that you might have sold me out, and then Annabelle turning up... Look, when you came back, we were in the middle of talking. I was telling her that she and I were over, apologising for making it seem like I was still with her, but making it clear it was only for the money. And she's not that bothered, it turns out, because I offered her my share of the money, and she took it, and she left.'

'And they say romance is dead,' I manage to joke.

'I can send you your share now, by the way,' Caleb says.

'Keep it,' I say with a shrug. 'I never really deserved it in the first place. Plus, I had an email from my editor, and I think her brain must have malfunctioned because I sent her my godawful book, and she reckons she wants to give me an advance for it. It makes no sense. I'm sure she'll realise her mistake in the new year.'

'Amber, wait, is that all she said?' Caleb asks.

'Yeah,' I reply. 'I think maybe she meant to send it to someone else or something, because she can't have meant it for me.'

'Or, maybe, it's because I sent my manuscript to my editor and told him that I had co-written it with you. That you had added the extra scenes. And then maybe I pitched our other idea to him, and he loved it, but I said we came as a team, so we would have to write it together,' Caleb explains.

'You did what?' I blurt. 'You did that for me?'

Caleb shrugs casually.

'Oh, I only did it so that you would be stuck with me,' he jokes. 'If you want to be partners in crime, that is.'

Imagine, not only getting to write the kind of books I want to, but doing so with someone like Caleb who is not only genuinely talented but a big enough name to get actual marketing, Tube adverts, TV spots – the works.

I grab him and give him a squeeze.

'I would love that,' I tell him. 'Thank you.'

'No, thank you,' he replies. 'I would have put out a crap book and it probably would've flopped. You've made it something special.'

I can't wipe the smile from my face.

'You didn't have to come to my mum and dad's weird party to tell me that,' I point out.

'No, I didn't,' he replies. 'But when Tom set me straight, saying you seemed like you might miss me, I knew what I needed to do, if I wanted to win you back.'

My breath catches in my throat, not that I let Caleb see that.

'You're here to win me back, huh?' I say.

'Yep,' he replies. 'I had hoped the book deal would do it but you're tougher than you look so, I don't know, name your price.'

'I don't have a price,' I tell him. 'I have a punishment. If you're serious then I want you to walk into that house and meet my parents and all their weird friends. If you survive that then maybe, just maybe, we can talk. What are you doing for Christmas?'

'No plans,' he says. 'I got a bit too distracted to make any, with any of my friends, so...'

'Oh, so you're here for a dinner,' I tease.

'You know I love a free dinner,' he replies with a smile. 'And I love a weird family party so, let me at them.'

'Are you sure?' I reply.

'I've never been more sure,' he tells me. 'Look, I don't want to get ahead of myself, but can I please kiss you already? I don't mind if you taste like a Scotch egg.'

'Shut up,' I say, pulling him close, making the first move.

Just like that, everything feels right again. It's like I've never been away from him, like I didn't feel a second of heartbreak. All that matters is now.

As our lips part, Caleb grabs my cocktail and knocks it back.

'Okay, show me the way to the parents, I am raring to go, and I can't wait to meet them,' he says, willing to boldly go where I have never dared to let any man go before.

We hold hands and leave the garage together, only to find Tom and my parents standing there, waiting for us.

'Caleb, hello,' Mum greets him.

'Great to finally meet you in person, lad,' Dad adds.

'Come on, come with us, we've got so many people we want you to meet,' Mum continues.

They take Caleb away, dragging him off into the crowd, and he almost vanishes like he's crowd-surfing, only this has to be much less fun. This will really test his commitment, that's for sure.

'Well, well, well,' I say to Tom, now that we're alone. 'You're a dark horse, aren't you?'

Tom just shrugs but his smug smile says it all.

'Who knew you were such a romantic?' I say.

Tom leans in and lowers his voice.

'I will deny this if you ever tell anyone I said it but sometimes the people who write the best love stories are the ones who need a little help writing their own,' he tells me, with a profoundness I didn't know he possessed. 'Now, get after him, and make sure those two nutters don't undo all my hard work.'

'Thank you,' I tell him, kissing him on the cheek.

I can't believe I'm saying it but perhaps Tom is right. Maybe I've been so busy trying to write love stories for the page that I've been thinking about my own all wrong.

Yes, this week has been messy, but the future is looking a little clearer now. And that's the best Christmas present of all.

49

EIGHTEEN MONTHS LATER

I'm currently on my knees, searching the carpet for my earring. One is in my ear, the other is nowhere to be seen.

I'm in a hotel room, and I was wearing it earlier, so there are only so many places it can be.

I thought this five-star room came with everything but, sadly, there is no way the concierge will send someone up here, to hunt for my earring – although, now that I've said it, I'm sure they would.

It really is gorgeous here. Plush cream carpets (that I'm terrified I'm going to cover in make-up), elegant mahogany furniture (that I'm also terrified I'm going to cover in make-up), and floor-to-ceiling windows offering a breathtaking view of London's skyline – which are actually covered in make-up, because the first thing I did when I arrived here was press my face up against the glass to admire the view.

Caleb emerges from the bathroom, looking dapper in his tux, holding my small gold hoop delicately in his hand.

'It was next to the sink,' he tells me. 'I was going to give you a lecture, on how it could have gone down the drain but, wow, you look beautiful.'

'Do you think so?' I ask, taking the earring from him.

I look in the full-length mirror, carefully putting it in my ear. The dress I'm wearing is a floor-length silky black gown that magically clings in all the right places and flows elegantly as I move. The dress is doing a lot – other dresses could *never*.

I smooth the fabric down, feeling a mix of nerves and excitement.

'You're going to knock them all dead,' he says. 'We both are – killing people is what we do.'

I laugh.

'It's okay for you to say, you've been to a million award ceremonies,' I point out.

Caleb smiles at me in the mirror as he adjusts his cufflinks.

'But this is my first book award ceremony,' he reminds me. 'And the first time I've been nominated.'

'At least we have that in common,' I say, my heart pounding.

It's still so surreal, that our book has been shortlisted for an award. Almost as shocking as the fact that it's topped every chart going and that it has already been optioned by a Hollywood production company. Imagine seeing our book on the big screen! And I love that we did this one together – it's our baby, and we've got another one on the way. A book, that is. You would definitely be able to tell if I had a baby on the way in this dress – you can almost see the outline of my lunch in my stomach.

'Oh, while I was in the shower, I thought of a way to seed our twist in Chapter One,' Caleb says, lacing up his shoes.

I laugh, loving how we can switch from typical couple talk to getting excited about plot twists, clever motives, and creative murders.

'Tell me about it later,' I say, glancing at the clock. 'We need to get going, or we'll be late.'

'Let's do it,' Caleb says, kissing me on the cheek, careful not to mess up my make-up.

We head down in the lift, towards the ballroom where the ceremony is taking place.

The grand chandelier-lit bar is packed with elegantly dressed people, all chatting and clinking their glasses, as they wait for the ceremony to start.

As we make our way through the crowded bar, a familiar voice catches my attention.

'Amber! Amber, darling, hello.'

'Oh boy, here we go,' I whisper to Caleb through gritted teeth as Mandy hurries over to greet us.

'Amber, darling, you look fabulous,' Mandy says, kissing me on both cheeks. 'And Caleb, wow, so handsome.'

He gets two kisses too.

Mandy is flanked by Bette and Gina, as always, who follow suit, saying their hellos.

'You two must be so excited,' Mandy says, widening her eyes with excitement.

'Everyone knows you're going to win,' Bette adds. 'Have you written a speech?'

'We're just going to see what happens,' Caleb tells her with a smile. 'And if we are fortunate enough to win, we'll speak from the heart.'

'Oh, he's so dreamy,' Gina says. 'Proper leading-man material. I'm surprised you're not firing out romance novels left, right, and centre, Amber.'

'Well, when I was writing romance, I mostly wanted to kill men,' I joke. 'Now that I'm writing about killing men, I'm all about the love.'

'Beautifully put,' Mandy says, laughing wildly. 'So witty.'

'This is why they're going to win,' Bette says with a nod. 'And we'll be cheering you on the loudest.'

Isn't it funny how success attracts more success? Now that I'm doing well, I have the respect of people I struggled to get it from before. When I visit my editor, she treats me like a VIP. And here, tonight, everyone is making me feel so special. I don't think my butt has ever been kissed as much as it has this year. I'm surprised I can sit.

'We'd better take our seats,' Caleb says. 'But it was lovely to see you, ladies.'

'And you,' Mandy replies. 'Come and see us for a drink later; we can celebrate your win.'

'They always seem so nice,' Caleb says quietly to me as we walk away.

'Yes, they're nice now,' I remind him. 'They think I'm cool now – thanks to you.'

'Oh, I'm just such a cool guy,' he jokes. 'You're welcome.'

Caleb might be joking but I do have a lot to thank him for. He turned up in my life at a time when I had no direction, no idea what I wanted, or what I was going to do, and it turned out he was everything I wanted – and my dream job was thrown in as a bonus.

Everyone is saying we're going to win this award tonight, and yes, it would be great if we did, but as corny as it sounds, I feel like I've already won.

This isn't the 'happy ever after' moment for Caleb and me, it's only the beginning of our story, and every time I turn a page, things just seem to get better.

ACKNOWLEDGEMENTS

Massive thanks to Nia, Amanda and everyone else at Boldwood for working so hard on my books. Thank you to Karen Cass, for always doing such a fab job with my audiobooks.

Thank you to everyone who takes the time to read and review my books. All your lovely comments and messages really make my day.

As always, I could not do any of this without my wonderful family. I'm so fortunate to have Kim, and Pino, and the amazing Aud. James and Joey, who always have my back, and Darcy, who is always by my side.

And finally thank you to Joe, my husband, who is an endless source of inspiration. I couldn't do it without you.

ABOUT THE AUTHOR

Portia MacIntosh is the million copy bestselling author of over 20 romantic comedy novels. Whether it's southern Italy or the French alps, Portia's stories are the holiday you're craving, conveniently packed in between the pages. Formerly a journalist, Portia lives with her husband and her dog in Yorkshire.

Sign up to Portia MacIntosh's mailing list for news, competitions and updates on future books.

Visit Portia's website: www.portiamacintosh.com

Follow Portia MacIntosh on social media here:

facebook.com/portia.macintosh.3

x.com/PortiaMacIntosh

instagram.com/portiamacintoshauthor

bookbub.com/authors/portia-macintosh

ALSO BY PORTIA MACINTOSH

One Way or Another

If We Ever Meet Again

Bad Bridesmaid

Drive Me Crazy

Truth or Date

It's Not You, It's Them

The Accidental Honeymoon

You Can't Hurry Love

Summer Secrets at the Apple Blossom Deli

Love & Lies at the Village Christmas Shop

The Time of Our Lives

Honeymoon For One

My Great Ex-Scape

Make or Break at the Lighthouse B&B

The Plus One Pact

Stuck On You

Faking It

Life's a Beach

Will They, Won't They?

No Ex Before Marriage

The Meet Cute Method

Single All the Way

Just Date and See

Your Place or Mine?

Better Off Wed

Long Time No Sea

The Faking Game

Trouble in Paradise

Ex in the City

The Suite Life

It's All Sun and Games

You Had Me at Château

LOVE NOTES

LOVE IN EVERY CHAPTER

WHERE ALL YOUR ROMANCE
DREAMS COME TRUE!

THE HOME OF BESTSELLING
ROMANCE AND WOMEN'S
FICTION

 WARNING:
MAY CONTAIN SPICE

SIGN UP TO OUR
NEWSLETTER

https://bit.ly/Lovenotesnews

Boldwood